RINGS OF SMOKE

Diane O'Toole

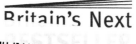

Britain's Next

D1513036

3179547

First published in 2015 by:

Britain's Next Bestseller
An imprint of Live It Publishing
27 Old Gloucester Road
London, United Kingdom.
WC1N 3AX

www.britainsnextbestseller.co.uk

Cover design by DARK IMAGINARIUM Art & Design.

Printed in Poland.

ISBN 978-1-910565-43-8 (pbk)

DEDICATION

FOR my mother-in-law, Nora O'Toole, who, as fate dictated, I never got to meet: for her profound love of the written word, and her desire to tell her own story, which, sadly, she never got to finish. For my Dad, for always being there, and for all those times you didn't know that I was hiding under my bed with a book, when I should have been at school! Coleen and Carole, no two friends can know me better – thanks for badgering me for so long to finish this story. But most of all, for my husband, soul mate, my best friend, Michael, who has supported, encouraged, even harangued me into continuing with what I often thought I couldn't achieve, the completion of my first novel. And, last but not least, I mustn't forget my young friend, Gemma Cahill, who pecked at my head for many a long month to finish this book so that she could finally get to read the end!

SUPPORTER LIST

Gemma Cahill, Julie Timlin, Coleen Connor, Carole Worley, Dawn Wetherill, Debra Jayne Shepherd, Jane Boardman, Christine Holt, Clare Sheehan, Rebecca Hodson-Ridgway, Gary Hodson-Ridgway, Anne Neal, Karen Hodson-Ridgway, Dave Channon, Alison Johnson, Pat Bennett, Debbie Jones, Julie Gaffney, Natalie Cotterill, Nikki Harwood, Matt O'Toole, Christine Beckett, John Hanmer, Nora Fryer, Lesley O'Toole, William Reibelt, Yvonne Perry, Kerri Hanmer, Jim Dobbs, Karyn Van der Walle, Benjamin Sawyer, Suzy Vermulm, Kayleigh Manock, Philip Westcott, Rachael Hodson-Ridgway, Gordon Hodson-Ridgway, Beverley Dalton, Caroline McKeague, Alan Currie, Wendy Trelfa, Elaine Sandbach, Sarah Gaffney, Nicola Doran, Andy Petrie, Suzanne Greenwood, David Fryer, Catherine Cook, Louise Neale, Alissia Cahill, Bill Entwistle, Peter Fryer, John Fryer, Shirley Lowe, Amie Hodson-Ridgway, Chris Brooks, Karen Woodhams, Justin Lanata, Francesca Lyons, Jessica Doe, Janet Noble, Nicholas May, Lauren Ridgway, Emma Brookes, Rebecca Hill, Francis Sapsford, Vagelis Makris, Julie Hill, Caroline Richardson, Linsey Payne, Brian D. Cook, Gordon Hodson Ridgway, Susan Chadderton, Gillian Smith, Bob Willis, Christine Jones, Helen Doublett, Alexis Makrus, Julie Gaffney, Barbara Henshall, Ryan Oldham, Michelke Brady, Joanne Hall, Margaretha van der Walle, Boral Brisbane Social

Club, Lisa Bush, Justin Lanata, Rita Thomas, Sandra Lanata, Jon Lawton, Angela Bogdou, Keith Robinson, Valerie Harrison, Steph Turner, Pete Burns, Julie Fisher, Lee Edwards, Janine Summers, Stuart Martin, Helen Robinson.

PROLOGUE

Lancaster, England 1945

L EONARD sat on the top step, looking down at the girls dancing in a circle. He was alone. He was always alone. Not of his choosing, that's just the way it was and the way it had always been for as long he could remember.

"Leonard Fitch is an ugly dick, doo-dah, doo-dah," they sang in unison.

"Look at that face dunnit make you sick, doo-dah doo-dah day!" The girls laughed hysterically. Taunting lanky Leonard Fitch was the highlight of their day. And as they ridiculed and tormented him he sat quietly, staring back at them, holding onto the thought foremost in his mind. He repeated that thought over and over in his head, *you may laugh now, but I will have my day, and you will all fear the name 'Leonard Fitch'.*

It was lunchtime at Lancaster Grammar School; the time Leonard hated the most. Not because the food was dreadful and inedible. Not because he was a loner, without a friend in the world. He had grown used to the loneliness, accepted it as his lot in life, and that's how he preferred it now. He hated it because it was the one time the boys from the Grammar and the girls from the adjoining High School mixed in the playground. It was an opportunity for those *whores in the making* to torment him.

His only enjoyment in life was reading. Books were his passion, and reading was where he found a release from his lonely existence.

Through books, he entered different worlds, became different people, acting out roles in the theatre of his mind. His reading material included the short stories of Algernon Blackwood after he found a copy of *The Listener* at the bottom of his father's wardrobe. Blackwood was one of the finest writers of ghost stories in his day, and he was also said to have been a member of *The Golden Dawn*, an organisation dedicated to the study and practice of the occult, something Leonard found intriguing and worthy of further investigation.

Despite his scientific leanings, he found books on fantasy a great release; a way of expanding his horizons, and nothing did that more than a good horror story, particularly those involving the brutal killing or sacrifice of young females. And if he couldn't find that in a book he would make up his own stories, even illustrating them with crude sketches. After reading *'The Pit and the Pendulum'*, he produced a comic book depicting a young female as the prisoner, tied down to a wooden table and a giant scythe swinging back and forth, but unlike the Edgar Allan Poe classic, in his story the scythe cut through the flesh and bone, opening up the chest of the unfortunate girl.

Being a great reader helped not only with his education, but also his imagination. He was top of his year in English. Straight 'A's all the way, in English language *and* English literature. And right now he was imagining what he could . . . *no not could, would* do to these bitches, in good time.

In post war Britain, life was hard and pretty grim. Many of the children had lost their fathers during the war, but Leonard was fortunate in that respect; his father had what they called a 'protected occupation', which in Leonard's eyes made his father special. Important even, like Mr. Churchill; *he* didn't have to fight, and neither did his dad. According to his mother though, his father was a coward – afraid to go and do his duty.

No, it wasn't the war that killed his father. It was his mother.

"Come along Fitch! Stop daydreaming, lad!" Leonard's form teacher yelled, giving him a slap across the back of the head. The girls laughed once more as Leonard rubbed his head. He slowly rose to his feet, unfolding his six-foot frame to its full height, still stinging from the slap received from his sadistic teacher. "You need to get those books out for the next lesson!" he shouted, looking back over his shoulder as he strutted across the playground, the tails of his long black gown flapping around his legs.

Oh, the joys of being a Prefect. Not only did the other kids hate you, the teacher's treat you like a slave.

Leonard glared back at the sniggering girls, and swore an oath to himself. *They'll regret this. Bitches! Every single one of them will plead and beg for me to show them mercy before I've finished with them.*

CHAPTER ONE

Bleazedale Forrest, Cumbria, September 1976

A SUDDEN rustling in the nearby trees brought Leonard Fitch to an abrupt halt. He froze, letting the knotted end of the coarse nylon bag slide silently from his long, bony fingers. With his back to where the sound came from, he reached out, grabbed the wooden balustrade and turned slowly, not daring to make the slightest noise. His small bald head and long scraggy neck gave him the appearance of a turkey as he leaned off the edge of the porch and peered into the darkness; his beady grey eyes screwed up tight behind round rimless glasses as he strained to see into the dark.

It was just after midnight and the clear night sky was lit by a full moon, the ghostly light clinging to the mist that cloaked the land around the isolated lodge deep inside Bleazedale Forest. Fitch had searched long and hard for such a remote property and the seclusion of a dense forest in the English Lake District was exactly what he needed for his work.

He looked into the trees and beyond, staring into a blanket of black velvet. Fitch knew this part of the forest well, better, he thought, than most of the wildlife. Nothing moved. The shadows from the porch light remained still. He waited and listened, and apart from the gentle chatter of running water from a nearby stream, everywhere was silent again.

It was mid-September and the country was enjoying an Indian summer, yet as the night wore on the temperature had dipped significantly. Fitch shivered even though he was covered in sweat from his exertions. Small droplets ran down from his bald head and into his eyes, the salty moisture stinging, blurring his vision. This kind of body heat made him uncomfortable and bad-tempered. It made him think of the woman whom he loathed and despised. The woman he had nothing but contempt for; the same woman he had the most profound misfortune to have been born to. There, she was back in his head again, derailing his carefully thought out plans.

Using the palm of his hand, Fitch swiped angrily at his forehead wiping away the moisture trickling down his face, as he tried to dismiss from his mind all thoughts of his mother. She wasn't important. Never had been. Never would be. Nothing could possibly change that. Yet, he could still hear her telling him, as a young boy, her greatest regret in life, "'I should have crossed my legs and chocked you to death at birth!'" *Shame she hadn't carried through with it,* he thought, *because you've no idea what I have planned for you!*

In addition to the regular beatings throughout his childhood and his teenage years, she abused him emotionally and mentally. Even today she was still there, taunting, tormenting and ridiculing him. If it was possible, she'd even made his life more of a living hell during her menopause years. It was her fault, all of it. Why he had to do what he was doing, why he was driven to do it and why he couldn't stop doing it.

He pulled a crisp white handkerchief from his trouser pocket, removed his glasses and rubbed vigorously at his eyes, before giving the thick lenses a quick wipe. He put them back on and squinted out into the darkness again – waiting for the slightest sign of movement.

He didn't have to wait long, though. A shrill cry followed by the loud, frantic flapping of wings shattered the unearthly silence. His mother instantly dismissed from his mind, he felt a sudden sense of relief. A thin smile spread across his small uneven teeth, his eyes almost disappearing into the back of his head. The predator had its prey.

Relieved, he started to relax again and the song, *that* song from his miserable existence of a childhood, played along his lips as he dabbed and mopped the salty moisture from his head and neck. His confidence renewed in the knowledge that he was still alone, hidden miles from anywhere and anyone, he began humming. But still he had to remain vigilant; he would not take chances, as the humming turned to singing, soft and low.

Hands clasped behind his back, he rocked to and fro on the balls of his feet, stretching and moaning, as he tried to hum away the onset of weariness that was beginning to creep into his muscles and his mind – today had been a long day for him, but his work wasn't quite finished – not yet.

A niggling ache in his lower back flared up again making him grimace in pain. He inhaled deeply and placed his long bony fingers against the bottom of his spine and massaged the troubled area. As he rubbed away at his pain, his humming gradually returned – the corpse lying on the decking beside him seemingly forgotten.

When it finally occurred to him why he was standing on the porch at such an ungodly hour, he looked down at the body and whispered, "Time we got a move on." He kicked the sack and said, "How about a little sing-song before we leave? What about your all-time favourite song, hmm? Lost your tongue have you?" He lashed out again at the sack and said, "I'll lead, and you can come in on the doo-dah-doo-dah!" And in a low mocking tone, he began singing, "*Camptown ladies sing that song . . .*"

He kicked repeatedly at the dead girl's body in the sack, his fury rising and with it, his body temperature. He was sweating again and he'd already had enough of that! Saliva running down his chin, he looked down and whispered "*Happy Birthday, bitch!*"

Fitch took hold of the large knot and dragged the sack down the steps pulling it behind him across the damp grass – and that was just the easy part. He struggled with the dead weight of the girl, and cursed as a pain shot across his lower back causing him to stumble and almost fall headlong over the barrow as he was heaving the body onto the flat steel base. He pulled himself up slowly to his full height, taking long deep breaths in an effort to control the pain.

He did this for a count of ten until the pain had subsided to a dull ache, then he turned and went back to the porch and leaned inside the entrance to the lodge, switched off the light and locked the door.

He made his way wearily towards the locked gate, took a key from his shirt pocket and released the padlock, pulling the gate open just wide enough to push the barrow and its contents out onto a path beyond the confines of the lodge. The path was on a slight incline making it easy for him to push the barrow through the narrow opening, where he stopped, closed the gate again, and put the heavy padlock back in place. *Don't take any chances Fitch old boy.*

He continued on his way along the winding path, ducking as he took a sharp left under the trees and into the dense woodland beyond.

CHAPTER TWO

THE pale misty moonlight falling through the trees helped to guide Fitch back to the grave he had dug earlier that day; his battery-operated lantern held in reserve for the graveside burial. After manoeuvring his weighty cargo along the well-worn path, he couldn't have been more relieved at arriving at the spot where he'd spent most of the morning – the trip back to the grave had taken its toll on him.

He lowered the barrow and stepped back to lean against a nearby tree, waiting for his breathing to return to normal. Sweat trickled down his back, so he unbuttoned his shirt and pulled it off. The relief was almost instant as the cold night air swept across his naked torso, cooling him down quickly as he rolled the shirt into a ball and began drying the moisture from his face, and upper body.

Shouldn't have left it so damn late. Wouldn't have mattered, I suppose, if she had spent the night in the freezer. His body temperature was almost back to normal, but not his energy levels, he was tired, so he allowed his entire weight to sink against a narrow hollow in the tree as fatigue threatened to consume him and render him useless for the task ahead. He had no choice. The job had to be finished.

Rested as much as he could be, Fitch tossed his shirt on the ground beside the barrow and walked along the edge of the grave, admiring his finely honed grave digging skills for this latest victim. *I must congratulate myself*, he thought as he surveyed his work. *Not bad at all!* He paced the length and depth of the grave, mentally gauging if more work was needed. *More than adequate for a small one,* he thought, *no animal will be sniffing around and unearthing this corpse for a free meal.*

As he approached the barrow, he squinted in the semi-darkness at his watch. *Half past midnight, another ten minutes or so should do it*. He was eager to get back to the lodge, and the comfort of his bed.

Fitch lifted the handles high and tipped the barrow up; the sack creaked as it slid off the steel base and made a soft thud on the ground. He knelt and untied the knotted end of the sack, reached inside, and pulled the body free onto the damp earth. He held the sack high, and shook it vigorously until the remaining contents dropped out beside the corpse – the girls severed feet.

He threw the sack back into the barrow and grabbed his shirt off the ground, pulling it on as he got back to his feet. Rubbing at the dull ache at the bottom of his spine, he stared at the dead girl.

Fitch had abducted Debra Johnson on her thirteenth birthday and had ended her life just a few hours ago on what should have been a celebration for the girl and her family, the day she turned fourteen. But, following a yearlong incarceration and a series of violent and sickening punishments during her confinement, today's birthday would be her last. It had become a ritual; Debra Johnson was not the first of his *Birthday Girl* victims and Fitch certainly didn't plan on her being the last. The next one had already been selected.

Johnson's naked body lay face down – Fitch couldn't take his eyes from it. Ignoring the ache in his back he got down on to his knees again and began stroking the cold flesh of her backside; the action seemed to sooth and relax him. The urge to lie down and rest became overwhelming, he gave into it, and like a newborn giraffe he shuffled around on all fours and finally managed to sprawl out beside the corpse in the sour smelling damp earth.

He fidgeted for a while until he found a snug position, resting his head in the hollow of the girl's back he stretched and yawned, clasping his hands together across the top his head, his long fingers covering his crown like a scull cap.

Fitch stared through the branches of the trees into the night sky, the weight of his body sinking into the ground; it was a wonderful experience, being able to relax. *Ten minutes should do it.* He sighed happily. And as he gazed into the blanket of stars flickering like candles on a far away ocean liner, he allowed his mind to wander. His thoughts strayed to the slender copper haired girl he'd seen walking along Bleaksedge Lane on his journey to the hospital. He used the route most days and she had first caught his attention two or three months ago. *You're next. All I have to do is wait; exercise a little patience for just a few more weeks, and then I'm coming for you.* He smiled as he remembered the day he had obtained those vital details; the details needed to fit in with his carefully planned MO.

* * *

As with many plans, luck plays a large part, and with this particular plan, his lucky day happened to be the day Erin Fallon had been brought into the A&E department at the hospital.

Fitch had been with one of his outpatients and making his way back to his office, he spotted her. The girl was still in her gym kit, and whom he presumed was her PE teacher was telling the Triage Nurse what had happened.

"She was playing netball when she clashed with an opponent," he overheard her saying. "She banged her head." Smiling at Erin the teacher added, "The other girl must be thick sculled; she's fine apparently. Hardly felt a thing."

"How do you feel?" the nurse asked in that sympathetic manner Fitch detested, taking the girl's hand and looking at the nasty lump forming on the side of her head.

"A bit sick," she murmured, "And I felt dizzy at first but it's not so bad now."

Fitch couldn't believe his luck, the incident and the timing, which had brought the girl to the hospital, could not have been better.

"I'll take over nurse," he said, asserting his authority and position. "I don't have any more appointments until this afternoon. Plenty of time to deal with this young ladies injury."

The nurse handed over the case notes to the eminent surgeon and turned to Erin, saying reassuringly, "You're in good hands, Erin. This is Mr. Fitch. He's the best in dealing with head injuries."

* * *

Whilst examining Erin Fallon's injury, as a matter of course, he had taken her name, address and most important for his current killing spree, her date of birth. The 6th November, a little over six weeks away.

The dead girl beneath him had been forgotten as he chewed on his lower lip and considered the only problem he foresaw. How would he abduct Erin Fallon? *That*, he thought, *is going to need a lot more planning than the others. They had been easy to take – but this one?* Whenever he had seen her she was never alone. Always with a long-haired youth who she appeared to be flirting with, throwing her head back and tossing her long copper curls from side to side as she laughed at, what he assumed, would have been smutty innuendo.

Fitch turned onto his side and whispered into the dead girl's ear, "You should have shown me at least a *degree* of respect, whore! You didn't, did you? None of you did. All you ever did was torment and ridicule me. I warned you didn't I?"

With a curious expression, he turned and gazed along the length of her body. He slapped her backside hard; his fingers tingled from the force of the slap. The pain thrilled him at the same time, so he slapped her again and again until his fingertips burned.

* * *

Debra Johnson had spent her fourteenth birthday bound and gagged on a hospital gurney in a small windowless room at the back of the lodge, where Fitch had abused her at every available opportunity. Her final day with Fitch fell on her birthday and, as birthdays should be, he intended to make it special. A day she would remember for the rest of her life, well, what she had left of her life, which he planned to be just a matter of hours, rather than days, weeks or months. She had served her purpose and it was time to move on to the next one.

Before gagging the girl, Fitch had begun by removing her teeth with pliers; the pain was excruciating for her and much to Fitch's annoyance, she blacked out. Fitch left her and went down the hall to the kitchen where he filled a large pan with ice-cold water. *This should do the trick. I don't have all day! Other tasks to be dealing with!* He went back to the room; the girl remained unconscious. Fitch stood beside her and poured the entire contents of the pan over her face.

"Wakey, wakey, Miss Johnson!" he shouted. The girl came to, terrified, choking and crying as she tried to pull herself up off the gurney. Fitch grabbed a roll of gaffer tape from the metal tray beneath and tore off a long strip, slapping it across the girl's bloodied mouth. Not satisfied with one strip, he applied two more for good measure.

He picked up the pliers again and pondered what he should do next by way of further punishment. She stared back at him with terror and pain filled eyes. He cocked his head on one side and said, "This is going to hurt – *a lot!*" He grabbed her nose between the pliers, twisting and tugging viscously; he had to resist the urge to break it, because that particular punishment he always saved for much later. He put the pliers down and reached for a clear polythene bag from the metal trolley at his side. Without hesitating, he pulled the bag over the girl's head, holding it firmly in place, long enough to cause as much distress and suffering as possible. Her fingernails tore at the vinyl covering on the gurney; her body convulsed as she struggled for air.

"Almost finished," he said in a cheerful manner. She was barely conscious. He could hear a low wheezing and gurgling, as tears still rained down the side of her face. He glanced at the clock on the windowsill; her brain would start to die within four to six minutes through lack of oxygen. He couldn't delay any longer what was his most sickening act of all. And like the other girls before her, he wanted her conscious for what he was about to do, so he removed the bag and tossed it into a bin.

Fitch took a small electric surgical saw from the trolley, walked across the room, and plugged it in. He went back to the girl, and stared into her eyes, seeing just a flicker of life remaining. He knew she had enough oxygen left in her lungs and her blood for her to be aware of the pain he was about to subject her to. He flicked the switch and the saw buzzed into action. He moved to the other end of the gurney, put on a pair of large plastic glasses, and covered his mouth with a surgical mask. As the blade cut through the thin flesh of her ankle, Debra's eyes bulged almost out of their sockets; her body tensed as she arched her back, and then fell limp.

Debra Johnson died before he had finished removing the first foot, but he continued oblivious to the fact until he had completed the amputation of both feet. Once that job was done, he lit a small acetylene torch and cauterised the stumps to stem the bleeding. He picked up the amputated feet and placed them either side of her head, the toes pointing towards the girl's ears; he stood back and admired the symmetry. The image was truly hideous, but with that came beauty. A hint of a smile danced in his eyes as she stared vacantly back at him, her face taking on a familiar appearance he couldn't quite place. *That's it, 'The Scream' by Edvard Munch. Wonderful!*

He stepped out of the room and returned a couple of minutes later with a Polaroid camera. He hummed quietly as he loaded the photographic paper and positioned himself at the foot of the gurney, considering the best angle for the shot. The picture had to have a harrowing effect, to traumatise and strike horror and revulsion in the mind of the girl's mother – a sight indelibly etched, never to be forgotten.

As a child Fitch had been fascinated by the artwork of John Newton Howitt, whose graphic drawings had adorned the front covers of American pulp magazines brought over by the same soldiers who gave those evil bitches *that* song. He used to imagine the girls in similar *'Damsel in Distress'* poses, being tortured by some crazed madman, or thrown from a speeding train, preferably both.

But even Howitt would not have attempted such a composition as this.

From the position he was to take the photograph he had

determined that, for full impact, the girl's head needed to be raised several inches off the gurney. He wanted her dead eyes to stare straight into the camera. He hurried from the room again and was back in seconds with a thick hardback book. He grabbed her hair, yanked her head up and placed the book at the base of her neck and went back to the foot of the gurney. The desired effect was achieved; her head positioned a good few inches above her shoulders, her eyes staring blindly back at Fitch. *Excellent.*

Satisfied, he moved to the end of the gurney and took a photograph of his work. Sixty seconds later, the picture emerged. He took hold of the corner and waved the photographic paper back and forth until the image was fully developed. He held the picture out to the dead girl. "Here, take a look at this. Look! Aren't you a sight? I have to admit, I'm becoming quite the creative photographer!"

He kissed the picture, making a loud '*mmmwwwaaaaa*' sound. Even in his warped mind, he had to admit the image was horrific and twisted. He couldn't wait to put the photograph inside the belated birthday card and mail it to the girl's mother. "How I would love to be a fly on the wall when you open the envelope and find out what I've done to your little precious."

As a final twist, he had forced the girl to address the envelope to her mother a few days earlier. This had become his signature on the killing of the last three victims, all part of his carefully planned modus operandi.

* * *

His thoughts returned to the job in hand. He stood and went back to the barrow and lit the lantern. With the dim light illuminating the scene, he gazed at the lifeless body. He couldn't help being fascinated by its beauty and youth.

The pain in his lower back returned, in truth it had never really gone away – he'd just blanked it out. The moon had moved across the sky and much of the pale light had gone. The lantern had also dimmed, so he had to work quickly before it became too dark to find his way back to the lodge.

As with the others, he had one final evil act to perform before he disposed of her. He reached for the spade, raised his arms high and brought it crashing down with full force into her face. In the quiet of the night forest, the loud cracking of bone sounded like tree branch snapping, as black treacle like fluid oozed into the earth from her crushed skull.

He stood for several minutes, fascinated by the ugly mass of mangled bone and tissue, and watched the dark fluid seep into the ground around her, turning her long blond hair black. "Not so pretty now, eh?"

Fitch used the spade to lever the corpse over the edge and into the dark hole. He picked up the severed feet and threw them on top of the body, then leaned over the grave to take in the scene for the last time, slapping the dirt from his hands before he began shovelling large piles of earth into the hole.

Fitch grimaced as he bit down hard on his lip and cursed his pain; it was becoming unbearable and difficult for him to work quickly. He had no choice though; he knew he had to work through it. The grave had to be filled before the dawn broke. He needed a distraction to take his mind off his backache, so he turned his thoughts to Erin Fallon, and how he was going to take her.

CHAPTER THREE

UNLIKE today, when Leonard Fitch had started his murder spree many years ago at the age of nineteen, he didn't have the means to hide and torture his victims as he'd wanted to, so he'd been careful to take them out quickly. He chose them cautiously, teenage schoolgirls and college students from all backgrounds, using various methods to take their lives and dispose of their bodies where they wouldn't be found for some time. He got a huge kick out of seeing the trail of devastation he left in his wake. Watching the pleading tear streaked faces of the girl's mothers on television begging and appealing for their little girls to be returned to them. Fitch alone knew they would not be coming back.

In April 1953, he killed for the first time. He was a student at the Queen Mary College in London, and although he didn't have the same problems he'd had at school, he still harboured a hatred for females of all ages. Despite this, he was attracted to them in a way he couldn't explain. He loved the beauty and the smell of an attractive young girl, a sucker for a pretty face. He never thought of himself as a paedophile – he wasn't into pre-pubescent girls, but he did like them in their early teens, before they'd had the chance to turn into what he regarded as *'God forsaken whores'*.

He didn't even know the name of the first one. A Fresher at the University of London, he met her at an end of term dance. Not a date, no. He never was the dating kind – his mother had made sure of that by destroying all of his confidence when it came to girls – but he had been watching this particular girl for some time having seen her around the campus. Not particularly beautiful, but with her long dark hair and striking blue eyes she attracted a lot of attention from the male students.

On the evening of the dance, he plucked up the courage to make a play for her. She was at the bar talking to a girl friend when Fitch walked up beside her. As she was a good eighteen inches shorter than him, he had to stoop to speak.

"Sorry?" she said, unable to make out what Fitch had said above the noise.

"I said would you like a drink?" Fitch repeated. "Err, with me I mean. I can see you have a drink, but would you like to have a drink with me?" Just at that point the music stopped and everyone around the bar turned to see who was shouting.

"With *you*?" the girl said in a strong Black Country accent. "You are jokin' aren't you?" She nudged her friend and burst out laughing. "You 'eard this Jules? He wants to buy me a drink!" The two of them laughed hysterically, as did all the other students hanging around the bar at the time.

The thought of committing murder had crossed his mind in the past. Often during lectures, particularly those concerning dissection, his mind wandered to the ways of taking a human life and disposing of the body bit by bit. He took an interest in drugs that incapacitated or disabled people – the perfect way to pick up girls when you looked the way he did, but he had never really considered using them on anyone. Not until that moment anyway.

Memories of those girls back in Grammar School swirling around in his head, Fitch picked up his jacket and left the party, and began plotting his revenge.

The girl's demise came only days later. Despite his medical knowledge, he decided in the end to go for brute force, so the police investigation would not be focussed on those in the medical profession. Death by strangulation was the verdict after the body was discovered a week after the event. End of term proved an opportune moment to hide a body, Fitch found out, giving him time to be well away from the crime scene and the police, who were clueless as to the perpetrator and motive.

* * *

Ten more victims followed, spread over many years, but since changing his modus operandi this last one was number four in the series; *'The Birthday Girls'*, the press called them. He liked that; he had always wanted to have a title for his killings. The random nature of his earlier murders meant nobody could see a pattern, and none of them were ever linked to this latest spate.

So now he had number five lined up, but first, some important business to attend to – preparations to make. The lodge needed a little tidying before his next victim could be brought along. It would be a diversion from his current plans, but a necessary one.

CHAPTER FOUR

Preston, Lancashire, July 1975

JOHN Fallon was bursting to tell his wife and children the good news. The family had just sat down for their evening meal. Whenever John Fallon was anxious or excited about anything, he couldn't keep his legs still and right now his legs were twitching like the clappers under the dining room table. Knife and fork at the ready, he waited impatiently for his wife to finish saying grace. She crossed herself, raised her head then nodded at the family to begin.

John didn't waste any time getting stuck in, he stabbed at a large gravy covered sausage, sliced off the end and scooped a pile of mashed spuds on top of it. He was eager to share his good news with the family, but just as eager to get stuck into his dinner. Fork on its way to his mouth, he said, "I have some excellent news for you, Helen!" then shoved the food into his mouth and began chewing loudly.

His children's heads sprung up quickly, they gazed excitedly at him, waiting to hear what he was going to say. His eldest daughter, Erin, shot a wide-eyed smile at her mother then looked directly at her father. She couldn't wait; "Are we going to like the news too, Dad?" His mouth was too full to answer her so he tapped the end of his nose with his knife and winked at his beloved Erin.

Neive, the youngest of his four kids, giggled, "Mum look! Dad's got gravy on his nose!"

"You're supposed to set an example, not behave like a pig at the trough!" She said, tossing a tea towel across the table at him. "Wipe your face!" She'd been brought up well and was a stickler for manners. Helen glared at him whilst he wiped the food from his face; the same cold expression in her eyes that John had seen all too often recently.

John looked away embarrassed, his eyes narrowed and his brow furrowed. No matter how hard he tried, Helen's attitude towards him was growing colder by the day. He'd hoped that she'd be in a better mood than she had been when he had left for work that morning but that clearly wasn't the case. He chanced a furtive glance at her, wondering what could be making her so ill tempered.

As John watched Helen absently pushing the food around her plate, a thought struck him, *Christ! What if she's pregnant again? Oh, Jesus God Almighty!* He couldn't cope with another child. They'd both agreed that four was more than enough. He broke into a sweat at the thought of baby number five. *Nah couldn't be, need to have sex for that to happen!* With the tea towel she'd thrown at him, he wiped his face and forehead and swallowed hard.

Desperate to cheer her up, he cleared his throat loudly, sat up straight in his chair and leaned toward her. Reaching across the table for her hand he said, "Well, Helen. Do you want to hear my news?"

The children stared from one parent to the other, waiting for their mother to answer. Neive's legs swung back and forth under the table. Helen looked up from her dinner plate briefly and pulled her hand out of his in the pretence that she wanted to continue eating. Feigning a cheerfulness she didn't feel, she said, "Come on then, tell us before you have everyone's dinner cold."

He tried to reach for her hand again but she'd tucked her elbows tightly against her sides now. Helen's cold demeanour and distinct lack of interest had robbed him of much of his enthusiasm; still, he tried his best now to sound cheerful. "The boss called me into his office today, and you'll never guess what?"

Helen was becoming more and more annoyed at his wanting to

drag out the mysterious news. She avoided looking at him as she mumbled, "For pity's sake, John, just get on with it will you?"

Another sideswipe. *What the feck is up with the woman?* He forked another piece of sausage and shoved it in his mouth, looking directly at Helen as she pushed her food around the plate. There was an uncomfortable silence at the table as the children stopped eating to look at each other.

At thirty-five, Helen still had her youthful looks, despite a hard life. She had fallen for John Fallon the moment she had met him, he was quite a catch back then. Glancing up at him now, she wondered what that attraction was. She saw the hurt expression on his face and even though his noisy eating made her want to shove his head in his plate, she knew that she ought to make an effort to show some interest in his tedious chitchat. She said in an apologetic tone, "Come on then, put us all out of our misery, John, we're dying to hear your news, aren't we kids?"

The four children nodded their heads vigorously as they looked at their father expectantly.

"I've been promoted." His tone was flat; she'd really upset him but not wanting her to know, he forced a smile and a nerve in his top lip started twitching uncontrollably, making his smile quiver, another obvious sign of John's anxiety.

John turned to his eldest son, Sean, who was sitting to his left, and playfully punched him in the top of the arm, "Son, you're dad is now the new works foreman at Preston Engineering!"

"Wow Dad! Does that mean that you're a boss?" Sean's eyes lit up.

"Yes. It certainly does, son!"

Glancing at his wife, he lowered his voice in a conspiratorial manner and said to the rest of his brood, "I have my own office now as well with my name on the door!" Then he added, in what he considered to be a posh English accent, "John P.W. Fallon. Works Foreman!"

"What do you think of that then, son?" Liam was still chuckling at his Dad's attempt at a posh English accent; the other three kids cheered and clapped.

"Enough! And mind your manners at the dinner table!" Helen said. The room fell quiet again. She looked away from her children's crestfallen faces, realising that she was being unnecessarily harsh with them; it wasn't her children that were making her unhappy. She forced a smile and said, "Let's have some quiet at the dinner table and your father can tell us all about his new promotion."

Her striking green eyes were suddenly alive again, and the swift change in her mood softened her features. She put her knife and fork down on her plate and clasped her hands together as if she was about to thank the Lord again.

"A promotion, eh? Oh, John, that's the most fantastic news I've heard in a long time. I'm pleased as our Lady herself! Will it mean that you'll be getting more money, then?" She was clearly interested now and it lifted John's spirits.

The kids chattered loudly across the table at each other again; this time it was their father who quieted them. He raised his hands, palm up, signalling for silence, and in a more serious tone he said, "Come on now. As your mother said, let's have a wee bit of order at the table."

"Sorry, Dad." Erin said, "It's just that we're so happy and excited for you." He winked and smiled at her "Thank you, sweetheart."

John turned back to Helen and said, "I've done the arithmetic, Helen. I'll be clearing roughly thirty pounds a week more than I'm bringing home now." She was stunned. Her body visibly relaxed and a huge smile of disbelief lit up her face.

John felt a lump in his throat. He desperately hoped that the change in their fortunes might bring them back together again, rekindle the love they'd shared for each other before they'd left Ireland thirteen years ago. Deep down he thought that she still harboured resentment toward him for having had to relocate them to England for the sake of a better job and a better standard of living, despite the fact that it was her desire for material things that drove him to that in the first place.

She broke into his thoughts, "John . . ." she sat up straight, elbows on the table, hands clasped together tightly under her chin, and gushed, "Oh, just think! We won't have to scrimp and scrape anymore! I can't believe it . . . thirty pounds a week more? Oh my, my!"

Helen's mind was racing as she gazed around the table at her kids and that was when the thought struck her. "John, I've just had a fantastic idea!"

He couldn't help smiling at her; he hadn't seen her look this animated in such a long time. "Go on, Helen, tell us."

"A new house, John! Do you think we could afford to move to a new house?"

Now there's a bolt out of the blue, he definitely wasn't expecting that. "A new house eh? That's thrown me. You'll have to let me think about that one, Helen."

He carried on eating as he gave some thought to what she'd just said – in fact he started to give it some serious consideration. *Perhaps a new house, better area, might be what we need – it might even put the spark back into our marriage.*

They'd lived in the small run-down three-bedroom semi in a rough part of Preston since they had come over from Ireland, when Erin had been just eighteen months old and she was now in her third year at the local high school.

He looked at his eldest child and for the first time he was genuinely shocked to realise that the apple of his eye was no longer a little girl; at almost fifteen, she was growing into a lovely young woman. He was pleased that she'd inherited her mother's good looks and petite build. He knew one thing for sure; she was going to break some hearts. She had stunning green eyes and long copper curls that framed a delicate heart shaped face. The pride he felt at that moment, he couldn't put into words if asked. Helen interrupted his thoughts again.

"Well, John? Can we?" Eager for an answer, she reached for his hand and lightly squeezed it.

"I think it's the best idea yet, Helen," he said. "And since you're asking, have you got somewhere in mind?"

"Hindthorpe! It's a lovely place and it'd be good for the kids to grow up somewhere decent and the schools would be better there, too."

"Aww, no!" Erin interrupted before her father got the chance to reply. "Please, Mum . . . we can't move all the way out there!" The whole family turned to look at Erin.

"That's enough, madam!" Helen snapped. Erin dropped her head and stared at her plate, her mother tutted loudly. Helen turned her attention back to her husband and said, "Can we go this weekend and have a look round? We could call in at the estate agents to see what properties are available for rent."

He nodded, another smile plastered all over his face. "Yes. Indeed we can!" And looking round the table at everyone he continued, "We'll all go. Treat it as a family day out, eh? What do you say, kids? And if the weather's nice we could take a picnic and have it down by the river like we did last time we were there, do you remember?"

"Yeah, last summer!" Sean shouted. "Liam fell in the river, didn't you Liam?"

"You pushed me in more like!" Liam said. Everyone laughed. Everyone that is apart from Erin, whose face turned to stone.

Her father noticed that she'd gone quiet. He said gently, "What do you think, Erin?" She couldn't bring herself to look at him for fear of bursting into tears. Seeing the expression on her face, he said, "You could even ask Caitlin if she'd like to come with us. You'd like that wouldn't you?"

He turned to his wife and said, "Helen, why don't you have a word and square it with Caitlin's mum?"

She glanced at Erin, rolled her eyes in annoyance and said non-too kindly, "I'll call and see her in the morning after I've seen the kids off to school" and then to Erin she snapped, "*MANNERS*, Erin! Your father has just asked you a question!"

Ignoring her mother, Erin looked directly at her dad and said; "I don't want to move to another town, Dad" Her emotions getting the better of her, she began sniffling. "If we have to go and live in Hindthorpe it means that I won't see Caitlin or any of my other friends again." Before he could answer, she burst into tears, jumped up from the table and ran from the room.

Clearly not impressed and showing no sympathy for her eldest daughter, Helen said, "Leave her . . . she'll come round to the idea as soon as she realises she has no choice in the matter."

Helen picked up her knife and fork again and pointed at Erin's plate. "Sean, take Erin's food into the kitchen and put it in the oven! She'll eat it later." She turned to John. "You've spoiled that girl rotten! It's no wonder she's sulking, she's used to you giving in to her all the time!" Pursing her lips, she shook her head and glared at him, "She has you wrapped around her little finger and you can't see it can you?"

He sighed heavily, "Yes, yes, so you keep tellin' me." Shoving his unfinished meal away from him, he stood and said, "Liam, you finish that if you want, son. I've lost my appetite!"

The nasty side of Helen had returned all too quickly, as she yelled at him, "Where do you think you're going? You've not finished your meal!"

"To get some fresh air, it's a bit stifling in here!" he shot back at her.

His anger was rising and as he got to the door he called out over his shoulder, "What you fail to see, Helen, is that she's a good girl, and you're far too hard on her . . . you always have been!"

CHAPTER FIVE

Preston, Lancashire, September1975

$\mathbb{A}$S Erin knew would happen, her mother got what she wanted and just eight weeks after her father's announcement about his promotion, a large removal van pulled up in front of the house and three men in brown overalls were given complete control as they began boxing up and loading all the Fallon's furniture and belongings on board for the twenty-two mile journey to the new house in Hindthorpe.

It was chaos downstairs. Erin could hear her parents shouting at her siblings to stop running in and out while furniture was being carried out of the house. Erin had no intention of helping with any aspect of the move. Instead, she stood impatiently on the landing outside her room, arms folded defensively in a gesture of defiance, as the last of her bedroom furniture was carried out by two of the removal men. "Right love, we've finished up here now. Why don't you go and have a last look, eh?" She didn't reply; she hated them.

She went into her room and closed the door quietly behind her and sat down on the floor beneath the window. It was a warm sunny day, yet her bedroom felt cold and depressing now. The tears she'd been holding back all morning finally filled her eyes and she began crying softly as she stared at the bare walls and the space where her bed had been less than half an hour ago, the indentations in the carpet reminding her of just where this and every piece of furniture had been. The two single beds, her dressing table, her favourite chair, the large double wardrobe she'd shared with Neive; all gone, just memories and ghosts now remained.

She crawled across the soft pile of the carpet and lay down on her side. The thought that she would never sleep in this room again brought more tears, raining down her face. Although she had had to share the room with Neive, she had always considered it to be *her* room, *her* bolthole; it had been for such a long time, at least until Neive had come along, her gorgeous, mischievous little sister.

Thinking about all the fun and the secrets she and her best friend, Caitlin, had shared when she'd stopped over, made her cry out loud, "Oh, God, I'm going to miss her so much!" She wept all over again. Erin had done nothing but cry since finding out that they were moving away. This room was where she had dreamt her dreams, where she felt safe and cosseted during long dark winter nights, year after year. He selfish mother had robbed her of her happiness, her friends, her home – everything!

Wrapped up in her childhood memories, Erin had no idea how long she'd been lying on the floor when she heard the bedroom door open, making a soft whoosh sound as it brushed along the pile of the thick carpet; her dad never did get around to planing the bottom of the door after he'd fitted the carpet. She and Neive had to give the door a bit of a shove before they pushed it open. The upside was, after the carpet had been fitted, her brothers couldn't sneak in anymore and scare her while she was completely absorbed in one of her books. Quickly wiping the tears from her eyes she looked over her shoulder and saw Neive standing there with a puzzled expression on her face, "What are you doing, Erin? Why are you lying on the floor?"

"Because I am. That's why!" She sniffed loudly, wiping her nose with the sleeve of her cardigan. "Now leave me alone and GO AWAY!" Neive didn't move, she turned and popped her head out and glanced quickly up and down the landing and then she pushed the door closed again. She went across the room and sat down beside Erin.

"Have you been crying, Erin?" She said, absently flicking her ponytail back and forth between her chubby little fingers, a frown creasing her smooth young brow. "I don't like it when you're sad, Erin."

Erin didn't answer; instead she looked away from Neive's questioning gaze and stared into the hazy sunlight streaming in through the bedroom window; the soft warm light touched her face, comforting her for a few fleeting seconds before the stark cold reality of why she was lying on the floor of her now vacant bedroom, struck her again. *I can't believe I'll never sleep in here again. I was happy here, and now she's gone and ruined everything.*

Neive interrupted her thoughts again, reaching out for Erin's hand as she gushed breathlessly in her little girl's chatter. "Dad's been looking for you *all over the place*, Erin; and mum's really cross. She said she asked you to help her pack the knives and forks and plates and cups and saucers and you didn't do it." Without drawing a breath she continued, "She's *really* cross, Erin, and she keeps shouting at me and Liam, and Sean, and we haven't *even done anything*! And it's not fair, Erin!"

Finally pausing for air, Neive got up on to her knees and gently tugged at Erin's hand, "*Will* you come down stairs, Erin? *Please?* If you do mum might not be mad at us and if you don't Dad might come to find you, and then he'll see that you're just lying on the floor and he'll be mad at you. I don't like it when Dad gets cross, Erin."

Erin couldn't argue with Neive's point, and knowing that she couldn't put off the inevitable, Erin forced a small smile and said, "Okay. Come on then." She dragged herself up off the floor. Neive scrambled up with her still clasping her hand, she gazed up at Erin, a worried expression in her big blue eyes. Neive adored her big sister and right now she was feeling more than a little worried that Erin might not go with them to the new house. Neive had overheard Erin asking Caitlin if her mum might let Erin move into their house with them. With this thought playing on her mind, Neive said, "Your bedroom at the new house might be better than this one, Erin. And if it is, do you promise not to be sad anymore?"

Erin looked down into Neive's lovely blue eyes and pleading

expression. Absently she brushed a few loose strands of hair from in front of Neive's eyes. She shrugged her shoulders and said, "No. It never could be, Neive. I just know that I'm going to hate it!"

They approached the bedroom door together, hand in hand. Erin turned and looked towards the sunlight coming in through the window, tears back in her eyes as she lingered for a moment just inside the doorway and said to herself, *Just one last look.* Swiping at her nose and the corners of her eyes, she sighed before turning and gently pulling the door closed for the final time. Erin followed Neive downstairs, nervously expecting a stern reprimand from her selfish mother.

CHAPTER SIX

Cumbria, September 1976

LEONARD Fitch collapsed on the bed. Much as he craved a long hot bath after his hard day's work he was simply too exhausted. He always felt this way after a kill, the emotional high after taking a young life only to be replaced by depression. Like a dog whose favourite toy no longer squeaked because of the relentless chewing, Fitch lay in the dark thinking about how good it had felt when he extracted that final breath, but no matter how hard he tried he couldn't get that feeling back. He knew there was only one way to achieve that high again and his mind wandered to the copper haired girl he'd seen on Bleaksedge Lane. It was time to put his next plan into action. He closed his eyes and said, *Erin Fallon, you're next.*

* * *

Violet Johnson poured herself another large gin and stared at the cards on the mantelpiece; her vision blurring through the tears and the alcohol she'd been drinking since getting up early that morning. It had been her little girl's birthday three days earlier but there were no celebrations this year. Debra had disappeared a little over twelve months ago, never to be seen or heard of again, but Violet always had hope, until that morning, the morning she had received *that* envelope.

Violet Johnson's husband was not there to catch her as she collapsed in the hallway of their home; he had walked out on her just after last Christmas. The stress of what had happened had put too great a strain on their marriage, especially when, as the stepfather, *he* was in the frame as one of the main suspects.

Violet was alone; trying to cope as best she could, refusing never to give up believing that Debra *would* be found safe and well, and would come home. "I know deep in my heart that she's still alive; call it mother's intuition. Call it what you will, but I just know that my little girl's still alive, she's out there *somewhere!*" She'd tell her husband countless times a day, day after day. "I know *deep down in my heart!* I know that she's not dead because I'd *know* if she was, I swear I would know it, Frank!"

Violet Johnson couldn't count the number of appeals she'd made on TV and in the press. "Surely somebody must know where she is, the whole country must have seen her picture by now, Frank!" Frank had grown weary of listening. He believed that Debra was dead. He would often complain to his workmates, "*How could a whole country be made aware of this missing girl and see her picture almost daily in the papers and on the news for God's sake, and not one single person come forward with some scrap of information as to her whereabouts? She must be dead! If not, she has to be living somewhere, with someone? Surely?*" But, in the end, he had grown tired of coming home from work to a dirty house, no food on the table and a drunkard for a wife who was always crashed out on the couch, empty bottle of gin on the floor beside her. So he had decided to call it a day. Before leaving for work one morning, just a couple of weeks before Christmas, he left Violet Johnson a short note telling her that he'd had enough and he wouldn't be coming back that night, or ever again.

A vacant expression in her eyes, and a heart laden with grief and despair, Violet Johnson slowly climbed the stairs up to the steam-filled bathroom. The bathtub was full to overflowing. She turned off the taps. Dense hot steam billowed up into her face turning her grey complexion a deep pink as the water cascaded over the top of the bathtub.

The bathroom used to be her pride and joy; it was the only room in the house to have had a complete makeover – it used to be, during happier times, her idea of heaven, where she went for a good long soak and some peace and quiet after spending all day on her feet at the foul smelling local abattoir. She'd worked there for fourteen years and yet she'd never got used to the vile stench of animal blood and guts. That stench still lingered in her nostrils, to this day.

She had stopped going to work after Debra went missing; her every waking moment filled with the vision of her only child and she had fallen into a deep depression which eventually cost her her job.

Violet Johnson placed her glass on the vanity unit, slipped off her dressing gown and, without even testing the water, stepped in to the piping hot bath. The water reached her chin as it splashed noisily over the side of the tub slapping loudly onto the linoleum floor covering. She picked up the card again. It had arrived that morning, three days after Debra's birthday, and recognising the handwriting as that of her daughter's, her heart hammered out of control in her ribcage, almost bursting with hope and joy in the knowledge that Debra was obviously still alive!

With trembling hands, she tore open the large pink envelope and pulled out the card. The greeting on the front said *HAPPY BIRTHDAY TO A VERY SPECIAL DAUGHTER*. Why would she send herself a birthday card? Is this some sort of a sick game? Disbelieving and confused, she opened the card. A look of horror and revulsion spread across her face as her clenched fist flew to her mouth. The macabre image in the picture, taped to the inside of the card, stared out at her; it brought Violet Johnson to her knees howling with grief like a mortally wounded animal.

She reached above her head to the glass tumbler full of neat gin and downed it in one before dropping it onto the floor next to the card. Then she picked up the packet on the side of the bath, unwrapped the razor blade and without hesitation slashed at her wrist three times, severing the artery on the final stroke

As her lifeblood spilled into the bathwater, turning it a deep claret colour, Violet Johnson closed her eyes for the last time; the picture of her little girl's lifeless eyes and her severed feet placed either side of her head, she was taking it with her to her own grave; her soul would never rest in peace – Leonard Fitch would be thrilled.

CHAPTER SEVEN

Hindthorpe, September 1975

A S the Fallon family pulled up outside their new home, Erin stared straight ahead and refused to join in the excited conversation in the car about how lovely the trees were and her mother's ridiculous gushing. "Oh and just look at the size of the garden, John, it's so much bigger than I remember!"

Erin glared at the back of her mother's head and silently mimicked her, '*Look at the size of the garden, John . . .*'

In a hurry to get in to the house before the removal van arrived, Helen pulled her oversized handbag onto her knee and began rummaging inside for the only set of keys the letting agent had handed to them the previous day.

She pulled everything out of the bag, hairbrush, scarf, a pair of tights and cosmetics bag along with countless envelopes and scraps of paper, which she tossed onto her husband's lap. John frowned, what the hell is she doing now? Panic creased her brow at the thought that she might have left the keys in the top drawer of the sideboard, which she realised, was now stored in the removal van, somewhere between Preston and Hindthorpe, "Oh, *no*! Please don't say I forgot to take them out!"

As she threw more of the handbag's contents at John, he said, "For God's sake, Helen! What are you looking for, woman?"

"The keys! I can't find – " her hand flew to her chest and she laughed, "Oh, here they are! Thank God!" She beamed at John as she gathered the contents of her handbag from his lap, shoving everything back in again, in no particular order, then she turned to the children in the back of the car and said, "Come on, kids! Let's go and see our lovely new home!" Giggling like a giddy teenager, she turned to her husband and playfully pinched his fleshy cheek and said, "That means you as well, John Fallon!"

The two boys scrambled out of the car, pushing and shoving each other in a scramble to get to the gate first. Neive sat squashed in the corner of the back seat next to Erin. Knowing how unhappy Erin was about leaving their old house, she tapped her big sister on the wrist and whispered; "Erin, look. It's so nice, there's a big garden too, look . . ." Erin shrugged her shoulders; she wouldn't look.

"Aww, *please* look at the house, Erin! There are lots and lots of trees!"

"I'm not interested, Neive!"

"Well I like it, so I'm getting out!" She struggled with the door, it was too heavy for her to push open, "Dad? I can't open the door. Will you help me, please?"

John looked at Erin through the rear view mirror and said, "Erin, help your little sister, and for the love of God, cheer up! It's not the end of the world."

Reluctantly, Erin leaned across her sister and pushed the door open so Neive could get out of the car. Erin didn't follow her; she remained in the back seat of the car arms folded tightly in a gesture of defiance.

Her father looked at her again through the mirror. He could feel her sadness, yet he didn't know what he could do to make her happy again. He was all too aware of what a wrench it had been for Erin to have to say goodbye to all her friends, especially Caitlin; they'd been almost inseparable since the day they'd started school together at four years old. He also knew how much she enjoyed being at the local high school with all the friends she'd made in the last couple of years, and for all those reasons he couldn't help thinking he was entirely responsible for how unhappy she was now. And seeing Erin so miserable and forlorn had put a real damper on what should have been a day of celebration for the whole family.

John sighed and, as if it was a huge effort, got out of the car and locked the driver's door. He stood for a moment taking in his new surroundings, before resting his gaze on the house Helen had insisted they had to have. No. 18 Florence Terrace was to be a fresh start, and the beginning of a brighter future for them – apart from Erin, it would seem. *Well,* John thought, *Helen said that Erin would come around to the idea in the end. She has to, because there's no going back now.*

His thoughts were interrupted when he heard, rather than saw, the removal van turn in at the top of the terrace and start making its way slowly towards the house. Florence Terrace was a narrow tree-lined road and the driver was inching along taking care not to prang any of the cars parked on either side of the road.

The burden of Erin's sadness weighed heavy on John's shoulders; what in the world could he do to make her happy again? He shook his head as he stepped to the rear passenger door and opened it wide. Holding out his hand he said, "C'mon, Erin'. You can't sit there all day. You've got to accept that this is our new home now. C'mon, sweetheart, give me your hand."

"I can't Dad. Will you take me home? Please?" She dropped her head against the back of the passenger seat, covered her face with her hands and sobbed.

John knelt by the car door and pulled Erin towards him, "Come on, sweetheart. This is your home now. There's no going back, Erin."

CHAPTER EIGHT

THE Fallon's new home was an impressive detached Victorian property with four imposing leaded bay windows facing out on to a huge front and side garden. Erin would later describe in a letter to Caitlin, '*it's a very grand house, Caitlin, and the garden's enormous! Neive and the boys love it here, but it's not home, at least for me it isn't and it never will be!*'

A variety of well-established trees surrounded the garden; twenty-three in total, Neive had counted them. She ran from room to room calling out to anyone who would listen, "We've got twenty-three trees and a *real Christmas tree* of our own!"

John and Erin trudged side-by-side along the shiny cobbled footpath to the front door. They could hear Neive inside the house, shrieking, "We've got a Christmas tree! We've got a Christmas tree!"

"Have you heard Neive? I bet she's flying around in there like a meadow sprite!" John said.

Erin forced a smile. "Well I'm glad someone's happy."

John pushed the front door open wide and standing aside he motioned for Erin to enter first. "Ladies before Gentlemen!" In no mood to be humoured, she lowered her head and stepped inside the doorway, making it almost impossible for her dad to get past into the large hallway. He rolled his eyes heavenward as he gently moved her aside. "The removal men are here sweetheart, we need to move out of the way."

The entrance was twice as wide as it was long and there were doors on both sides all the way to the end of the hallway. The first two doors opposite each other opened up into large *reception rooms* – that was how her mother had described them after viewing the house for the first time, and Erin could see at least another three doors along the length of the hallway.

The sound of shouting and laughter echoed down the hallway from the other end of the house, and John pointed to where the noise came from. "Right down there is the kitchen and there's the cloakroom and the pantry, and the cellar door is in the recess just before the kitchen."

"Oh . . ." Erin said, not the least bit interested.

"C'mon, Erin, I'll do the guided tour with you, and then you can choose your bedroom, eh?"

As she entered the first of the two reception rooms, her surroundings were not lost on her, the first thing to capture her attention was the high ceiling painted silver, of all colours, and her gaze swept down the dusky pink walls to the elaborately designed marble fireplace. She began to wonder if her parents had gone mad. *How can we afford to live in a place like this?*

She pulled her chunky Aran cardigan around her as she shivered and wrinkled her nose as she sniffed the stale air. "Smells damp."

"It'll be fine when we get that fire going. Just look at the size of that thing, we could build a bonfire in it!" Still no smile from Erin.

He stepped across the room to the large bay window where he looked out onto the garden, admiring the variety of well-established trees. Erin walked across the room and stood beside him. "Dad, the size of this place, it must be costing you a fortune. Can we afford it?"

John turned to her and smiled, "Darlin' we can *more* than afford this house. So if that's what's troubling you, Erin, you can put the thought right out of your pretty little head."

He put his arm around her shoulder and hugged her close, thinking he'd give anything to see her look happy again. Still not convinced, Erin gazed up at him as he continued, "I'm making a lot more money now, which is why we're able to afford a bigger house in a decent neighbourhood. And, trust me sweetheart, you'll make lots of new friends –" He felt Erin's body stiffen so he added quickly, "And I don't have to tell you that Caitlin's welcome to stay over with us whenever she wants and as often as she wants, provided her mum's okay with that. Now, let's go and have a look at the bedrooms. You can have your pick. You won't have to share with our Neive either because you'll each have a bedroom of your own here. How's that, eh?"

"Okay, I suppose . . ." Again that note of indifference in her voice,

Erin trailed her father back into the hallway, up the wide curving staircase leading to a broad landing with numerous rooms off it. Erin could hear her mother downstairs at the other end of the house shouting at Liam and Sean to stop arguing and to come and help her unpack the boxes the removal men had just carried through to the kitchen. "And, Neive, for the love of God! Will you stop counting trees and come and lend me a hand in the kitchen!" It hadn't gone unnoticed by Erin that her mother hadn't even bothered to ask where she was.

Erin peered round the door of the first room; she didn't give it a second glance. She muttered, "No. I don't like it." She followed her dad to the next room; again she peered round the door and after a cursory glance, shrugged her shoulders and nodded her head. John began to wonder if she might insist on sleeping in the car overnight. Winning Erin round was turning out to be much more difficult than he had anticipated. Crossing his fingers inside his coat pocket and uttering a silent prayer, he led her along the landing to the third room.

He pushed the door open and stood aside. Arms still folded tight against her chest in a defensive stance, she stepped past him and stood in the doorway. A strange feeling swept over her as she stared at the magnificent round leaded window. Outside the window was a majestic looking tree with spectacular burgundy and copper coloured leaves. The strong autumn sunlight shimmered through the leaves, dappling the entire room in a gorgeous crimson glow. Erin was dazzled. She let out a long, deep breath. Her shoulders relaxed and the tension she had felt all day seemed to be slipping away. The room was bathed in an array of warm pinks and deep scarlet; the effect was that of an otherworldly, enchanting place.

John stepped inside the doorway and watched her, waiting for her to turn about and walk past him with another sullen rebuff. He was about to suggest they look at the next room when she turned to face him.

John was taken aback at the wonder on Erin's face. In a split-second, his mind went back in time to when Erin was just two years old. It was Christmas Eve and after Helen had finished dressing the Christmas tree she had gone up stairs woke Erin up and brought her down to see the tree. Helen had spent all evening dressing it, John remembered remarking to Helen that it was the grandest tree he'd seen yet; *even better than those expensive trees in Lewis' and Debenham's store windows.*

Helen had put Erin down just inside the living room and John had watched Erin, her little bear tucked firmly under her arm, totter towards the large tree in the bay window. He had been completely overwhelmed by the wide-eyed innocence of his child; her little mouth open wide, forming the perfect 'O' as she turned and looked from one parent to the other, her blue eyes full of tears and wonder, shimmering like sapphires. He had looked away as he tried to swallow the lump in his throat and hide the emotion in his own eyes.

Now almost fifteen years old, Erin stood facing her dad with that very same look of wonder in her eyes. John Fallon was surprised and shocked at his emotions; nearly thirteen years on and she was doing it to him again, a different tree, a different place this time, and he had to swallow the lump in his throat that threatened to reduce him to tears.

Unable to make direct eye contact with his daughter, he peered over her shoulder out the window and all he could think of saying was, "I know, it's beautiful. Japanese maple."

"Dad, I love it!" She crossed the room, her movements light and relaxed, as she took in every nook and cranny before turning to her father and asking, "Can I have this room . . . *please?*" The sudden and unexpected change in her mood was remarkable.

John couldn't deny that his relief, at seeing the apple of his eye smiling again, was overwhelming. *Thank you, Lord, thank you!* He stepped across the room and ruffled Erin's long curly hair, "Of course, you can, sweetheart. I want you to be happy, Erin. And you will be. I promise. Now, convince me I didn't imagine it and let me see that smile again, eh?"

She hugged him close, "Dad, I love you lots but it doesn't mean that I'm going to be happy here. I can't tell you how sad I feel about not being able to spend time with Caitlin every day, and I'm dreading starting at the new school mum's enrolled me in."

John rested his chin on the top of Erin's head as he stroked her hair, gazing through the window, deep in thought. He loved his kids but, although he would never admit it, Erin was his favourite, his first-born, his pride and joy, the apple of his eye. And as he held her close he hated the fact that he'd taken something special away from her, her best friend and the security of the place she had called home, the only home she had ever known. She was growing up into a wonderful, caring and intelligent young woman. The knowledge of what a wrench it had been and how much it hurt Erin to have left her childhood friends behind, tugged hard at his heartstrings.

Still struggling to keep his emotions in check, John held Erin away from him and said, "No more tears, Erin, or you'll make your old dad cry and we can't have that!" Taking her hands in his, he said, "Erin, listen to me. Nothing in life stays the same. And now that you're growing up, you'll find some things change for the better and some not and you'll have to deal with the emotions – happy or sad – that change brings."

He cleared his throat noisily, something he did when he was nervous. He started again, "The thing is . . . well . . . erm . . ." Unable to find the right words, he paused and turned away for a moment then said, "You see, Erin . . . it's like this, you have to adapt and deal with the changes, you know, like when you're faced with a challenge, something you have to overcome."

He was getting the hang of it now so he continued, "What I'm trying to say is that you should always try to turn a bad situation on its head, so that you come out on top . . . so to speak." The expression on Erin's face said it all. *She thinks I've lost the bloody plot!*

He ruffled her hair again and smiled, "Think about it, Erin, you're a bright young woman, I'm sure you'll get the gist of what I'm trying to say – albeit not very well! I'm not very good at this sort of thing," He laughed, "the look on your face is confirmation of that!" Changing the subject now, he said, "And, Erin, you can still Caitlin. Like I've already said, she's welcome here *anytime*. She can stop over at weekends and if her mum agrees, she can stay during the school holidays as well."

"I know. Thanks, Dad."

She pulled away from him and stepped back to the window and said, "Dad? This room is beautiful and you know what mum's like; what if she decides she wants this one?"

He wagged his finger playfully. "Stop worrying. You leave your mother to me. And anyway, if I'm not mistaken, I think she said she prefers the room at the other end of the landing, next to the bathroom."

"Believe it or not, the room your mum's chosen is even bigger than this one. Although I've got to admit, this is a fair size!" He rubbed his chin thoughtfully as he took in the high ceiling and the ornate art deco fireplace. *What on earth have I let myself in for, agreeing to take on a house of this size?* He crossed the room back to the door and said; "Heaven knows how she's going to fill these rooms, and the rest of the house for that matter. God help me, she'll probably want new furniture throughout!"

He held the bedroom door open and motioned for Erin to go through it, "C'mon, let's go and help your mother with the unpacking. I don't know about you, sweetheart, but I could do with a cup of something warm and sweet"

CHAPTER NINE

THE Fallon family settled with relative ease into their new home and town. Helen was pleased with her choice of school for Sean, Liam and Neive; they loved it. Although Thomas Evans Primary school was a bus ride away it had by far the best reputation of all four primary schools in the area. The local authority had been difficult at first, objecting to her insistence at having her children enrolled in that particular school, advising her it would be better for her children to attend one of the schools much closer to home, but Helen had dug her heels in. Her kids were all good achievers and she wanted it kept that way; there was no compromise as far as their education was concerned.

All three soon formed new friendships at the school and in their new neighbourhood; it was as though they'd lived in the area all their lives. Erin was a different matter, though. Helen had enrolled her into the local Girls High School and when John asked Erin, as he often did, if she had settled in and if she was enjoying it, she'd simply shrug her shoulders and say, "It's okay." She was in the fourth form now; an important year, and John had hopes of her going on to college or University. She was bright enough, no doubt about that, but would this move and the necessary change of secondary school have a detrimental effect on her? Before the move, Erin had been a happy and popular young girl. And now her lack of friends and quiet demeanour, troubled John, he didn't know what to do or how to make things better for her. When he'd raised his concerns with Helen, she'd commented that, "it's her age, she'll come around in time. She's just a moody teenager!" then Helen would change the subject completely. It was clear to John that Helen wasn't interested in their daughter's happiness. No matter how hard he tried to get Erin to open up about school and friends, she simply wasn't interested; she made it obvious to him that she had no desire to enter into a discussion on the subject.

As far as Erin was concerned, it should have been enough that she at least went to *that awful school* every day; she never feigned illness or gave excuses not to have to go and it was her choice to come straight home every afternoon to spend time in her bedroom reading, or writing to Caitlin and the other girls she considered as being the *only* friends she needed and wanted to spend time with.

John gave up trying to talk to Helen about Erin. Helen would become impatient and irritable if he tried to discuss Erin with her. Erin was, and always had been, a Daddy's girl; and over the years as she was growing up, it hadn't gone unnoticed by Helen. In fact, the strong bond between father and daughter had become a festering sore. Helen was jealous of Erin.

It was for this reason that John struggled to make any progress in understanding how Erin was truly feeling since moving away from Preston. His wife's lack of interest and coldness towards their eldest child deeply saddened John; it wasn't as if he'd ever given his wife reason to make her feel that he'd ever put Erin before her, or cared more for his daughter – he loved his children in equal measure, but most parents know, even if many would be unwilling to admit, that their first born is always that tiny bit *extra* special.

CHAPTER TEN

WITH the kids out at school all day, Helen had lots of time on her hands and she finally found something that interested her and she could throw her time and energy into, their new home. Wife and mother came all too naturally too her, after all, it was all she'd ever known since marrying and all she had known since the birth of the first of her four children – but that wasn't enough, not anymore, in fact it hadn't been for a long time. She wanted much more out of life, and a large house in a much sought after location was just the beginning. After all, John owed it to her, and not before time, either.

Spending money on transforming No.18 Florence Terrace into the standard of home she had always known she deserved was fast becoming an obsession with her. Helen was dipping into the joint bank account on a daily basis without a second thought as to how much she was spending, or even whether she'd left enough money in the account for John to be able cover the rent and other household bills.

She began shopping for wallpaper – lots of wallpaper, in fact, rolls and rolls in various colours and designs. None of the cheap end stuff would do either, she'd had years of having to 'make do', well not any longer! So she spent hours trawling through countless sample wallpaper catalogues at the various stores in the town centre, until she found what she was looking for, and that just happened to be at the high end, expense wise – nothing less than she deserved in her opinion. She wanted every room in the house finished before all the new furniture was delivered. Helen estimated it would take about four weeks to have the house painted and decorated from top to bottom. A tall order by anyone's standard, so she hired a couple of painters and decorators to undertake the work. Of course, she had no idea how much *that* was going to cost. *John will deal with that aspect of things,* she thought.

Although he didn't say anything, because he didn't want to dampen Helen's enthusiasm for her their new home, John was becoming mildly irritated with Helen's pre-occupation with the house and the fact that she wanted everything brought up to date, and she wanted it done now! *Christ, has she found a bloody money tree amongst the twenty-three trees Neive counted?* Helen's shopping sprees had spiralled out of control, forcing him to put in extra hours at work. He was tired and Liam even accused him, at breakfast that morning, of being grumpy all the time. John left for work thinking about what Liam had said; "*You never used to be grumpy in the old house Dad. You always played with us and made us laugh.*" It was on his mind all day.

By the time he arrived home from work, his mild irritation at Helen's spend, spend, spend attitude had spilled over into something verging on seriously annoyed, and when he opened the front door and stepped into the hallway to find Helen unwrapping boxes of matching bedding *and* curtains, he decided it was time to put a stop to all this madness.

Thoughts of how he would approach the matter had been running through his mind all day. *Now look Helen, I know you want to make this place a nice home for us, but don't you think you're rushing into things a little too fast? And I was thinking, maybe if you got yourself a part-time job . . . Yes that's it, if she got herself a job, it'd help with the up-keep and she'd have less time to plan all this decorating nonsense.* He needed to pick his time and words carefully, something he was not renowned for.

That evening after the kids had been packed off to bed, John and Helen were sat in the lounge in front of the fire. The BBC's Nine o'clock News was on the TV. Helen curled up with her feet tucked beneath her in the oversized armchair with a Country Homes magazine in her lap. John was sat at the far end of the couch watching the news – or so Helen thought – his feet resting on the worn coffee table they'd brought with them from their old house. The scene, a warm fire burning brightly in the hearth and soft lighting hiding the threadbare carpet and bare walls, was a stark contrast to what was about to erupt – a full blown and bitter argument between the two of them.

John glanced at Helen idly leafing through another posh interior design magazine. *What's she thinking of buying now* he thought, unable to control his rising anger.

John stood up and went to switch off the television. Reaching for the TV's on/off switch he hesitated, thinking, *best leave it on. The kids might still be awake. I don't want them to hear us arguing.*

John went back to the sofa and sat down again. He cleared his throat as he always did when he was about to make a statement of some importance. Helen looked up from her magazine and waited for him to say something, when he didn't say anything, she went back to her magazine thinking, *he's probably preparing one of his speeches about God knows what.* She waited for him to get it out in the open – she could tell by John's mood he was building up to saying something that was probably going to piss her off.

Not sure how to broach the matter of her getting a job, John blurted out, "Helen, you do know don't you that we're supposed to have permission from the landlord before we redecorate any of the rooms in this house?"

Her attention still on the magazine, she didn't bother to look at him as she said, a bit too casually for John's liking, "I've already done it. It's all organised, decorators, the lot."

"Done what? Organised what?" John was confused, "Helen? *What* exactly have you *done* and *organised*?" Before she had chance to answer, he leaped off the sofa and paced back and forth in front of her, "You've no right, Helen! What in the hell do you think you're playing at, and just how much is all this going to cost?"

Helen slammed the magazine down on the arm of the chair and

said, "Keep your voice down! You'll upset the kids!"

Cutting across Helen's protestations, John said, "I've had a feckin' promotion, woman! I've not won the Pools. I *do not have* bottomless pockets you stupid selfish . . . " John was lost for words.

Helen stretched out her legs from beneath her and got out of her chair. She picked up the magazine she'd been pretending to read, rolled it up deliberately, and tucked it under her arm. She stood right in front of him, the heat from his body radiating out to her, and matching his steely expression she said, "Stupid? Selfish? That's rich coming from you, you big feckin' Eejit!" She pushed past him and headed to the door, and without looking back at him, she said, "Don't you ever speak to me like that again! I'm going to bed now. I'll sleep in the spare bedroom. Don't think about joining me, I don't want you near me!"

As she stepped out of the room into the hall, John called out to her, "You'll have to find yourself a job, Helen, and pretty sharpish, too! Because, believe me, I have no intention of footing the bill for this lot on my own. You're costing me a fortune, and quite frankly I've had enough!"

Helen stopped dead in her tracks. *What did he just say?* She turned around and headed back to the lounge and stood in the doorway. John was standing in front of the TV, his back to her. She said, "So that's it is it? You're forcing the mother of your four young children to go out and find a job?" She waited for John to say something.

In truth, he didn't know what to say, everything was falling apart between the two of them. He couldn't turn around and face her, so he kept his back to her.

Helen said, "You should be ashamed of yourself, John Fallon. But if my getting a job is what you want, then so be it. You'll damn well regret it, though!" She turned and quietly closed the door behind her.

He'd handled it all wrong. *Jesus Christ, what a mess!* He sat down hard on the chair Helen had vacated just minutes earlier, running his hands through his hair, rocking too and fro. The move to Hindthorpe was turning out to be a big mistake and was costing him dearly, in more ways than he could have imagined. *What am I going to do? Maybe I went too far telling her she has to go out to work.* Then of course there was Erin. Although she appeared to have finally settled down in their new home, he sensed she was still deeply unhappy, lonely in fact. Erin went to school and came home, that was it. She never went out and she never invited friends home, as she'd always done in the past, before they'd upped sticks at Helen's behest and moved to Hindthorpe. She was a changed girl. She had become quiet and isolated; choosing to remain in her room after school and spending most of her weekends up there too. No amount of cajoling or treats for his lovely Erin had made a difference to how she felt. *Another major fuck up because of this fucking promotion!*

He had deceived himself and he knew it now. His elevated position at work and the substantial increase in his salary should have been the answer to all his problems; it was supposed to have made everything right between him and Helen. Their relationship had been rocky for some time; he put that down to money being tight and Helen not having a social life or any friends to speak of. *How wrong could I have been?* He got out of the chair and switched off the television. He had never been a drinking man but right now he would have given anything for a large whisky or three. Instead, he turned off the lamps and headed upstairs to bed. He couldn't remember a time in his entire life when he'd this unhappy.

When John entered the bedroom he realised, with a sickening jolt, that Helen had meant what she'd said. The room was dark and cold and their bed was empty. She didn't want him near her, that's what she'd said.

John and Helen were deeply in love when they married seventeen years ago and, apart from short stays in hospital when she was having the children, they hadn't spent a single night apart. He couldn't bare the thought of her not being by his side when he woke in the morning. He closed the door quietly and moved across the room in the dark. He lay down on top of the bed and gave way to his emotions.

CHAPTER ELEVEN

HELEN was determined to make John suffer for attacking her about spending *his* money. She didn't waste any time in finding herself work. In fact, she was surprised at how quickly she landed her first job in fifteen years.

The morning after their bitter exchange, Helen had seen the kids onto the school bus and set off on the long walk to the Bus Station at the other end of Bleaksedge Lane, where almost an hour later she caught a bus to the centre of Hindthorpe. She had used the yellow pages to find the addresses of Employment Agencies in the main town and it was there she was heading, hell bent on getting a job, any job! She was determined to rub John's nose in it and make him suffer.

Helen had made a list of four agencies advertising both permanent and temporary clerical vacancies, and it was the second agency on her list that she arrived at within minutes of leaving the bus station.

Before Helen entered the recruitment office she scanned a number of vacancies displayed in the window, three or four of which she knew she would be more than capable of filling.

After checking her reflection in the window, she took a deep breath and walked into the office where a young girl who was busily scribbling notes on a pile of forms greeted her with a smile. "Good morning, can I help you?"

"Erm, well yes. I hope you can." Helen glanced round at the

other staff in the office and continued, almost apologetically, "I'd like to enquire about any clerical vacancies that I might be able to apply for?" It came out as more of a question than a confident statement. The young agency employee was quick to take control; she picked up her pen and notepad, "No problem. Are you already registered with us, Miss? Mrs?

"Fallon. My name's Helen Fallon, please call me Helen and, no, I'm not registered . . . do I need to be . . . registered, that is?"

The girl stood and pointed to a small desk and two chairs in the corner of the office by the window and said, "Yes, you'll have to register first and then we can have a look at some suitable vacancies. So if you'd like to take a seat over there, I'll bring the registration forms over for you to complete." Helen found the cheery sing-sing tone of the girl's voice irritating, and hoped it didn't show as she smiled back at her.

Helen sat down at the desk as instructed and waited as the girl walked over to the filing cabinet. "Now where are the forms? Ah yes, here they are." That voice again. She was probably only twenty at the most, Helen thought. *Just starting Primary School when I last had a job.* "If you would fill these in for me . . ."

While Helen completed the lengthy forms about her personal details, career history and experience, the agency worker gathered a number of small reference cards, each listing details of vacant clerical posts then went and sat down opposite Helen. "Almost done?"

"It's just this last bit about referees . . . I haven't worked since I left Ireland thirteen years ago . . ." Helen said, her confidence draining by the minute.

"Don't worry too much about that for now, I'm sure we can get around that somehow. What about character references? You can provide at least two of those can't you?"

"I've just moved into the area and I don't really know anybody I could ask?"

"Okay. What about where you lived before? Were you a member

of any local societies or committees, Mother and Baby groups, School Board, voluntary work, that sort of thing?"

Helen thought she'd blown it and didn't have a hope in hell of getting any sort of paid work, so she picked up her bag to get ready to leave and said almost apologetically, "I'm afraid not. I've been a housewife and mother for the last fifteen years and I rarely go out . . ." She looked directly at the capable and confident young girl, shrugged her shoulders and said, with a note of defeat in her voice, "except with my husband, that is, shopping, the usual stuff, you know . . ." she turned away from the girl's sympathetic expression and stared out through the window, continuing, "well perhaps you don't, you're young . . . I only ever went out with *him*, I mean my husband, or when I took the children to school. And met them off the school bus at home time, that sort of thing." She shrugged and started brushing imaginary bits off the bottom of her skirt. She imagined she must appear quite pathetic to this young girl. "I suppose you could say that I lead a very dull and boring existence."

She turned sideways and pulled her jacket off the back of the chair and started to put it on.

"Hold on, don't dash off before I've at least had a chance to look through your registration." The agency employee picked up the forms Helen had been completing and said, "I'm sure we can fix you up with some clerical work." She quickly read through the details about Helen's past employment and experience, and then she surprised Helen when she said brightly, "Actually, we have quite a few positions here that I think you might want to consider . . . in fact . . ." she flipped through the cards until she found what she was looking for, "Here we are, this one came in this morning," she was smiling as she handed the card to Helen, "I think you could be just the person they're looking for!"

Helen took the card and read it. The vacancy was for a part-time receptionist at a busy dental practice in the town centre, and when she'd finished reading through the details she looked up and said with genuine confidence, "I could do this!"

"Great! But they need someone to start straight away, are you available for an immediate start?"

Helen was shocked at this turn of events. Things were going a little faster than she anticipated. She shook her head, bewildered and said, "What? You mean now? Today? This morning?" For some reason, she found the idea quite comical and couldn't help smiling; in fact she was almost giddy at the prospect of returning home and telling John that she had found herself a job, quite a nice one at that. She almost laughed out loud.

The agency girl said, "Well . . . if you're available right away, I could give them a call and ask if they'd like to see you this morning. Would that be okay with you?"

Helen hadn't been prepared for this; her mind had gone into overload. It had been years since she'd had a job interview. *Oh my God*, she thought, *what if I flunk it? What if I can't even get through an interview for a receptionist position? Perhaps I should aim lower? Ask her if she has any cleaning jobs. I've got more than enough experience in that area!* The panic was clear in her voice when she said, "But what about experience? Do you think they'll agree to see me if you tell them that I haven't worked for so long?" She appeared to be more than a little worried now and continued defensively, "I'm certain that I could do the job just as well as the next person" then, almost pleading, "and I'm a very fast learner, all I need is for someone to give me the chance to prove myself."

"Erm, let me see . . ." The girl picked up the card with the job details, reading it once more. "They've not been specific about level of experience. The job is mainly dealing with telephone calls and booking appointments into the diary, pretty bog standard really" she looked up and said reassuringly, "I'd say that you're as good a candidate as any." She reached for the phone, "OK. Let's give them a call then shall we?"

CHAPTER TWELVE

ALTHOUGH she hadn't worked since just before Erin's birth, her long absence from the jobs market and lack of experience hadn't proven to be an obstacle.

The senior partner of the practice had agreed to see her that morning and when she arrived for the interview an hour later, she was greeted by an elderly looking lady whom Helen assumed to be the incumbent receptionist. Late fifties, grey hair tied back in a severe bun and horn-rimmed glasses, she gave Helen the impression of a School Ma'am. For a portly woman, she was quite nimble on her feet, and wasted no time in showing her into a small meeting room off the main reception area.

"Please take a seat. Mr. Karapialis will be with you in a few minutes," she said in a no nonsense manner, without any introductions. She openly eyed Helen up and down, lips clamped firmly together with a look of derision on her face and then without another word, she turned and left the room, closing the door behind. *Nice to meet you too*, Helen thought.

Helen sat in the small meeting room gazing at posters on the walls depicting decaying teeth and diseased gums. She shuddered and looked away before the images became engrained on her mind for the rest of the day.

The self-assurance she had felt earlier that morning was rapidly deserting her to be replaced with a feeling of uneasiness. The last thing she had expected when she left the house just a few of hours ago was to be sat in a meeting room waiting to be interviewed. She couldn't believe that she'd let the young girl at the recruitment office talk her into it so easily. *Stupid Eejit, why did I go along with it, allowing some young kid to set me up in an interview when I haven't held a bloody job down in donkey's years? Jesus, she couldn't have been much older than Erin! Maybe I should leave now? Quit while I'm ahead.* She looked at her watch. *How long have I been sitting here? I should just get up and leave now. But then again the experience will do me good. And if I fail embarrassingly, at least I never have to see these people again.*

The gruff receptionist had made her feel like a delinquent schoolgirl who had been called to the Headmistress's office for some misdemeanour of sorts. Helen fussed with her skirt, smoothing it and pulling it over her knees. She buttoned then unbuttoned her jacket and fluffed her hair, her nerves getting the better of her. She began rummaging in her handbag for her lipstick when the door flung wide open.

Helen almost jumped out of her skin. She looked up quickly and locked eyes with the olive skinned male who stepped into the room. Self-conscious and feeling guilty, of what, she had no idea; she leaped out of her seat. Her handbag fell out of her lap, the contents spilling noisily onto the floor.

She looked down at her belongings scattered beneath the table, blushing all the way down to her toes. "OH! Sorry . . . urm, very sorry." Unable to think of another intelligent thing to say and desperate to hide her embarrassment, she stooped down and began retrieving her things from the floor.

He closed the door and placed some paperwork on the table, "Here, let me help you. I'm sorry, I didn't mean to startle you."

As he handed her purse, a small hairbrush and lipstick to her, he tilted his head to one side in an effort to make eye contact with her, "I think that's everything, yes?"

She hadn't intended to, but her embarrassment had got the better of her, and she snatched the items from him, and said, "Yes. Thank you."

It was evident to Vlasis Karapialis that he had caught Helen off guard, the fact that her hands were shaking as she was putting everything back into her bag was an obvious give away. She wouldn't make eye contact with him either – *beautiful eyes they are, too*, he thought – so he stood up and nodded his head towards the chair she had been sitting in and said, "Please, take a seat."

"Thank you" she said, and sat down on the edge of the seat, placing her handbag on the table in front of her.

He sat down opposite. "Shall I start by introducing myself?" It was more of a statement than a question.

Still unable to make eye contact with him, she said to her handbag, "Erm . . . yes. Thank you." *God, why do I keep saying thank you? I've got to get out of here.*

Pre-occupied with how she was going to make her escape, she slid her handbag off the table into her lap, then she realised her interviewer had stopped speaking and was staring at her, as if waiting for her to say something. It struck her then that she'd hardly heard a single word he'd said. *Did he say his name was Mr Vlassie? What sort of a name's that?* She finally managed to look at him; from his colouring and complexion she assumed him to be Mediterranean, probably Italian or Spanish. "Urm, sorry, did you say your name is Mr. Vlassie?"

He laughed now, relieved that she could indeed string a sentence together. "Yes, that's right. My name is Vlasis, I am Greek." He waited for her to continue but she just sat and stared back at him.

Her mouth was slowly opening and closing like a goldfish. *Think! Think! What was he saying to me?* Her hands were clammy and she shuddered as beads of perspiration trickled down her back, *oh my God! This is the worst day of my life.*

Vlasis leaned across the table towards her, a look of concern on his face, "Are you alright?"

She blinked rapidly; *of course I'm not all right! What sort of a stupid question is that! Get a grip, Helen! Get a grip!* Sitting up straight in her seat she looked at him directly, "Yes. Sorry. A little nervous, that's all."

He smiled and she noticed that his eyes danced mischievously; she shifted in her seat and looked away. The fluttering in her stomach was something she hadn't felt since her teenage years.

"So, Mrs . . . erm," He thumbed through the paperwork he'd fetched in with him, "Excuse me . . . ah, yes, here it is . . . Fallon, Mrs Fallon," He settled back in his seat, looking relaxed and oozing confidence as he continued, "Mrs Fallon, please tell me a little bit about yourself and why you think you'd like to join our dental practice."

That charming smile, again. He was arguably the most attractive man she had ever met and she couldn't help being drawn by those deep brown eyes that twinkled playfully when he looked at her.

Helen got up, clutching her bag in front of her, the chair scraped loudly against the tiled floor, "I'm so sorry! I don't think I should be here, I don't want to waste your time . . ." She glanced at the door toying with the idea of making a run for it yet knowing that wasn't an option. Instead, she addressed the wall above his head and said, "I've not had a job, urm, well . . . what I mean is that I haven't worked for fifteen years and I don't have any experience of working in a dental surgery! I'm sorry for wasting your time, but I think I'd better leave . . . urm, now, I'd better go now." But she didn't move, she wanted to bolt for the door but it wasn't happening, her legs wouldn't do their job!

Vlasis was baffled and mildly amused by her outburst and her behaviour, "Have I said something to upset you, Mrs Fallon?"

"Oh no, no you haven't!" She looked him square in the face, but only for an instant before talking to the wall above his head, again. She spread her arms wide not really knowing what it was that she was trying to indicate by the gesture . . . *ground open, swallow me up, beam me up, Scotty, anything, just get me out of here!*

"Look, why don't you sit down and we will start again." She didn't have a choice really. She wanted a job, but not half as much as she wanted to rub John's nose in it! And she was already here. *Might as well get it over with. He might offer me the job. And I might holiday on the moon later this year*. She shrugged again and looked around the room before deciding to sit down and continue with what was after all, quite a farcical situation.

"Alright then . . . Thank you." She said.

Although he was enjoying what was so far a very entertaining meeting, he decided to get on with the interview. "Experience is not that important, Mrs Fallon, so please don't let that put you off. If you can manage a diary, the appointments system, and deal confidently and professionally with telephone calls and enquiries, then I would be happy to give you a chance, to prove yourself, so to speak."

Helen was flabbergasted! *What? Did he just say that he'd be happy to give me a chance?* She shook her head slowly, "Are you serious . . . I mean? Really? You don't mind that – " *That smile, he's doing it again!*

"That you have not worked for a number of years and that you have not been employed by a dental practice before? No. I don't. I'm prepared to offer you the position on a temporary basis, say six weeks? And if we are both happy with the way things are going at the end of that period, then the job will be offered to you on a permanent basis. What do you say?"

Her smile lit up the room. "Yes! Thank you so much! I really don't know what to say. I'm speechless . . ."

Great teeth as well, in fact the whole package is fantastic, he thought. "So, we are agreed. That is settled then, but I will need you to start as soon as tomorrow morning. Mrs. Faversham can show you the ropes. So would you be available to start in the morning?"

"Oh, no. No! I mean, yes, yes. Tomorrow morning's fine. Yes, yes, I'll be here." She didn't really know if it was fine or not because she hadn't expected to get a job so quickly, her head was spinning. "Mrs. Faversham, is that her name? Her confidence returned. "Cheerful soul isn't she?"

Vlasis laughed. "Miss Marple, we call her, although not to her face. She's fine when you get to know her."

He stood up and gathered his paperwork off the table and glancing at his watch again he said, "If you like, I can show you around now and we can discuss your hours of work, etcetera, before my next patient arrives."

He held the door open for her and as she walked ahead of him out of the small meeting room, he couldn't help admiring her long luscious copper hair, shapely legs and small waist. He pursed his lips and nodded in approval. *She'll be a real asset to the Practice*, he thought. *And what an immense pleasure it would be to have her in my chair, literally;* he smiled and wondered how long it would take him to do just that.

Back in the main Reception area, Vlasis pointed out the five treatment rooms before leading Helen into the back office where all the filing cabinets and other office paraphernalia was stored, finishing the small tour back in Reception, where she had begun her ordeal just over half an hour ago. Seeing her to the door, he said "tha doúme ávrio"

Helen frowned and said, "Sorry?"

"See you tomorrow," Vlasis translated for her, following up with "Sas ypérocho gynaíka"

"Yes," Helen replied, "thank you and the same to you." She laughed nervously.

Behind the reception desk, *'Miss Marple'* peered over her horn-rimmed glasses. "I take it she got the job?"

"Yes, I thought I would give her try, Miss . . . sorry, Agnes. She will start tomorrow. If you would be so good as to show her the ropes?"

"Yes of course Mr Karapialis. Perhaps I should teach her a few Greek phrases as well. And you're right she is very beautiful. Also married, I believe."

Vlasis looked down sheepishly and walked back towards his surgery. If he were capable of blushing he surely would have done. He'd forgotten the old bat spoke Greek.

* * *

Helen left the interview feeling ten feet tall; she couldn't stop smiling to herself, she was thrilled. The senior partner of the Dental Practice had been clearly impressed with her, she had to put her hand over her mouth as a giggle bubbled up inside her. He'd openly flirted with her during the interview and she had been shocked and surprised at how attractive he'd made her feel.

On her way back to the bus station, she strutted along the high street and couldn't resist admiring herself as she caught her reflection in store windows. When she arrived at the bus station she still had a half hour wait so she popped into the station's small cafe and ordered a pot of tea and as she waited for her bus to come in, she began to go over the previous night's argument with John and his demand that she get a job. Sitting by the window that looked out onto the busy main street, she gazed into the distance. *I'll show him. No one gives me ultimatums.* She finished her tea and left the café just in time to see her bus pulling up

CHAPTER THIRTEEN

AS the weeks passed, things got steadily worse at home; Helen began going out three or four evenings a week and the relationship between her and John now seemed beyond repair. John spent more and more time at work, putting in exceptionally long hours and as a result, the two of them spent little time in each other's company, apart from meal times and a couple of hours at the weekend when they were forced to be civil to each other for the sake of the kids.

John had no idea how to fix what had gone wrong and on the rare occasions they were alone and he attempted to talk to her about it she dismissed him abruptly, saying there was nothing to talk about anymore and to leave her alone.

Apart from Erin, both her brothers and sister appeared to be blissfully unaware of the gaping cracks in their parent's relationship. Erin spent most of her home time in her room, reading or writing letters to her old friends. She hated the atmosphere in the house and she hated the way her mother was treating her dad. It broke her heart to see how unhappy and tired looking her dad had become. She knew that her mother's job was to blame for the trouble between her parents. Because ever since her mother had gone to work at the dental surgery she had become a completely different person, not the mother Erin knew, in fact, she didn't look like their mother anymore, either, she looked . . . different somehow, changed.

CHAPTER FOURTEEN

Hindthorpe, April 1976

IT was unusually warm for early April and, uncharacteristically, Helen had readily agreed to let the boys and Neive play out for an extra hour. "Not a minute after seven o'clock, do you hear?"

Sean stamped his feet, "Aww, but, Mum, it's the holidays; it's not like we have to get up early for school in the morning."

"I said seven o'clock, Sean! Don't argue with me or you'll come in now and go to your room." He turned and stomped out down the hallway. Helen continued brushing her hair, humming as she did so.

Erin looked up from the book she was reading and smiled at her mother's reflection in the mirror. "You're in a good mood tonight, Mum. Are you going out again?"

Helen turned and gently yanked at Erin's long auburn ponytail, and mimicking her husband's soft Irish accent, she said, "Cheeky young minx, so ye are! I'm always in a good mood!" She turned back to the mirror and began pinning her hair up in a messy but very chic looking bun.

Curled up in the corner of the sofa with her book open in her lap, Erin watched her getting ready for yet another night out and as her mother was putting the finishing touches to her make up, Erin couldn't help thinking how beautiful she was, especially when she wore her hair pinned up; her make up wasn't overdone, just enough to bring out her stunning green eyes and the red lipstick accentuated her small mouth and perfectly shaped lips. She was wearing a very fitted black sleeveless silk dress that showed off her figure perfectly – it was new and looked very expensive. *Another new dress*, Erin wondered where on earth her mother was getting the money from to buy so many new and expensive looking clothes.

Unaware of her daughter's attention, Helen turned her head from side to side, making sure that she'd not overdone the blusher and then she ran her tongue across her teeth cleaning specks of lipstick away, she smiled at her reflection, pleased with the finished look.

"Where to tonight Mum?" Erin asked.

"Oh, the usual, you know."

"Bingo again?"

"That's right."

"With, erm, what's her name?"

"Brenda. Now what's this, twenty questions?"

Helen had become quite friendly with the cleaning lady at the practice, apparently the woman, called Brenda, went to bingo with Helen three evenings a week – something Erin knew her dad was definitely not happy about. *It's all her fault, encouraging Mum to go out all the time spending money gambling.*

Erin had heard her parents arguing time and again about it, but her dad had lost that particular battle. Helen had argued that it was the only time she got to herself, and after all didn't she keep a nice home and go out to work as well, surely she was entitled to a bit of fun now and again?

Erin had met the new *friend* on a number of occasions whilst out shopping with her mum. At Brenda's insistence, she and her mother had gone back to her house for a cup of tea and a chat on a couple of occasions. Erin didn't like her at all, Brenda was what her dad would call *common* and the estate where she lived was really rough. Erin couldn't quite say why, but she felt ill at ease in the woman's presence. She definitely wasn't the sort of person she imagined her mother to have as a friend, it was quite an odd friendship really. The woman was much older than her mother and when they went back to her house, they would stay in the kitchen talking very quietly while she was left in the grubby living room to watch television. Above all, she hated going on to the estate; it was very run down and both times they'd gone back to the woman's house there had been gangs of youths fighting in the street and neighbours shouting and swearing loudly from their doorsteps at their kids. *Dad would go mental if he knew where Mum was spending a lot of her time* she thought.

Yes, things had changed in the Fallon household and not for the better. Helen no longer seemed to care very much for her family; it was increasingly obvious to Erin that her mother cared more about her job and her new friend.

"Mum, can I ask you something?"

"Hmmm . . .?"

Erin sat up straight, pulled her denim skirt over her knees and moved to the edge of the sofa, unsure of how her mother would react to her question. She took a deep breath and came straight out with what had been playing on her mind for quite a while, "Why do you get so dressed up when you go out in the evening – without dad, I mean? And . . . well, you know . . . you wear . . . perfume and stuff?" Determined to finish what she'd finally had the courage to come out and ask, not wanting her mother to interrupt before she had finished, she continued hurriedly, "Why didn't you bother with all that stuff when you used to go out with Dad? And why don't you two go out together anymore? All you do is argue and fight with each other all the time, why, Mum?"

Almost breathless after her outburst, she sat back and huddled in the corner of the sofa again. *There! That's it! I've said it!* Her face was bright red, she was anxious, she looked down at the book in her lap and waited for her mother to say something.

Completely thrown off guard by Erin's outburst, Helen shot a glance at her through the reflection in the mirror. Helen hadn't been prepared for so many direct questions from her teenage daughter. She was too shocked and too stunned to think of a quick answer.

Avoiding eye contact with Erin, Helen was suddenly nervous

and hoped the slight tremor in her voice didn't give her away, "Erin, for God's sake! You do ask some strange questions!" Unable to face her daughter's questioning gaze, she grabbed her handbag and stalked out of the room. She couldn't wait to get out of the house.

CHAPTER FIFTEEN

ERIN sprawled across her bed gazing out of her bedroom window at the cloudless blue sky. Chewing the end of her pen, she was thinking about whether she should tell Caitlin that she was going to ask her mum and dad if she could stay for a few days with Caitlin's family during the school holidays; she wanted to see her old friends again and she didn't want Caitlin to come to Hindthorpe because of the obvious tension between her parents. Erin had decided that her mother's idea had been wrong all along, if they hadn't moved from their old house in Preston, perhaps they'd still be the happy family they used to be.

She was half way down the second page of the letter she was writing to Caitlin when she heard her parents shouting at each other, again. She slid off her bed, tiptoed across the room and quietly opened her bedroom door, just a crack; she wanted to hear what this latest argument was about. They were constantly at each other's throats and Erin was seriously worried about what might happen if they didn't sort things out soon.

It was her father's voice she could hear now, "I'm telling you for the last time, Helen, you're keeping something from me and I want to know what it is; I wont have secrets between us!" There was a pause, and then he continued, "I don't trust you anymore, Helen! I think you're lying to me about where you're going on all these nights out you're having. You've changed since you started working at that surgery. What the hell's going on?"

Her mother was talking now, but Erin couldn't hear exactly what it was that she was saying. Her ear pressed hard against the crack in the doorway, she waited for her father to speak again, but everything went quiet. It seemed that this argument was over pretty quick, unlike all the other rows they've been having.

Erin stood by the door a little longer, she wanted to be certain that they'd stopped arguing. Eventually she breathed a sigh of relief and mumbled, "Thank God." She closed her bedroom door quietly and climbed back on to her bed with the intention of returning to the letter she was writing to Caitlin, but she was distracted by what she'd heard her dad say to her mum, she couldn't concentrate.

Chewing at the hard skin on the side of her fingernail, Erin couldn't stop worrying about what was going to happen to the family – should she tell Caitlin? As she lay on her bed considering whether or not to tell her best friend about her concerns, her thoughts were interrupted by the sound of the front door slamming.

Erin shot up off her bed and looked through the window; her mother was already out of the garden and hurrying away from the house, in the direction of Bleaksedge Lane. Neive spotted her and ran after her. Erin watched. Her mother stopped and waited. As Neive caught up with her, Helen bent down and said something to her before hugging her and pointing back towards the house. Neive turned around and slowly headed back.

Head hung low, dragging her feet, Neive stopped a couple of times and called out to her mother but Helen either didn't hear her or deliberately chose to ignore her little girl; in fact, Helen never looked back that night. Neither Helen nor Neive noticed the dark blue car parked a little further along the road on the opposite side to the Fallon's home.

Leonard Fitch watched the exchange between mother and daughter and waited until the little girl had reached the garden gate when his patience was finally rewarded.

As Neive came closer to the house, Erin could see that she was crying. She slid off the bed and rammed her feet into her slippers, then ran downstairs and straight out the front door.

Neive was standing by the gate now looking in the direction her mother had gone, she was sobbing, tears streaming down her face. Erin went to her and said, "Neive, what's the matter?" She knelt in front of Neive and brushed the tears from her face with the pads of her thumbs. Neive didn't answer, she sobbed loudly, hiccupping with each sob.

Erin tried again, "Neive, did mum tell you where she was going?" Too upset to answer, Neive shook her head slowly and continued crying.

Erin hugged her again and looked out in the direction her mother had gone – she was nowhere in sight now, it was as though she'd vanished into thin air.

Just as she was about to take Neive back inside the house, Erin noticed a big and *expensive* looking car parked on the opposite side of the road. The engine was running idly and there was a man sat in the driver's seat, staring directly at the two young sisters – Erin suddenly felt very uncomfortable and for some reason she couldn't explain, *scared*.

Turning quickly from the stranger's gaze, Erin hurried Neive inside the gate and along the garden path straight into the house. Before she closed the door behind them, she looked out over the hedge and saw the car drive very slowly past the house – the driver, a gaunt, ugly looking middle-aged man, stared right at her. Erin slammed the door and stood with her back to it. She shuddered. *Where have I seen that car before?*

CHAPTER SIXTEEN

NEIVE finally settled down and joined her brothers in the living room watching the cartoon show, Wacky Races. Erin was in her bedroom reading when her dad called to her from the bottom of the stairs, "Erin? I'm going to pick your mum up. Can you come down and keep an eye on things until we get back?" Erin came out of her bedroom and leaned over the banister, "Okay, Dad. See you later."

As he pulled on his coat he looked up at her and said, "I'll be about half an hour or so. And remember, don't open the door to anyone while we're gone, okay?"

She smiled, "No. Of course I won't, Dad."

About twenty minutes after leaving the house, John Fallon drove onto a badly run-down council estate searching for the address Helen had given him. Normally she would come home in a taxi or he would pick her up outside the bingo hall, but this estate? He couldn't understand what on earth she would be doing in a place like this. He shook his head in disbelief as he passed a burned out car and as he drove on a little further he noticed rolls of chicken wire around the windows of the local corner shop. He made the mistake of slowing down to take a good look when a gang of teenage boys standing outside the shop shouted something at him and began throwing bottles and other missiles in his direction. A pint-sized Heineken bottle bounced off his bonnet. He instinctively ducked as he saw it coming.

He wound down his window and screamed at them, "You bunch

of morons!" The lads laughed and hurled obscenities at him as they began to throw more missiles, some even picked up bricks and began chasing his car. He panicked and put his foot down on the accelerator, anxiously keeping an eye in the rear-view mirror as his car gathered speed.

He couldn't wait to pick Helen up and get off the estate, *I'll have to find a different way back though, don't want to risk another encounter with that gang of eejits, he* thought.

The very idea of Helen walking these streets outraged him; he punched the steering wheel several times thinking, *You stupid bitch, Helen What the hell got into you?* He realised at that moment that he didn't know her anymore, *what the hell is she doing hanging about with people on an estate like this?*

Relieved and a little shaken, John finally pulled up outside the address Helen had given him earlier that day. Before he got out of his car, he had a good look at the house, it didn't look as scruffy as most of the others and the small garden appeared to be well maintained, unlike the neighbouring houses.

He pushed the gate open and made his way to the front door. He stood for a minute trying to regain his composure. Taking a deep breath, he rang the doorbell. There was no answer so after a few seconds he banged on the door with his fist. "All right! All right! I'm coming!" It was a woman's voice. He was still surveying the neighbouring houses when the door opened and a woman, who looked to be in her early forties, leaned against the doorjamb and took a long drag of her cigarette. .

She eyed him up and down. "Can I help you?"

"I'm Helen's husband," he said as he strained to peer over the woman's shoulder and down the hallway into the house. She moved into the middle of the doorway, intentionally blocking his view.

She grinned and said, "Oh?"

He didn't like her one bit, she made the hair stand up on the back of his neck, "Would you mind telling her I'm here, please?"

She leaned out off the doorstep and looked up and down the road and said, "She didn't stay very long; her friend picked her up a couple of hours ago." Before John had a chance to ask the woman what she meant by *her friend*, she turned to go in and said "Sorry you've had a wasted journey!" before slamming the door in his face.

Speechless and shaking from head to toe with anger, the realisation dawning on him that *the friend* the woman referred to must be a man. It was the sly way in which she had stressed the word *friend*. John turned away from the door and made his way back to the car. He did not remember getting home that evening, nor the fact that he'd made it alive.

CHAPTER SEVENTEEN

JOHN Fallon's children were still sat together on the sofa watching the television when the front door slammed, startling them. Their father stormed into the living room and roared, "*Go to your rooms, now! All of you!*" Erin had never seen her dad so furious before.

Shocked and confused, Erin grabbed Neive's hand and dragged her up off the sofa; "Liam, Sean, Come on! Quick!" Neive tried to scramble ahead of the others, she was whimpering, "Erin, what's wrong? Where's our mum?" Erin hesitated, something was seriously wrong and she needed time to gather her thoughts. All four children ran upstairs, frightened and crying. Erin ushered them into her bedroom, "Wait here until I tell you to come out!" She pulled the door shut and sat down at the top of the stairs. Wringing her hands and rocking back and forth, she tried to gather her thoughts amid the sudden mayhem.

Erin couldn't stop shaking as she listened to her father, demented with rage, smashing the house up, breaking furniture and anything else he could turn his fists and his feet to.

After what seemed like an eternity, everything finally went quiet downstairs. It was dark now and Erin, still sat at the top of the stairs heard her dad sobbing in the kitchen. It broke her heart to here her dad's gut-wrenching sobs. Tears rained down her face, "Oh God, Mum, what have you done?"

* * *

Weeks and months went by without a word from Helen. The police were notified but didn't take much interest; it was clearly a case of an errant wife.

The Police Sergeant in charge of the case had relished sharing some of the gossip that was making the rounds down at the station.

"A real stunner and, by all accounts, did she know how to use it to her advantage. Earned herself a bit of a reputation for being not just easy on the eye, if you get my drift!"

Rumours abounded. The dentist she worked for denied any affair. "She became jealous when I told her my wife was pregnant, and I was thinking of going back to Greece for the birth. She quit shortly after that." His story stacked up in terms of the dates, but didn't agree with the statement by Brenda Thomas, the cleaner at the surgery.

"They were at it like rabbits," she told the police. "But when she left her husband he got cold feet. Didn't want his wife to find out so he gave her money to leave, out of town I mean. Last I heard she moved in with one of the patients there, a young Irish lad over on the other side of the estate."

The case was eventually closed so that more effort and resource could be spent on the high profile case of 'The Birthday Girls'. It was now late September, and the suicide of Deborah Johnson's mother following receipt of her daughter's photograph and birthday card, had raised emotions in the town, with the Chief Constable calling for more effort to find the perpetrator.

CHAPTER EIGHTEEN

ERIN wasn't being completely honest when she told her dad she hadn't made any new friends. She had made a couple of friends at school, but not the kind she could relate to like Caitlin. They all seemed so grown up, with their short skirts and make-up. It wouldn't have been allowed at her old school, and she was often ridiculed for her more modest appearance.

But there was one person she had taken a shine to. Billy Ashcroft; he lived just a few minutes away from the Fallon family and would often hang about to catch her leaving in the mornings so that he could walk with her to the bus stop. Billy was a few years older than Erin and worked as a Hospital Porter at the local Infirmary.

Erin hadn't minded Billy walking with her because she had been glad of the company, especially when the days began to get shorter and the mornings were still dark – and secretly because she had a bit of a crush on Billy. He was a good-looking young man, despite his pock marked skin from early bouts of teenage acne. He was popular with the girls and had a bit of a reputation for leaving a trail of heartbreak in his wake. But Erin knew that wouldn't happen to her because although she felt flattered by his attention, she was too young for him to be really interested in her.

On one occasion, John Fallon arrived home from work and found Billy at the front door talking to Erin. John wasn't happy about the lad hanging around Erin and he told her so later that evening, "I don't like that Ashcroft fella, Erin. He's a bit of a jack the lad by all accounts and he's got a reputation to go with it, and besides he's too old for you. I don't want to see you with him again, is that clear?"

"Dad, he's just a friend that's all. We just have a bit of a laugh together, nothing more. And I know he's a lot older than me."

"Yes well think on, Erin. It's not the right time for you to be thinking about lads. You need to work hard at school if you want to go on to University." And as an afterthought, he ended his little lecture by adding, "Concentrate on your school work, Erin. Boys are an unnecessary distraction, the last thing you need if you're going to get a good education."

Despite her father's warnings about keeping away from Billy Ashcroft, Erin continued to allow Billy to walk her to the school bus stop every morning, until the morning he tried to kiss her. After that the shared walks came to an abrupt end on. Billy had been telling Erin some of his tales from the Infirmary, which had Erin in stitches; Billy couldn't help being captivated by her youthful loveliness.

Erin stopped laughing when Billy turned to her smiling and brushed her hair away from her face, saying, "You know, Erin, you've got beautiful eyes."

Erin blushed, "Oh I bet you say that to all the girls,"

"No, I don't. Anyway, I don't have a girlfriend at the moment," he said. "I don't know that many girls, I've only been out with a couple – nothing serious or anything like that. I've not found the right one yet."

Now Erin knew he was lying. She laughed. "That's not what the girls in 4B tell me,"

"Why what have they been saying?"

"Oh, you know, 'Girl stuff'. The stuff we never tell boys about." Now Erin was doing the teasing.

"Orr come on, you can't leave me in suspense. What have they said? If it's that slag Carole Meredith, don't believe a word she says. I wouldn't touch her with a barge pole."

"Actually it wasn't Carole Meredith, but I'll be speaking to her later today."

Billy laughed, then turned to her again and put his hand on her shoulder, and much to her surprise and disgust, he pressed her none too gently against a tree and tried to kiss her, shoving his tongue into her mouth!

"Urgh!" She tried to push him away before wiping her mouth vigorously with the back of her sleeve, "Urgh! Stop it! That was disgusting! Get your hands off me!"

Struggling wildly to free herself from Billy's grip, she screamed in his face, "If my dad finds out what you've just done, he'll kill you, Billy Ashcroft!"

Billy was still holding her firmly against the tree when she remembered what her dad had told her to do if she ever found herself being attacked by a man, so she did it; with all the force she could muster, she slammed her knee up hard, right between Billy's thighs. His hands went straight to his crotch as he fell to his knees clutching his testicles and moaning in pain.

Erin panicked, she hadn't really intended to be so brutal, but he had asked for it. She set off running and didn't stop until she was nearing the top of Bleaksedge Lane, nor did she look back once to see if Billy had recovered and was coming after her. As a parting shot she had yelled to him over her shoulder. "My dad was right about you! I never want to see you again, you pervert!"

Billy struggled to his feet, "Erin, wait! Wait! I'm sorry! I didn't mean to offend you!" His apology did nothing to convince her to stop running and that was the last Erin saw of Billy on their walks along Bleaksedge Lane.

CHAPTER NINETEEN

Hindthorpe, November 1976

SATURDAY, November sixth, Erin's sixteenth birthday. It was just after seven in the morning when Erin got out of bed. Shivering like mad, she dressed quickly in a pair of jeans, polo neck sweater and pulled a cardigan on over the top – 18 Florence Terrace might have been a very grand house, but it was also freezing cold during the wintertime. And today was no exception. She left her bedroom and crept to the bottom of the stairs where she sat down, waiting for the postman.

Erin rubbed the sleep out of her eyes and yawned, she had tossed and turned all night, hoping and praying that she'd receive a birthday card from her mum; at least that would prove that she was still alive even if it didn't mean that she still loved and missed her family.

She'd been sitting there for some time, huddled tightly in her mother's oversized cardigan and had begun to doze off when the rattle of the letterbox startled her awake. She jumped up and ran down the wide carpeted hallway to the front door, gathered up the mail and ran back to the bottom of the stairs, plonking herself down again.

Her hands were trembling as she clutched the mail against her chest; she closed her eyes and silently prayed that *one* of the envelopes she was holding would be from her mum – she was too scared to look, and so she prayed.

There were eight altogether, three envelopes were addressed to her dad, *probably bills*, Erin thought. The other five were addressed to her. She knew straight away from the handwriting that they were from her friends: Caitlin, Emma, Colleen and Sophie, the fifth envelope had been sellotaped to a small jiffy bag. She recognised the spider-like hand writing immediately, it was from her Nana in Ireland. Flicking frantically through the envelopes again she started crying. "*Where is it?*"

Still believing that her mother would *never* forget her birthday, Erin put the mail down on the floor at the bottom of the stairs and ran down the hallway again to the front door. She checked the spring-loaded letterbox thinking that there might be another envelope trapped on the outside. Nothing. She opened the front door and looked down at the step, again nothing. Her eyes followed the length of the garden path right up to the gate and back again. Perhaps the postman had accidentally dropped some of their mail on the way to the front door? He hadn't. As she turned to close the door, she whispered, "*Surely, you can't have forgotten?*" With a sense of utter rejection, she sat down with her back against the door, dropped her head into her hands and sobbed. *Oh, Mum! How could you? How could you forget so easily?*

It was almost seven months to the day since Helen left, and Erin had never given up hope of her mother coming back, never! In one letter to Caitlin she wrote, '*Why wouldn't she come home? She has four children who love her so much. She knew that surely? She must know how much Liam misses her?*' Liam was her mother's favourite. Erin knew that. Whenever they had cuddled up as a family on the large sofa in the sitting room to watch a favourite TV programme, it was always Liam who snuggled up tight against their mum, and she held him close, gently stroking his hair and kissing the top of his head. The whole family were affected badly in so many different ways by Helen's disappearance, but Liam seemed to be struggling most.

Still sat with her back against the front door, crying softly, Erin heard a bedroom door open. She held her breath and waited. It was her dad going to the bathroom. Not wanting her dad or her brothers and sister to know that she'd been crying, she wiped her eyes and face on the sleeve of her cardigan and got up off the floor. She went back to the bottom of the staircase to collect the envelopes and jiffy bag and waited until she heard her dad close his bedroom door again. It was still early, but she didn't want to go back to her room, so she crept down the hall into the kitchen.

Erin flicked the light switch and entered the kitchen. The fluorescent tube broke the silence as it buzzed loudly. After Helen disappeared, it was Erin who was always first downstairs each morning. She got breakfast ready for the family and, the large house having no form of central heating; it was down to Erin to light a fire in the kitchen and the main living room – a job she hated with a passion. It was a dirty job and one that involved going out in the dark and freezing cold to fetch coal from the bunker at the bottom of the back garden. Still, if she didn't do it, it was unlikely her dad would bother. He didn't do much around the house any more. He got up, ate breakfast in silence, and went out to work and when he came home he always carried his meal into the sitting room where he preferred to eat alone before disappearing to bed with only a grunt of a 'goodnight' to his kids.

November had arrived with a bitter chill making the house feel absolutely freezing first thing in the morning and, for that reason, it was a nightmare for Erin to get Sean, Liam and Neive out of bed for school – it invariably resulted in their father bawling at them to get a move on. But this was a Saturday, so no rush to get the kids up. She had to make breakfast for her dad, who still had to work – more so at the weekends now – to pay off the debts her mother had racked up.

She went across the kitchen and lit one of the gas burners on the stove, before filling the kettle with water and putting it on to boil. Any form of heat was a blessing this morning so she turned on another burner to help warm the room up. She couldn't stop shivering as she placed the mail on the kitchen table and turned towards the fireplace the thought of having to go out in the backyard for coal made her shiver even more. Maybe she should go and get back in bed for a bit, she looked up to see what time it was and saw four envelopes with her name on placed along the mantelpiece. Reaching up on her tiptoes she took them down and placed them on the kitchen table with the others she'd received. She thought about opening them now but her teeth were chattering with the cold so she pulled her mum's cardigan tightly around her and went back into the hall to the small cloakroom. She pulled on her dad's heavy overcoat, slipped her feet into a pair of his work boots and headed back into the kitchen and out the backdoor to fill the coal bucket. She'd get the fire going first. Wait until the kitchen was warm and cosy then she could sit down and open her birthday cards.

The first envelope she opened was from her dad. It was beautiful; it had a picture on the front of an angel, 'To a Very Special Daughter' and inside he'd written, '*To my Angel, Happy Birthday, Erin. Love you lots, Dad. xxxxxx*' She swiped at a tear as it slipped from the corner of her eye. He'd put a five-pound note inside the card. She was surprised because it was a lot of money and she knew that her dad was still paying off Helen's debts. She would spend it wisely; let her dad know what she'd bought with it. After all, he had to work very long hours lately and she wanted him to know how much she appreciated it. It was certainly more than enough to buy the latest Fay Morgan novel, her favourite writer of the moment. She'd still have more than four pounds left. *Save the rest! Show dad that that I'm sensible and responsible. That's what I'll do; I'll put it in the Building Society account Nana opened for me last year!* She smiled at the idea of having a building society account.

Next, she opened the cards from her brothers and her sister; she was moved by their thoughtfulness. Neive had drawn a picture inside her card of a little girl holding up a bunch of flowers to an older girl. It was cute; Erin thought she was really lucky to have such a lovely sister and two wonderful brothers.

She put the parcel from her Nana to one side and then opened the cards from Caitlin and her other friends, they'd all written messages of how much they missed her and hoped that she has the 'Best Birthday Ever' and what a lovely best friend she still was to each of them. She smiled again.

Finally, she opened the parcel from her Nana. It contained a lamb's wool scarf with matching hat and gloves. The colour was lime green, unmistakably, lime green. She held the soft wool against her face, thinking at the same time that people would probably see her approaching from a mile away, and then quietly concluded that her friends might make fun of her, particularly if she wore the hat. Perhaps she could get away with the scarf and gloves, but the hat? "I doubt it!" she said to the empty kitchen. She spun the hat round on her fingers and said out loud, "Nana, where did you get this from?" She laughed, "I'll never get away with it. I'll look like one of those new fluorescent ink pens!"

"Erin, my head hurts and I feel sick." She almost jumped out of her skin. She hadn't heard Neive come into the kitchen.

Her hand flew to her chest, "Neive! You minx! You almost scared the life out of me." She put the hat and gloves down on the table and went to Neive, taking hold of her hand she walked her straight out of the kitchen, down the hallway and into the main living room, "Come on, lie down. Do you want me to get you a bowl?" The living room was freezing so she pulled a heavy tartan blanket from the back of the sofa and started tucking her in tightly, "Well, Neive, do you?"

Neive looked away sheepishly, "Erm . . . I don't think so, Erin."

She knelt in front of the sofa and placed her hand on Neive's forehead, just as her mother used to do when any of her kids complained that they didn't feel well, "Hmm, you don't feel too hot, Neive. I don't think you have a temperature or anything." Knowing full well that Neive hated milk of magnesia, and if she were genuinely sick she wouldn't argue with her, Erin said, "What if I get you some milk of magnesia? It'll make the sickness go away."

Neive sat bolt upright and said quickly, "OH! No, Erin, I really don't feel so sick now, just my head hurts that's all now."

"Hmm, I thought as much, you little sod!" She covered her up again and kissed the top of her head then said, "Oh, and thank you for my lovely birthday card. You're very clever you know!" She pinched the end of her nose and laughed, "I like the flowers, and you've made us both look really pretty!"

She settled down on the thick rug beside the sofa and began stroking Neive's forehead. As if she didn't know, she said gently, "So come on, tell me . . . what's really bothering you, Neive?"

Reaching for Erin's hand Neive pulled it underneath the blanket and whispered in her little girl's voice, "When's our mum coming back, Erin? I wish she'd come home . . ." She began crying, "What if she never comes back ever, Erin?"

Sighing deeply, Erin got up onto her knees and hugged her, "I don't know." She looked down at her worried little face and said, "But I promise you this . . . I will find her and, yes, Neive, she will come home. I promise you. Do you believe me, Neive?" Not sure if she did, she nodded and gripped Erin's hand tightly under the blanket.

Still cuddling Neive, she stared out into the garden. A heavy frost had blanketed the trees and a pale sunlight was just beginning to break through the dawn mist, making the branches sparkle as a gentle breeze lightly brushed against the naked branches.

She compared the garden, now, to how it was the night her mother had left; it had been a blaze of colour then, trees and flowers sprouting and budding, the Japonica showing off their striking lavender and pink flora, and the baby soft pink of the Cherry tree in full bloom. She remembered a saying she'd heard somewhere, '*And everything is rosy in the garden . . .*' she hugged Neive closer and whispered, "*But not in this garden . . .*"

CHAPTER TWENTY

SUDDENLY, the peace and quiet in the house was shattered. Liam and Sean were knocking ten bells out of each other at the top of the stairs. Erin leaped to her feet and said to Neive, "Stay here!"

As she reached the bottom of the staircase, she heard her dad yelling, "Pack it in you stupid pair of eejits or I'll give you both a good hiding!"

Liam came tearing down the stairs. He pushed past Erin and stormed down the hall into the kitchen, she could hear him cursing and crying. Sean disappeared back into his bedroom, slamming the door behind him.

She popped her head round the living room door and said again, "Stay there, Neive, while I sort this out."

She hurried down the hallway into the kitchen. Liam was rubbing his shin. She tutted at him and shook her head as she started putting bread under the grill and as she busied herself making breakfast, she said, "If you two don't stop trying to kill each other, you're going to cop it off dad for sure!"

He glared at her back and bawled, "*I hate him and I hate her as well!*" He kicked the chair to the side of him almost tipping it up, "And I hate all of you!" He picked up the tea towel that was lying on the table and began crying into it, "You're a feckin' load of . . ."

Erin spun round, "Enough! Don't you dare use language like that again or *I'll* give you a hiding, never mind dad!"

She snatched the tea towel from him and, leaning towards him almost nose to nose, she said, "Anymore of your feckin' an fuckin' and fighting and God help me, Liam, I'll murder the pair of you!" Liam's eyes were wide with fright, he'd never heard Erin swear before and she'd certainly never threatened him before either.

She registered the shock in his face and stood up straight with her hands on her hips, "Now, sit here and be quiet until I give you permission to speak. Understood?" She went calmly across the kitchen to the stove and lit the grill.

Liam stared at her with disbelief and tears in his eyes, he couldn't believe Erin had just threatened to murder him, *and she means it as well!* He muttered under his breath, "Feckin hell! She's mental, the whole lot of 'em in this house is mental!"

Absently kicking at a small tear in the lino under the kitchen table, he said at last, "I'm sorry, Erin. It was Sean who started it; he dragged me out of bed and I banged my head" Sighing heavily, Erin sat down beside him and taking hold of his hand, she said softly, "Alright. I'll have a word with him. Are you okay now?" He shrugged and nodded, looking down at the big red mark on his shin.

She ruffled his hair, "You've got to stop fighting. Do you hear me, Liam?"

He shrugged again and mumbled, "I know. I know. But it's always Sean who starts it, he won't stop picking on me, Erin." He looked at her, his big doe eyes brimming with tears.

They hadn't heard their father come down stairs; he came straight into the kitchen and slapped Liam across the head, "If you two eejits don't quit the fightin', I'll feckin' kill the pair of you" Liam burst into tears again and ran from the kitchen. John looked at Erin, shook his head and muttered something under his breath. He turned back towards the kitchen door then stopped and said to Erin, "Where's the other one? " Before she could answer, Sean shouted from the living room, "I'm in here Dad, with our Neive!"

He roared, "In here *now*, Sean!" As Sean came into the kitchen he instinctively raised both hands to protect his head and ran past his father, ducking to avoid the inevitable slap; but he surprised Sean. Instead of slapping him across the head as he'd done with Liam, he kicked him up the backside. Erin turned away, chuckling at the surprised and shocked expression on Sean's face. The kick up the backside wasn't what he had expected. About *time*, she thought, Sean deserved a kick up the arse. He was turning into a bully and was getting far too big for his boots since their mother had left.

After John had finished rollicking Sean for fighting he turned to Erin and said, "Happy birthday sweetheart." Erin noticed how drawn and sad he looked. She went to him and hugged him, "Thank you, for the lovely card, Dad, and thank you for the money. I'm going to buy a book with it and put the rest in my building society account." He pecked her forehead and said, "You're a good girl, Erin, and a very sensible girl, too. Now, make us a cup of tea and some toast will you sweetheart, while I go and get ready for work"

She loved her dad with all her heart and couldn't understand why her mother had deserted them. She asked herself time and again what they could have possibly done to make her dump her husband and kids for another man. It wasn't as if her dad was a bad man; he loved her mother dearly and he'd always given her what she wanted if it was within his reach to do so and he was a fantastic dad who'd do anything for his kids.

Erin had heard some of the girls at school whispering about her mother and her boyfriend, the dentist. She swore to herself for the hundredth time that she would see her again and she'd tell her how much she hated her for the pain and heartache she'd brought to the family. John came back into the kitchen and sat down at the table to tie his bootlaces. He looked at Erin, she seemed deep in thought, pre-occupied and he could smell the toast burning. "Erin, I think that toast is about to ignite."

"Oops, sorry Dad! I was just thinking about the English exam I've got next week. Mock 'A' level."

" You're not nervous about it, are you? Because you'll pass with flying colours, I've every faith in you!" He didn't wait for her to answer as he pulled his coat, snatched a piece of toast that Erin just finished buttering, "Back in a couple of minutes, I'm just going to scrape the ice off my windscreen." As he left the house he was thinking, *A levels eh? Who'd have thought a daughter of mine would be taking A levels?*

"Fat bastard!" Erin spun round and slapped Sean across the face so hard that he banged his head against the kitchen wall,

"What have I told you? That's enough! If I hear you say that again about Dad, I'll kick your backside so hard you won't sit down for a month!"

It was Sean's turn to be stunned, rubbing the side of his head, he shouted "Aww, Erin, that feckin' well hurt! I feckin' hate my dad and my mum and I hate you too, Erin!" He jumped up and ran from the kitchen and she heard the front door slam for a second time that morning.

Neive appeared in the doorway and asked Erin, "Where's Liam and Sean, Erin? And where's dad gone?"

Erin went to her and took hold of her hand, "Come on, come and have something to eat. Dad'll be back in a few minutes, he's just sorting out the car before he goes to work."

CHAPTER TWENTY-ONE

SEAN knew where to find Liam and just as he expected he was down by the river skimming stones. Sean went and sat down beside him. Nudging him in the side he said, "I'm sorry, Liam. Can we be mates again? I don't like us to be fightin' all the time, it's all Mum's fault." Liam wiped his nose with the sleeve of his sweater. He'd been crying again and Sean, being two years older, felt responsible. He knew that he should go a little easier on his brother; it's just that he couldn't help feeling angry all the time and wanting to lash out at everyone.

"Aww, c'mon, Liam, I really am sorry." Liam wouldn't look at Sean he just shrugged his shoulders.

Sean tried again, "Are you hungry? Erin's made breakfast and dad'll be gone to work by now so we don't have to worry about coppin' another crack off him!" He stood and pulled Liam to his feet, "C'mon, Liam, I'm freezin'! I'll race you home and the last one back has to give up next Monday's dinner money!" Liam, not one to miss out on his food, didn't hesitate, he was off like a rocket, the fight seemingly forgotten.

Sean was remorseful about bullying Liam. He didn't mean to pick fights with him; he never used to, not when their mum was at home. He was sad and lonely and wondered if things would ever be the same again, he wished so hard every single day that she'd be there when he got home from school or playing out with his mates. He longed for her to hug him and ruffle his hair, just like she used to do when she tucked him in at night. As the eldest boy he felt he had to be tough, and not to cry. *Crying's for babies.* But he was hurting, just like everybody else, and when he felt hurt he lashed out. It was always poor Liam who was often first in the firing line. *I should go easier with our Liam; it's not his fault that our mum's run off with another man.*

The boys let themselves in quietly through the back door. Erin was still in the kitchen trying to encourage Neive to eat a slice of toast. It was Sean who peered round the door. He whispered nervously, "Is dad still here, Erin?"

"C'mon in you pair of eejits. Give me a minute and I'll make you some tea and toast and then I want you to tidy your bedroom before you go out to play, okay?" Sheepishly, both boys nodded their agreement.

* * *

As she was pouring tea for her brothers, she couldn't help watching Neive. She was concerned about her, she didn't look well and had become withdrawn and wasn't eating properly. Erin didn't know what to do, her father was too preoccupied with trying to find their mum and couldn't see what was happening to his kids and she didn't really have anyone else to turn to. Her nearest relative was Nana and she was all the way over in Ireland . . . *perhaps I should telephone her and ask her what to do?*

Worried sick about Neive, and now the boys, she made up her mind there and then to pay a visit to her mother's friend on the Woodsend council estate. The thought made her shudder. Erin had met the woman a few times and didn't like her; there was something about the woman, she wasn't to be trusted. Still busy hurrying her siblings with their breakfast; she planned what she'd say to her mum when she found her. She thought through all kinds of scenarios, from the indignant "How could you do this to us?" to the pleading "Mum, we miss you, please come home." What she really wanted to do was slap her across the face and drag her by the hair back home, just like she would have done to her had the situation been reversed.

She placed the teacups on the tray with several slices of toast dripping with butter, and carried it to the table where the boys and Neive were seated. They looked up at her, and Erin felt the weight of what should have been her mother's responsibility, on her young shoulders. She was the only one who could fix this, and that is what she would have to do.

CHAPTER TWENTY-TWO

IT was Monday the eighth of November when she finally decided to go in search of her mother. Bleaksedge Lane is the only route that leads into the main town of Hindthorpe. The long tree lined road has no shops, or houses along it. Apart from the school bus, there was no public transport service available along the route, just the occasional car or lorry, and if you didn't have anyone to tag along with, it could be a lonely and daunting journey.

That morning, just like any other, she saw to it that Sean, Liam and Neive caught the bus to their school before walking along Bleaksedge Lane to catch her school bus. Except that this morning, Erin wasn't going to school. She was going to the Woodsend estate to ask Brenda where her mother had gone.

Erin set off knowing that if she walked briskly it would take her about twenty minutes to get to the bus station at the other end of the lane. She didn't mind the walk during the summer months but today was different; it was a bitter cold November morning and a thick icy fog had begun to descend.

Determined to see her plan through, her emotions all over the place, she was finding it difficult to get her thoughts in order, and as she hurried along the deserted road she couldn't shake off a feeling of uneasiness, of fear – of what? She didn't know.

On previous occasions she'd had the company of Billy Ashcroft. Today, having to walk that lonely road made her realise how much she really missed Billy, she wished now that she had apologised to him for the way she had reacted to that aborted kiss. She had often thought about that kiss and was actually glad in some ways that she didn't bother with boys because if that's what kissing was like she would happily do without boyfriends for the rest of her life!

But she was sixteen now, and she felt the changes inside her own body. Without a mother to discuss these things with, these strange feelings, she felt it difficult to come to terms with it all. The other girls at school talked about boyfriends and sex openly, many were taking contraceptive pills and virgins were becoming the minority. Another reason why Erin felt isolated there.

Apart from her dad and two brothers, Billy Ashcroft was the only male she had become close to. There wasn't much opportunity to meet boys, her being in an all girl school, and she rarely socialised, so she didn't really see how attractive she was to the opposite sex. The odd beeping of the horn from lorry drivers as they passed was the only inkling she had. Billy had told her she had beautiful eyes, and she was flattered, but then he tried to kiss her and ruined the moment. She now wondered if he was to try that again, would she have acted any differently? *Most definitely*.

CHAPTER TWENTY-THREE

ERIN was still only half way along Bleaksedge Lane when the fog descended; a thick, freezing cold blanket of nothingness and it had all too quickly become difficult for Erin to see much further than a few feet in front of her. It was quiet; eerie in fact. She started thinking that perhaps she should have waited until a little later in the day when the weather might have improved. *It's a bit too late now; I'm halfway there.*

She pulled her lime green scarf securely over her ears and buried her gloved hands deep inside her coat pockets. Lost in thoughts of how she would react and the first thing she would say to her mother if she found her, she was unaware of the car that was parked out of sight at the back of the derelict petrol station, engine purring quietly, ready to move.

Just as Erin was passing the petrol station, the car appeared out of the thick fog right along side her. She was stunned, rigid with fear, like a rabbit caught in headlights. The driver was leering and mouthing words at her that she couldn't make out. He leaned over into the passenger seat, his hooknose almost touching the window as his dark bird-like eyes drank in every inch of her. He waved at her beckoning her to the car.

Erin tried to scream but the freezing cold air took her breath away, nothing came out. She set off running for her life and as she ran she could still hear the hum of the car's engine but couldn't tell whether or not he was coming after her; she was too terrified to look back and so she just kept running. The ice-cold air burned the back of her throat and her lungs as she gasped for breath.

From out of nowhere she was grabbed from behind and lifted off her feet, then a hand came across her face and she almost chocked as the pungent smelling rag was pushed and held firmly against her mouth and nose. The Chloroform was fast; it took less than a minute to do the job. She was out cold – Fitch had his next victim; a little older than most of the others, it couldn't be helped, he'd wanted this one badly and although he'd missed her birthday by a couple of days this time, he'd make sure that her birthday card reached it's recipient on time next year.

He lifted her effortlessly over his shoulder and carried her to his car, the engine still running quietly, he opened the boot and dumped her inside. Not a single vehicle had passed down Bleaksedge Lane to witness the abduction – it was so much easier than he had anticipated – just perfect! He chuckled as he slammed the boot shut and climbed back inside his vehicle.

She'd be unconscious for a couple of hours or more, long enough for him to get her back to the lodge and settled in. He slowed as he drove past the girl's house for one last time wondering what the girl's mother was doing inside. *Well, whatever you're doing, your little girl won't be coming home today, or ever again.* The car sped up and disappeared into the fog.

CHAPTER TWENTY-FOUR

ERIN woke up on a foul smelling mattress in the corner of a room she didn't recognise. Her head was aching badly. She tried to pull herself up but a wave of nausea forced her to lie down again.

There was no light other than the pale yellow stream of moonlight that lit the other side of the room. It was very quiet. She started to shiver uncontrollably and in a small, terrified voice, she called out into the dark, "Is anybody there? Please! Help me . . ." The only sound that came back to her was the echo of her voice, then an empty silence.

She waited as her eyes began adjusting to the darkness; she could just about make out the layout of the room. She was lying on a thin mattress in the corner of the room. There was a window on the opposite wall and a large desk beneath it with an armchair to the side. There was a door to the right of the window – the door was wide open and all she could see beyond that was pitch black – she was absolutely terrified!

Again she tried to pull herself into a sitting position and, as she struggled, a strong sour smell wafted over her and she realised that the blanket wrapped around her was covered in her own vomit, but something more sinister caught her attention. Her shoes were missing and so was most of her clothing, all she had on was her bra and pants and a large metal shackle around her ankle, which was attached to a long chain. She started to whimper, a low childlike moaning. Where was her dad? She wanted her dad! Spluttering through tears she moaned, *"Dad? Oh, please Dad. Please help me."*

There was nobody there.

She tried to crawl to the window, but only got as far as the desk before the chain restrained her. The pain shot up her leg as the shackle dug into her soft flesh. She yanked on the chain but it wouldn't budge – she was trapped, like a performing bear in a cage.

CHAPTER TWENTY-FIVE

SEAN, Liam and Neive stuck rigidly to Erin's rule about coming home from school. They were to come home together, always, on the same school bus. Erin had drummed it into her two brothers; they must make sure they were always on time to meet Neive at the school gate. *Under no circumstances must you let Neive make the journey home alone – you're her big brothers and you must make sure you always take care of her!*

Erin had repeated the same instruction to her brothers on an almost daily basis, saying that it wasn't safe; it was dangerous, particularly for girls on their own, and so it was their duty, as brothers, to look after their little sister.

It was getting dark quite quickly and the fog hadn't lifted all day. Standing outside the school gate, Neive stood patiently, stamping her feet and blowing into her little gloved hands to keep warm while she waited for her brothers to collect her. Sean spotted her and called out, "Neive! Come on!"

Neive ran towards them and because the weather had turned bitterly cold and icy the three of them ran all the way to the bus stop without speaking, just in time to see the bus idling along the road towards the large group of unruly school kids.

They boarded with about twenty other children who were pushing and shoving, some even breaking into scuffles while other kids were still trying to board in an orderly manner, but this didn't last for long.

The bus driver going mad, he hated the school run; in fact, he hated kids full stop. Liam thought he heard the driver mutter, '*Little bastards.*' Sean managed to thrust his arm between a couple of the brawling youngsters, dropped the exact fare into the drivers tray and shoved Liam and Neive all the way to the back of the bus out of the melee that was taking place at the driver's end.

Liam, seemingly oblivious to the circus, asked if they knew what Erin was cooking for their tea. "I'm starving and I could eat a scabby horse between two back gates."

Neive kicked him in the shin and told him he was disgusting. "No one could be *that* hungry that they'd want to eat a *mangy ole' horse.*"

Liam swung round and yanked hard on Neive's ponytail. "You cocky little fecker, Neive! If you kick me again you can find your own way home in future."

Another fight broke out, this time at the back of the bus, this time between the two brothers. Sean jumped up, grabbed hold of Liam and pulled him under his arm into a headlock, pummelling him hard in the face. "I'll smash your teeth in if you do that to our Neive again, you little shite!"

Liam struggled, shouting and cussing as he tried to break free from his brother's grip. The bus driver peered into his rear view mirror and shook his head, he muttered to himself; "*Christ, it's like feedin time at the Zoo!*" It was the second fight Sean and Liam had that day. Neive began crying.

After getting off the bus, the three of them trudged the rest of the way home down Bleaksedge Lane in complete silence. As they turned in at the bottom of their avenue, Neive stopped short, causing Liam and Sean to bump into her and almost topple over. Liam pushed her and said, "You stupid cow, Neive! I nearly fell on my feckin' face!"

Neive ignored him; instead she pointed towards the house and said to Sean, "Look, Sean! No lights on in the house." She turned and stared up at her big brother and then back at the house. She whispered, "*Where's Erin?*" All three set off running at once.

Desperate to get inside, Sean struggled with the key and Liam tried to push him away. "You stupid eejit let me do it!"

"Stop it! Stop it!" Neive yelled as she tried to squeeze between them. "Stop fighting you two or I'll tell Dad." The door swung open and Sean fell through it with Liam on top of him.

She scrambled over her brothers who were wrestling on the floor and ran down the hallway into the living room. It was dark, cold and silent; she called out, "Erin! Erin! Erin, where are you?" She ran from room to room calling out, "Erin, where are you?" Increasingly distressed, tears streamed down Neive's face.

She pushed the door open into the kitchen; it was dark in there too, no fire burning and no sign of Erin. "Sean? Liam? She's not here . . . *Erin's not here!*" The two boys immediately stopped fighting.

Pushing Liam off him, Sean stood and ran up the stairs two at a time. "Maybe she's ill and gone to bed."

He went straight to her bedroom and flung the door open wide but the room was empty, cold and dark just like the rest of the house. Then, like Neive, he ran from room to room. There was no sign of Erin, or any sign of her having been there since early that day. He went to the top of the stairs; Liam and Neive were standing at the bottom looking askance at him. He started down the stairs, slowly, and said to Liam, "Have you looked in the back garden and the outside bog, Liam?" Liam shook his head and said, "She's not here, Sean."

He ran down the rest of the stairs and pushed past Liam and Neive, running into the living room. He searched frantically along the mantelpiece and along the shelf above the sideboard, "What're you lookin for, Sean?" Neive had followed him in to the room and was standing beside him.

Ignoring his little sister, he said, "Liam, where's that Cocoa tin Erin keeps our dinner money in?"

Still rummaging amongst the clutter on the shelf, Neive pushed him to one side and knelt in front of the sideboard.

She opened the bottom drawer and pulled out a pile of neatly folded tea towels.

The Cocoa tin was at the back of the drawer; Neive lifted it out and handed it to her big brother, "What're you gonna do with it, Sean?"

"I'm goin to the 'phone box at the end of the road to phone dad's works. He'll have to come home quick."

"Can I come with you, Sean?"

Sean gently pushed his little sister aside, "No, Neive. You'll have to stay here with our Liam until I get back."

Liam slumped against the wall, a vacant expression on his face. Sean forced a smile and said, "Liam, I need you to stay here and look after Neive, will you do that for us? I'll be back in a few minutes . . . okay?"

Liam nodded, his eyes beginning to fill with tears. He couldn't bear the thought of Erin leaving them; he loved her so much and didn't know what he would do if she didn't come home. Too upset to answer, he looked away, took hold of Neive's hand and nodded again to Sean.

* * *

In the quiet of his office, John Fallen replaced the receiver in its cradle and sat staring at it, bewildered, thinking; *surely she wouldn't still be out in the dark and freezing cold?* He had picked up on the panic in Sean's voice. *First Helen and now this.* His stomach sank.

Thinking about telephoning Erin's school, he glanced at the clock on the wall and realised it was probably too late, everyone would have left by now. It was just after half past four. He couldn't sit there a moment longer, so he grabbed his jacket off the back of his chair and ran from his office, not stopping to speak to anyone as he fled through the factory and out into the car park. His hands were shaking as he tried to get the key into the ignition but eventually he managed to start the engine and, with a screech of wheels, set off to find his daughter.

On the off chance, he pulled up outside Erin's school, but the place was in darkness and the gates were locked. He didn't have a clue where to go next and he began to hate himself for not knowing a single friend of Erin's – how the hell had he let this happen! He turned the car round and put his foot down, heading for home. He hoped and prayed, *please, God. Let her be there.*

* * *

It was half past seven and there was still no sign of Erin; John Fallon paced back and forth, repeatedly rubbing his forehead and cracking his knuckles, something he did when he was extremely agitated. He called the Police as soon as he arrived home two hours earlier, and was *still* waiting for them to arrive. His three young children watched his every move, anxiously.

CHAPTER TWENTY-SIX

THE two police officers introduced themselves as Sergeant Paisley and WPC Julie Gaffney, but John wasn't paying attention. "It's been over two hours since I called, where the bloody hell have you been?" he yelled at them, "What if Erin has had an accident and is lying somewhere in a ditch desperately in need of help?" The thought of it sickened him, as he fought to maintain control of his emotions. It was almost half past eight and the temperature outside was well below freezing.

"Could you provide us with some details, Mr. Fallon?" It was the softly spoken WPC who led the questioning.

"She just turned sixteen last Saturday, she's a *vulnerable young woman*! For the love of God, can you not get out there and look . . . "

"Has she done this sort of thing before?" the Sergeant interrupted, his Glaswegian accent evident despite his attempts to sound the English gent.

"No! She would never do anything like this. She's a good girl."

"And you've not had an argument or disagreement over something?" the WPC responded. John leapt to his feet.

"Now look, I know what you're trying to say, but I'm telling you – "

The Sergeant interrupted again. "We're only trying to rule out the usual reasons young girls sometimes go missing. Perhaps she's at a friend's house and got carried away, lost track of time. You know what girls of that age are like, Mr Fallon, all they're interested in is fashion, makeup and boys."

John exploded, rounding on the officer. "Now you listen to me and listen good! Erin's a good girl! She doesn't have time for messing about with boys and I certainly wouldn't allow it either! She's too young and she has responsibilities here at home taking care of her brothers and sister." He pointed towards his three children, "*They* are Erin's priority. She's not some air head bimbo whose only interest is in tarting herself up and putting herself about!"

During this highly charged and emotional exchange, John Fallon's children sat huddled together in absolute silence. It was only when their father finished shouting at the police officers and there was a moments silence that Sean quietly spoke up, "Dad, I know who might be able to find Erin. Billy Ashcroft. He likes our Erin and he's always asking me about her. He might know where she is, Dad."

John slowly sat down and stared at Sean. In a quiet voice he asked, "What d'you mean, son?" Sean looked from his dad to the Police officers, he looked very nervous, so John prompted him, "What's *Billy Ashcroft* been saying about her, Sean?" Sean struggled to sit up straight, to release himself from the grip of Liam and Neive.

"Billy's brother Phil is in our class and he met us at the bus stop after school." Sean hesitated, looking at the two police officers.

"Go on Son, we're listening," his dad said.

"Well, it's like when our Erin walks down Bleaksedge Lane to school. Billy asked me; you know . . . he asked me if Erin would be walking by herself or if she had friends to walk with. He said he likes our Erin and he doesn't want her to walk along that road on her own. He told me that some girls have gone missing; so I must be sure to let him know if Erin was going that way."

WPC Gaffney sat down next to John and, looking directly at each of the children in turn, she said in a gentle tone, "Think now. Can any of you remember anything else that Billy might have said, or asked you about Erin?"

The children looked at each other in silence and then at their father. Neive dropped her head to her chest, tears spilling down her soft rosy cheeks, she whispered, "Billy was trying to hurt Erin, that's why she ran away from him, Dad." Sniffing loudly and wiping her eyes with the back of her hand, she continued. "Emma Graham told me, 'cause she was in her dad's car going to school and she said that she saw them. She said Erin pushed him and he fell over."

John leaped up off the sofa, "*When Neive?* When were Billy and Erin fighting?"

In between gulping sobs Neive said, "I don't know, Dad." She nervously twisted and pulled at the cuffs of her cardigan, "Emma's my friend at school. She told me about Billy and Erin. But I don't remember. Honest, Dad, I can't remember when it was!"

The two police officers exchanged a knowing look. Paisley nodded at his colleague, who stood and walked over to Sean, kneeling beside him. "Sean, where does Billy Ashcroft live?"

Sean glanced towards his father. John nodded for him to continue. "He lives at the bottom of Eskdale Street, I think it's number twelve. The big terraced house in the corner."

She turned to John Fallon, "We'll start there first, see what Mr Ashcroft has to say for himself. I'm sure she'll show up, Mr. Fallon." Before he could say anything, she added quickly, "Mr Fallon, are you sure that Erin went to school today?"

John was outraged again, "*What do you mean by that?*" She was about to answer when he angrily interrupted her, "Of course she went to bloody School! I'd have known about it if she hadn't!" Truth known, John Fallon had no idea whether his kids skipped school or not – he was too wrapped up in self-pity.

WPC Gaffney blushed, and asked for the name of Erin's school. "Look, we'll contact the head teacher first thing. Maybe she was in some sort of trouble and didn't want to tell you. It happens to the best you know."

John was about to explode again before the Sergeant stepped in. "Mr. Fallon, with respect, we see this all the time and invariably the child turns up with their tail between their legs when it's gone past their bed time."

John pushed past the officers and walked out of the living room and down the hall to the front door. Opening it, he signalled for them to leave. "Just get out there and find Erin!"

As they stepped out into the front garden, John said, "I won't rest tonight. I expect to see you later this evening with my daughter, do you understand?" Not waiting for an answer, he slammed the door behind them and muttered some obscenity that only he heard. He walked back down the hall and into the neat and tidy living room and turned his attention to his three children. They looked wretched and lost – *where the hell is that bitch of a mother of theirs . . . and now this, Erin missing. Dear God, please bring her back safe, tonight.*

They were still in their school uniforms and he knew that they wouldn't have had anything to eat since lunchtime. He was at a loss as to what to do, Erin did all the cooking and she was very good too, not that he told her often. *She learned well from that mother of hers, proper Irish, simple but plenty of it.* He realised at that moment just how much his daughter had taken on, and so young. His feeling of guilt was only overshadowed by his fear of what may have happened to his darling little girl.

He couldn't think about eating right now, he felt physically sick. "Son can I trust you to look after your brother and sister while I go out and look for Erin?"

Eager to please his dad and to prove to him how grown up he was, he gushed, "Course you can Dad! And is it okay if I make us some supper? And can we wait up until you get back, Dad?"

For the first time since their mother had left, John took a proper look at his son and it frightened him when he saw just how much the boy had changed; he'd been too wrapped up in his own pain and pre-occupied with his search for Helen to notice his children. He'd left everything to Erin. He looked at Liam and Neive in turn, and in that heart breaking second he wanted to drop to his knees and hug them close and never let them out of his sight.

The painful realisation hit him hard now, that Erin had been holding this broken little family together and, selfishly, he'd left her to it. It was only now that she was missing he realised just how precious she was to him and his children. For months on end, he had wallowed in his own self-pity and hadn't given any thought as to how his kids might be suffering and dealing with their loss. They deserved so much more from him.

He was struggling with so many emotions and now added to those was an intense feeling of shame and inadequacy. He should never have allowed Erin to shoulder the burden of running the home and being an emotional support for her brothers and sister. She was after all only just sixteen and he had burdened her with so much, forced her to grow up before her time. He was devastated; he couldn't bear the thought of her being in any danger or lying hurt somewhere in the cold and dark.

Sean couldn't make out what was wrong with his dad; he had a strange, faraway look in his eyes, one that Sean hadn't seen before. Still waiting for an answer, he whispered, "*Dad?*"

Shaking his head, John said, "Sorry, son. You three must be hungry. Yes, of course it's all right. Can I trust you to make beans on toast without burning the house down, Sean?" He smiled and ruffled Sean's hair but Sean noticed that the smile didn't touch his dad's eyes and it made him want to cry.

Then to Liam and Neive John said very gently, "Sean will make supper and then I want the two of you washed and in bed by nine o'clock okay?"

Wanting to wait up until her dad came home with Erin, Neive was about to appeal when John said; "I don't want you to be late for school in the morning, and, don't worry; Erin will be here when you get up tomorrow. Now sit and watch some telly while Sean gets your supper ready."

He turned and started to walk slowly from the room before stopping in the doorway, and saying to Sean, "Don't forget, son, don't burn the house down – be very careful in the kitchen, all right?"

"Don't worry, Dad, you can trust me and as soon as we've had supper I'll make sure Liam and Neive go to bed. Anyway, Dad, Erin might come home while you're out looking for her."

His father didn't answer, he was staring at a photograph on the mantelpiece; it was a picture of Erin standing to attention in her Brownie uniform. Sean waited. Looking for reassurance, he prompted, "Dad?"

His mind clearly in another time and place, he tore his tormented gaze from Erin's picture and said, "Sorry, yes . . . I hope so, son. *God help us*, I hope so!"

Sean wasn't sure who was trying to convince whom.

John turned and walked out into the hallway, took his coat from the stand by the front door, and walked back into the living room. His kids hadn't moved; they were still huddled together in front of the unlit fireplace, "Think on now. Do as Sean tells you and when you've eaten, get washed, brush your teeth and in bed for nine o'clock. No arguing"

Neive started crying and ran to him, throwing her arms round his waist. He bent down, wrapped his strong arms around her and hugged her tight then kissed the top of her head, choking back his own tears, "C'mon, sweetheart, stop crying. Erin will be here when you get up in the morning." He pulled her away from him, "Watch some telly while Sean makes your supper, eh? I've got to go out now."

As he turned to leave the room, Sean said, "She will come home, won't she, Dad?"

Tears welled in the big man's eyes, he couldn't bring himself to turn and face his son. He walked out of the room and, a little sharper than he'd intended, his voice gruff with emotion, he called back to him, "Yes! Of course she will!"

* * *

John was about to open the front door when he caught sight of his reflection in the mirror by the coat stand. He was shocked to see how haggard he looked. His wife's disappearance and now this, his beloved Erin was missing. The past months had taken their toll on him and now he didn't know whether or not he could survive if Erin didn't come home.

He looked away quickly and opened the front door, and as he stepped out into the cold dark night, the tears he'd been holding back started to rain down his face. Not knowing where to begin his search, he walked desolately to his car and once inside he broke down and wept inconsolably. His huge frame heaved as he gave vent to gut wrenching sobs. It had taken every ounce of courage he had not to let his kids see how scared and broken he felt.

The depth and pain of his despair was almost physical. He choked and spluttered through his tears, *"Oh, God, please take this pain away! Please bring her back to us!"* The very thought of not being able to find her and bring her home with him that night was incomprehensible, but deep down he couldn't shake off a terrible feeling that she wouldn't be coming back.

He knew his daughter better than anyone and he also knew that she would never stay away from home without speaking to him first and letting him know where she was going and whom she was with.

Something bad had happened to her. He felt sick with a grief so intense that it tore at his heart. As he wept, he continued praying to God to keep her safe, to bring her home . . . but still that nagging doubt remained . . . what would he tell his kids if he returned without her? He'd promised Neive that Erin would be there in the morning. *Aww, Jesus Christ Almighty what did I do that was so bad that you'd make my children suffer like this.*

He had never felt such profound despair in all his life and he wished at that moment that he could end it all. He didn't know which way to turn; he had no one now. His father was dead and his mother was over in Ireland and she couldn't remember her own name these days, let alone her son who hadn't visited her in years. Yes, he was truly alone . . . he had to find Erin; he needed her to hold his precious family together.

CHAPTER TWENTY-SEVEN

A S WPC Gaffney drove the police car away from the house, she glanced sideways at her colleague and said, "What do you think Sarge? Another disgruntled runaway teenager, or something more sinister?"

The sergeant was reading through the notes he took while talking to the missing girl's family, "Hmm, I can't say for sure, but something tells me that we might be looking at a more serious matter of abduction. From what her father said, she doesn't seem to fit the bill of a rebellious teenager." He stared out the side window into the cold dark night.

"You're right about that. From what he's told us, she seems to be a real levelheaded young lady. Pissed off teenager rebelling? Somehow I think, *not this one.*"

"I'm worried that I have to agree with you there. If she's not found in the next forty-eight hours and it becomes public knowledge, which it's bound to do, I think it'll whip up a hell of a storm with the press and media. What's worrying me even more right now is that the Fallon girl could be another one to be added to the growing list of the missing girls – cases still unsolved!" He looked straight ahead, shaking his head slowly.

"I can't help thinking about those three little kiddies of his, they looked so scared and lost."

Paisley wasn't listening. He was thinking about the girl that went missing last year, the one the press labelled as another missing

Birthday Girl, and the poor mother who took her own life when she received a card only a matter of weeks ago. He looked at the WPC side on, "Let's pray she turns up tonight – unharmed! It's bad enough we weren't able to locate that so-called missing *wife* of his; and now this. Jesus Christ! No wonder he wasn't exactly enamoured with us when we turned up tonight."

"Missing? My arse! Come on, Sarge. It's a well-known fact that the woman was at it with that Greek bloke . . . dentist wasn't he?" She didn't wait for him to answer, "It's a cruel excuse for a mother who dumps her kids for a bloke!"

"Hmm, beats me." Paisley remarked in a pre-occupied fashion. Looking over his shoulder at the road sign he said sharply, "Turn around!"

Confused, she shot a sideways glance at him, "What?"

"Turn the bloody car round, woman! We're going to pay young Ashcroft a visit! We're no' waiting 'til tomorrow."

He pulled his notebook out of his breast pocket and flipped through a couple of pages, "Number twelve Eskdale. That's the address the wee laddie gave us."

CHAPTER TWENTY-EIGHT

MRS Ashcroft was annoyed. As she waddled from the kitchen down the wide hallway to answer the door, she called out to the two men watching telly in the living room, "Yes, that's right, you lazy pair of buggers, just sit on your useless fat arses and let me get it!"

She swung the door open ready to give whoever it was a mouthful for calling at such a late hour.

The police officers stepped back as the heavy door swung wide and a small dumpy woman appeared ready to do battle with the caller.

Noting the angry expression on the woman's face, Sergeant Paisley wasted no time and enquired, "Mrs Ashcroft?"

"Yes. What's wrong?"

Removing his cap, he introduced himself and his colleague, "I'm Sergeant Paisley and this is WPC Gaffney."

"And?"

"We're here to speak to your son. Billy. Can we come in, please?"

She popped her head out and glanced up and down the street, stood to one side and nodded for the officers to come in. Impatiently she said, "Come on, come on. Don't hang around out here! You'll have all the neighbours gossiping, nosey bunch of arseholes at the best of times!"

She closed the door quickly, "What do you want to speak to him about?"

WPC Gaffney smiled and said, "We believe Billy's a friend of Erin Fallon? We'd like to ask him a few questions about when he last saw her"

Bernadette Ashcroft suddenly felt nervous and rattled, *what's he been up to now?* She replied with a barrage of questions, "What do you mean, when he last saw her?" Like a machine gun. Ratatatat! "Erin Fallon? Do you mean the little auburn haired girl from Florence Terrace? Why? What's he got to do with her? What's he supposed to have done?"

Slowly edging backwards down the hallway in the direction of the living room and wringing the corners of her apron, she became angry at the intrusion. The police were not frequent callers at her house and she began to worry about what that good-for-nothing son of hers had been up to. The officers couldn't get a word in edgewise.

"What's he done?" Her hand flew to her mouth, "Oh, Lord! She's not pregnant is she?"

Sprawled out in front of the fire, the two men in the living room were oblivious to the visitors and the conversation taking place in the hallway; they were still watching the telly when Bernadette Ashcroft peered round the door and hissed, "Billy! Get out here now!" All bravado gone, she was wringing her hands, "The police are here! They want to ask you some questions!"

The officers were now halfway down the hallway and were standing outside what was usually referred to as the parlour in these grand Victorian terraced houses – well that was according to Bernadette Ashcroft, anyway. "We'd like to speak to your son in private if we may, Mrs Ashcroft." The sergeant inclined his head in the direction of the parlour, "In there, if that's all right with you?"

Billy appeared in the hallway, both hands stuck down the front of his jeans, a blue check shirt unbuttoned to his waist, his dishevelled shoulder length dark curly hair appearing as though it hadn't seen a comb in days. WPC Gaffney took all this in at a glance. Despite his scruffy appearance, he was a good-looking young man and it was easy to understand why he might be popular with the girls.

Mrs Ashcroft moved down the hall again, pushed past the officers and flicked the light on in the parlour. She turned to her son and, shoving him none too gently, she hissed, "Get in there!"

Unperturbed by the surprise visit of the police and the angry tone of his mother, Billy didn't say anything; he just looked blankly at the officers and then at his mother, shrugged his shoulders, and did as he was told. Hands still down the front of his jeans, he casually sauntered into the parlour and stood in front of the unlit fireplace; the puzzled expression on his face gave nothing away. The officers followed and Sergeant Paisley closed the door before Mrs Ashcroft had a chance to join them.

Not wanting to waste any time, Paisley turned to the lad and said, "You're a friend of Erin Fallon, is that correct?"

Still standing and, in a cocky, couldn't care less manner, Billy replied with a smile, "Yep, I know her."

"No. That's not what I asked. Answer the question, please. Are you a friend of Erin Fallon?"

The sharp, no-nonsense, tone of the Sergeant suddenly unnerved Billy and he wondered what the Police could possibly want with him. He hadn't see Erin for weeks. A little less cockily, he said defensively, "I was! I mean, I am a friend of Erin's but I haven't seen or spoken to her for about three months," he lied. "Why? What's this about?"

WPC Gaffney sat down at the large dining table in front of the window and was making notes. Wanting to gauge his reaction, she looked up and said casually, "Mr Fallon has reported his daughter missing. Do you have any idea where she might be or why she has gone missing?"

Billy looked genuinely shocked now, his demeanour changed. He stepped across the room to the dining table and sat down opposite the WPC.

Sergeant Paisley noted the immediate change in Billy's manner. He thought the lad looked convincingly surprised at the news of Erin's disappearance. *Good little actor, this piece of shit*, he thought.

WPC Gaffney finished scribbling notes and, notepad and pen ready to go again, she said, "Billy, we want you to tell us everything about the last time you saw Erin and what exactly happened between the two of you on that occasion?"

"Why? I've not done anything! I told you, I've not seen Erin for months!"

Sergeant Paisley was becoming a little impatient, he interrupted, "Tell us about the fight you had on Bleaksedge Lane with Erin Fallon!"

Startled, Billy looked from one officer to the other. *Shit.* Mouth wide open, he raised his hands as if surrendering to a charge. Shaking his head wildly, he protested, "Whoa, whoa, hold on a minute! Erin and me did not have a *fight!* I don't know who told you this, but we have never fought. I liked her a lot. I'd never have hurt her, and that's the God's honest truth!"

Paisley pulled out one of the dining chairs and sat down directly in front of Billy, so close he could smell the lad's breath, clearly intending to intimidate him. Billy's discomfort was evident as he tried to move out of the way, but from his position in the bay window he found he had no room for manoeuvre. The Sergeant had him hemmed in as Billy tensed.

Paisley sensed the tension. He had him cornered and leaned in even closer, causing Billy to bang his head against the window.

"You were seen, Billy! Erin was spotted running away from you in tears! And it wasn't months ago, it was a matter of weeks, wasn't it, Billy?"

In an attempt to scare him further, he added, "If you don't tell the truth, you've as good as booked yourself a night in a cell. Now, have I made myself clear?"

Mrs Ashcroft had been outside the door the whole time, listening to the officers questioning her son. But what the officer had just threatened was too much, she couldn't hold back any longer.

She barged into the room, shouting, "That's enough, d'you hear!

What is it that you're trying to accuse my son of doing?"

Billy jumped up and said, "Okay! Okay! I'll tell you what happened, but we *did not* have a fight, I can explain, *honest!*" Sergeant Paisley doubted he knew the meaning of the word.

The room fell quiet as Billy stood up and moved away from the dining room table, wringing his hands as he began pacing up and down the room. "I've always had a soft spot for Erin. I used to walk her to the bus stop at the top of Bleaksedge Lane when she was on her way to school. I wanted to make sure that she was safe, you know?" He looked at each of the officers and then at his mother.

Still taking notes, Gaffney said, quietly, "Go on then. What else?"

Running his hands through his thick curly hair, he said guiltily, "I tried to kiss her, that was all. I think I must have scared her because she pushed me, started yelling at me, called me a pervert. It was only a kiss, for fu – "

"Billy. Language!"

"Sorry mum. *I did not and would not – ever, hurt Erin!*"

His audience waited for him to continue; his mother's mouth was open as though about to speak but she said nothing, she just continued staring at him.

"Carry on. We're listening," the sergeant said.

"Well, I never intended to upset her or scare her, I ended up on my arse because she kneed me in the bollo – testicles! Christ, it didn't half hurt! I felt a right prick! She ran off in tears and I called after her. I shouted after her that I was sorry and to wait for me, but she just kept running. I never caught up with her. That's it. *That's the truth.* I've not seen Erin since, like I said, it's been months – err weeks."

"And you've not spoken to her at all in that time?" WPC Gaffney asked.

"No, honest. I've not spoken to her since then. I warned her about walking up there on her own."

"Oh, and why's that, Billy," the sergeant said.

"Well, you know, these girls that have gone missing over the last few years."

"Tell me, Billy, what would you know about that?"

"Now look," Mrs Ashcroft interrupted. "If you think this lad has been abducting schoolgirls since the age of twelve – "

"No I'm not suggesting that," the sergeant said, defensively, "but he certainly knows this one, *doesn't he*?" Sergeant Paisley stood up, motioned to Gaffney and walked towards the door. "We'll leave it there for now," then turning to Billy, "but we'll be speaking to each other very soon laddie. Very soon."

As the two police officers left and the front door slammed shut, Billy exhaled. His mother went back to the parlour. "You'd better be telling the truth!"

"I am!" Billy protested. "There is on thing though."

"Go on." Mrs Ashcroft said in a doubting manner.

"You know that *Birthday Girl* killer they were talking about in the news?"

"What's that got to do with it?"

"I think it was Erin's birthday last weekend."

CHAPTER TWENTY-NINE

Bleazedale Forest, May 1977

ERIN was doing what she did everyday – when *he* wasn't there. She was sat in front of the window searching the shadows, watching and waiting. Maybe *somebody* – a group of hikers, perhaps, might stumble across the lodge and catch sight of her through the barred window. Every day was the same, at least four or five days out of every week and those days were randomly chosen by her jailer. Left alone, she maintained her vigil and would not give up hoping, no matter how exhausted and sick she was feeling, so she sat for hours on end peering through filthy aluminium window blinds that were covered in dark spots, the remnants of countless flies and other dead insects. Some had been caught in the spider's webs on the grimy dust covered windowsill, others had either been brushed out of sight or lay dead and decaying behind the cluttered desk. She moved the stacks of old newspapers and medical journals out of her line of vision and settled in for another epic watch.

A loud buzzing nearby interrupted her thoughts. Probably another disgusting blue bottle, the only things she had for company; the lodge was always full of them, she hated them – filthy things flying around her food and the squalid living space she occupied. She even woke sometimes to find the insects feeding on the open wounds on her hands and feet

She picked up a magazine from the pile on the desk, rolled it up, and launched it at the window blinds. The buzzing stopped, but only for a few seconds and then it began again, only it seemed louder this time, more deliberate. The disgusting insect knew that she had tried to kill it so it taunted her, flying around her face and head. The constant drone was like an alternative form of Chinese torture. If he would only bring her a can of insect repellent, but that would be too much to hope for. She would use it on *him* too; aim it straight at his eyes, keeping her finger on the nozzle until the can had emptied in his face. She could blind and choke him to death with it. But he probably already knew that because he did nothing to get rid of the insects.

During the first few days of her captivity, she had searched every inch and every corner of her limited living area desperate to find something, *anything* she could use as a weapon against him. But he had made sure there was nothing, nothing at all that she could attack him with.

She had once dared to ask him if he would bring her some canned soup or canned beans instead of the cereals, cartons of milk and dried fruit he left her each week. "And if I did, how would you heat the soup up? Your chain isn't long enough to move beyond the water closet and this room." He had smiled slyly as he waited for her to answer.

She had already prepared for that particular question and said "I don't mind eating cold soup, I used to eat cold peas straight from the tin when I was at home." She dared to think that she might have convinced him.

"How disgusting you are. You will eat what I choose to provide you with and canned food will not be on the menu, ever!" And that was that, end of conversation. He turned and left, locking the lodge door from outside. It wasn't the canned food itself she wanted; it was the idea that she could use the sharp tin lids as weapons. It had taken a lot of courage to ask him for something, she had even anticipated receiving an extra beating for daring to speak to him. She didn't care, though; it would have been more than worth it. She had fantasised for so long about how she would conceal the metal disks on her and when he removed the ankle iron and chain she'd lash out at him, slash his face and throat repeatedly – he would bleed to death and she would be free, free to leave the lodge and run for her life. There wasn't much more he could do to hurt her. She was sore and in constant pain from the physical abuse and torture he put her through each time he came to the lodge. Another battering from him would have made not the slightest difference.

Stretching her arms above her head, she yawned loudly; it seemed very strange hearing her own voice. It sounded as if it belonged to someone else. She hadn't heard her voice in months; maybe it was somebody else? She turned from the window and looked around the room, "Hello? Who's there?" She was greeted by silence, empty lonely silence. It was her voice.

Looking down at the navy plaid skirt she was wearing and the matching navy cardigan, she wondered about the girl who had once worn them. Had she escaped? Did the mad doctor let her go when he was finally finished with her? Maybe there had been other girls here who had worn these very same clothes? She looked at the pile of clothing in the corner near her mattress. Those clothes had been there since her arrival; so many pairs of shoes, dresses, ribbons, underwear. How many girls had there been before her? She shuddered and turned back to the window.

CHAPTER THIRTY

WITH the stealth of a hungry animal targeting its prey, Fitch entered the lodge at the rear and positioned himself behind the kitchen door. By peeping through the small hole in the middle of the upper panel he had a clear view of Erin seated at the desk in front of the window. He stood for several minutes, rigid, not wanting to make a sound. He didn't want her to know he was there – not just yet, anyway – and how easily he could come and go without her knowing.

As he stared through the small hole he couldn't understand why he felt a tiny spark of admiration for this particular young girl. When she dared to speak to him, which was rare, she did so respectfully and he liked that. There was something else about her too which he couldn't quite fathom. It wasn't just her physical beauty. Yes, she had that certain . . . je ne sais quois? Whatever it was, it set her apart from the others. He enjoyed watching her, particularly as she was now sitting very still, head held high, feet crossed at the ankles, her hands clasped prayer like beneath her chin. She had a grace and refinement about her and was by far the prettiest of all the girls he'd taken. Yes indeed, she was different, special.

He pulled the syringe from his coat pocket and looked at his watch, he wasn't due at his office for another three hours, plenty of time to do what he'd planned. He heard her sigh as she brushed her long copper hair from the side of her face. Her hair had grown considerably and was much longer now than when he first brought her to his little hideaway. With his weekly supply of provisions, he had made sure she had toiletries and shampoo – he wanted to keep her clean and fresh for when he decided to take out his frustrations on her weakened body and he made sure that she always had enough food to keep her alive but not enough to give her the strength to resist.

He tightened his grip on the syringe overcome with a sudden urge to grab a fistful of her hair, yank her out of the chair and throw her small body about like a rag doll. He tapped the door lightly. The noise behind her made her freeze. *Oh, God, he's here!*

Terrified of turning around, she sat absolutely still and waited. He would probably grab her from behind, as he often did. A cold sweat raised goose bumps across her scalp and down her entire body. Teardrops sprang free and rained down her cheeks. She was paralysed with fear as she waited to feel his long bony fingers grip the back of her neck. She didn't realise that she was holding her breath until she exhaled loudly above the deafening thud of blood as it throbbed loud and hard in her ears. What is he doing? Where is he? She couldn't stand it any longer; she had to face the monster. She turned slowly and peered over her shoulder at where she thought the sound had come from.

Nothing. No sign of anyone. Nothing appeared out of place. Yet her instincts told her that he was in there with her, she sensed his ominous presence. He was playing with her, terrorising her before he attacked.

Gripping the edge of the large oak desk she pulled herself up out of the chair. Turning slowly, she began to move towards the sitting room door, the heavy chain dragging along behind her letting him know that she was moving about. As she crossed the floor, she felt and heard the creaking of the floorboards beneath her birdlike weight; the sound cracking the stale air. She prayed silently, *Dear Lord God help me. Please help me!*

She moved towards the open door, the chain rattling along the floor as she went. Her teeth were chattering. She stopped just on the edge of the hallway between the kitchen and the sitting room and dared to look up the dark stairway. She looked away quickly, she didn't think the noise had come from up there, it had sounded much nearer, so she edged out towards the kitchen door and craned her neck inside, scanning the large room. There was no one there and nothing out of place.

She had a sudden need to run for the bathroom when she realised she had already lost control of her bladder, her legs were warm and wet. Ignoring her mess, she turned towards the stairs again and looked up. She called out into the dark shadows of the upstairs rooms, "Hello? Who's there?" She couldn't control the trembling as she stared into the darkness, *why won't he answer? Show yourself you sick bastard!* Fitch smiled at the fear in her voice, he was enjoying this.

Her hand flew to her chest and she clutched the top of her cardigan, pressing it hard against her body as her heart pounded so hard and so fast she thought it was going to burst through her ribcage. She wanted to throw up. She knew he was there; she could feel his presence. She could smell him. And then his warm breath came through her hair and touched her ear; *he was behind her.*

"Disgusting little bitch!"

Grabbing a fistful of her hair, Fitch thrust the syringe into the top of her left arm. The effects of the drug were almost instant. A scream caught in her throat as her body started to go limp. Her arms and legs went numb and she slumped at the foot of the stairs. Twisting her hair repeatedly around his fist he used it to pull her to her feet then he shook her violently, the long chain rattling against the floor as he yelled in her ear, "Stand up, bitch! Stand up!!"

Still conscious but unable to feel her arms and legs she was unable to fend off the blows that rained down on her, a pain shot across the back of her head where he was shaking her violently by the hair. She tried to plead, to beg him to stop hurting her but she couldn't speak. With savage force, he threw her down again hard against the foot of the stairs and kicked her repeatedly in the ribs and stomach yelling at her.

"Get up!"

Erin attempted to pull her knees up to her chest to avoid the blows to her stomach and ribs but her legs were useless, he had paralysed her.

It started to go dark and his voice began to fade. Her father's kind face looked down at her. She tried to raise her arms to reach out to him but they wouldn't move, they were useless, *Dad? Help me, please!*

He took a small key from his trouser pocket and unlocked the shackle around her ankle; the chain fell away as he began to drag her mercilessly up the staircase, deliberately banging her head hard against each step.

Erin came to in an upstairs room. She knew that he was going to take her to the brink of death and she would have given anything for him to take her over the edge, to end it once and for all. A small lamp was placed on top of a box in the corner of the room and the intense glare from the naked bulb hurt her eyes, forcing her to struggle to focus and that's when she saw a large nylon sack in the corner of the room, it was writhing and she could clearly hear clawing and squealing sounds coming from it. *He'd fetched Rats!* Her blood ran cold as she wondered what hideous insane game he was going to subject her to. Looking up she saw the ropes hanging from a beam in the exposed roof space. She screamed but nothing came out.

Fitch came back into the room with a roll of gaffer tape in his hand. He looked down at Erin and said, "I don't think you're going to enjoy this. But I'm quite sure I will."

CHAPTER THIRTY-ONE

JOHN Fallon was determined not to allow the police to give up searching for his daughter. For months after she had gone missing he kept her in the forefront of the nation's mind. He regularly spoke to newspaper reporters and used radio and television to air his pleas to whoever had taken her not to harm her, to let her go.

John also appealed to the viewing public not to let the police forget Erin, and to the person responsible for taking Erin he said, "If you're watching, please know that Erin is a very gentle and caring girl, she's precious . . ." Struggling to hold back tears, he continued, "Whoever you are, I beg you, please don't hurt my little girl – we just want her back!" He swiped at the tears he couldn't hold back anymore and said, "She has two brothers and a wee sister, Sean, Liam and Neive, they need her . . . she's all they've got . . . please!"

The sight of this giant of a man publicly displaying his grief and heartache was too distressing for many parents and the general public and it resulted in hundreds of people wanting to volunteer their support, assisting the police searches of open fields, woodland, derelict properties. School grounds, churches and other public buildings were subjected to the same rigorous searches but not a single trace of any of the five missing girls was found.

John Fallon continued to harangue the police week after week, month after month demanding a blow-by-blow account of what was being done; how much of the town was still to be searched. He was never going to give up on Erin and he made damned sure the police knew it. For reasons he couldn't explain, he knew in his heart she was still alive and until she was found he would fight with every fibre of his being to have her back – safe.

The police stepped up their search again for the missing mother in the hope that when they found her, they'd find Erin. John always maintained that Erin had set off to find her the day she disappeared, and their investigations led them to Ireland.

Kevin Monahan, a twenty four year old carpenter, was the last person to catch Helen's eye after a series of appointments at the dentist where she worked. On the morning of the ninth of March, the police arrived on the doorstep of his stone cottage on the banks of Dogs Bay, Roundstone in County Galway. Helen was in the kitchen cooking breakfast.

The young Irish officer spoke first. "Mr Monahan? Kevin Monahan?"

"That's me. Can I help you?"

"Reserve Garda O'Sullivan, and this is Constable Shepherd from England." Monahan shook the hand of each in turn.

"Pleased to meet you both. And what brings you to this remote part of the world?"

Shepherd held out a photograph. "We believe you know this woman." Monahan took the picture and smiled. "Helen Fallon?"

"Indeed I do." Holding up the picture outside the doorway to catch the natural light, he added, "And a beautiful woman she is too. Would you like to speak to her?"

"She's here?"

"Well now, last time I checked she was in the kitchen, and my nose tells me she's busy cooking breakfast. Would you like to come in? Can't guarantee a rasher sandwich but there's a pot of tea brewing if you want a cup."

The policemen entered the cottage as Helen came out of the kitchen carrying two plates stacked high with bacon, eggs, tomatoes and fried bread. With her hair scrunched up in a bun and no make-up, she didn't resemble the photograph, but her striking looks left no doubt as to her identity.

"Oh, I didn't realise we had company." Helen said as she put the plates on the table.

"Indeed we have, Helen, and they're here to see you. You did remember to return those library books didn't you?"

"Kevin! Can you be serious for just a few minutes in your life?" Helen said, turning to the policemen. "What can I do for you?"

Shepherd took over proceedings. "Mrs Fallon, I'm Constable Shepherd of Lancashire Constabulary. I don't know if you heard, but your daughter, Erin . . . "

"Yes, what about her?"

"She disappeared last November." The unease was evident in Shepherd's voice.

Helen pulled a chair from under the table and sat, resting her elbow on the bare wood, her hand supporting her head as she eyed up the young Englishman. "Disappeared last November you say? That was . . . five months ago!"

"It took some time to find out where you'd gone, Mrs Fallon. Your friend the cleaner, Brenda Thomas, was quite protective."

"Brenda? Ha! I'm surprised she could keep her gob shut about anything. T'was her that spread all those rumours about me and that dentist."

"I'll go and make the tea." Monahan decided it was time to make himself scarce.

"Mrs Fallon, I know this is difficult, but do you have any idea where Erin might have gone?" Shepherd continued. "We have reason to believe she left home with the intention of finding you. Did she try and make any contact with you at all?"

"He spoiled her rotten, the stupid eejit. Her daddy, John. I told him but he wouldn't listen. Why would she come looking for me when it was him that gave in to her every time?"

"Did she confide in you at all? Was there somebody she may have – "

"Look. She was the apple of her daddy's eye, she told me nothing about anything. If you want my opinion, she probably ran off with some Gypsy feller 'cause she got pregnant and couldn't face her dad."

At that moment, Monahan returned with a tray full of cups and a pot of tea. "Sugar and milk's over there gentlemen," he said, as he placed the tray on the table.

Helen pushed back her chair and stood. "They won't be needing it, Kevin. I've told them all I can. Now if you don't mind . . ." she motioned towards the door. "Only our breakfast is getting cold."

* * *

PC Shepherd returned to England with the unfortunate duty of advising Sergeant Paisley that the journey was a waste of time, not to mention the taxpayer's money and a big chunk of *his* budget for the year. It was becoming the most perplexing case Paisley had ever worked on and his frustration was heightened when the Chief Superintendent announced he was handing the case over to the local CID, which with the recent changes in policing in the region, amounted to a team of two!

CHAPTER THIRTY-TWO

'OFFENDER PROFILING' it said on the front of the dossier on Detective Constable Mike Jones's desk. He had just been assigned to the '*Birthday Girl*' case along with Detective Sergeant Ken Harris. From what Mike Jones had gathered, the case spanned over four years and had been covered by two police authorities in that time but apart from a few photographs, there had been no tangible leads.

Jones had recently been promoted from the rank of Trainee Detective Constable after serving as a uniformed officer for three years. At the age of twenty-five, he was one of the youngest detectives in the force and showed great potential.

Harris, on the other hand, had been around the block a few times. Although only fifteen years his senior, he looked a lot older than Jones. He had every right to. As a war child, he was evacuated from his home in Liverpool to Oswestry in Shropshire. His father was called up for duty, never to return and his mother died in a farming accident when he was only six years old, leaving him to be raised by his Aunt and Uncle in Preston once the war was over. Harris joined the force after leaving college and slowly worked his way up the ranks to become a Police Sergeant in the Lancashire Constabulary in 1966. Two years later he made the switch to the CID where he thought he'd found his true vocation. Unfortunately, others didn't see it like that and his career stagnated. He should have moved on, he knew that, but he liked it where he was. It felt comfortable.

"What's this about?" DS Harris thumbed the first couple of pages and smiled. "More new fangled ideas from the States?"

"Actually it's not that new. The first criminal to be *'profiled'* is said to be Jack the Ripper." DC Jones replied. "Thought we might use some of the ideas on the 'Birthday Girl' case. Let's face it, the uniform brigade haven't turned up any leads have they?"

Harris shook his head impatiently, "Look it's simple; this fellow's a Cadbury's fruit and nut case. He takes young girls, does unspeakable things to them, and then disposes of their bodies. Our job is to find him before he takes another." DS Harris was pretty much no-nonsense Old School. He continued, "How long's that Fallon girl been gone now?"

"Ten months I think." DC Jones fumbled for his notebook. "Yes, she went missing on the 8th of November last year."

"And there've been no more since. What was the time lapse between previous disappearances?"

"Just over a year apart. Gemma Cahill was the first, we think; 25th June '72. Wendy Hilton 16th July '73, Natalie Critchley 9th September '74, and Debra Johnson 24th September '75."

"And then on the 8th of November 1976 he takes Erin Fallon. All apart from the last one, taken on their birthday."

"Hence the name of the case, Sarge."

"*Yes I know that.* The point I was making was that the last one *wasn't.* Never mind the *'Offender profiling'* rubbish, this man is meticulous. He knows his victims; he knows when they were born, he even dictates when they are going to die. But Fallon, he missed her birthday by two days, that's sloppy. Get your coat Jonesy, we're going for a ride."

"Where to Sarge?"

"Bleaksedge Lane."

CHAPTER THIRTY-THREE

Hindthorpe, September 1977

CAROLE Worsley was an attractive, young looking middle-aged woman, dainty in stature, with cascading locks of blond hair. She was often mistaken for a young girl from behind – a cause of jealousy with some of her female colleagues. As a long-term employee of the National Health Service, she had marked out a good career over the years, and had made many life-long friends as a result. She had joined the service at sixteen as an office junior in the medical records department at Hindthorpe Royal Infirmary after leaving school with no formal qualifications. Realising how fortunate she was to have landed her first job at a large hospital, and with much encouragement from her parents, she determined to get on and work her way up within the organisation, so she enrolled in evening classes at the local college where she trained as a Secretary.

Married and divorced twice, with two grown-up children by her first marriage, she had spent all her working life at The Royal and worked her way up to what was deemed by many as being a very coveted position within the hospital administration. Carole, on the other hand, would beg to differ. Although she kept her misgivings to herself, she enjoyed the kudos that her role as senior PA to one of the medical professions most highly respected consultants afforded her . . . but that was soon to change.

She had been working as PA to Leonard Fitch for six years and, given the close one to one association, she'd never been able to form anything more than a strictly professional, no-nonsense working relationship with him; Mr Fitch this and Mrs Worsley that. There was never any light-hearted exchanges between them and he had never once asked her about what she'd done at the weekend, how her family were, where she was going on holiday – the usual sort of banal banter between boss and employee. In truth, they knew very little about each other. Carole often described him to her closest colleagues as *someone who is unable to express any kind of emotion, a cold and peculiar individual,* but then to be fair to him, she'd put that down to his profession – working with pain and death day in and day out – maybe that was why he was such an *oddball*?

The fact that he didn't have a wife, or a long-term partner, didn't surprise her either. She knew he was intensely uncomfortable around women – particularly, if there were no males present. One thing she was sure of was that he wasn't *queer*, well not in the homosexual sense of the word. She couldn't exactly say why she new this, perhaps it was woman's intuition, but that was her theory and she was sticking to it.

She was deeply curious at Fitch's obvious discomposure when in the presence of women – whether it was female nursing staff or the female relatives of his patients; she wondered if they picked up on the disdain he seemingly harboured for them. He was definitely out of his comfort zone where women were concerned. Served him right, he'd made her feel uncomfortable enough at times, especially when he'd deliberately gone out of his way to put her down, to make her look stupid and incompetent in front of male colleagues, ridiculing her over the smallest administrative error. He was a bully of the worst kind and she didn't know how to hit back; it was at times like this that she genuinely despised him.

The only reason Carole tolerated his attitude towards her was because of the money. In what was a glorified secretarial job, she wouldn't get the same salary working anywhere else.

PA to *Mr Leonard S. Fitch, MB ChB MRCS MD* carried a prestige with it and she was aware that many of the other secretaries at the hospital looked up to her. She enjoyed the elevated position and reputation she had worked hard to achieve; it made her feel very important given her humble beginnings within the Health Service.

Fitch's pattern of attendance at work was never set. He often worked long hours. Sometimes he would go for days without leaving the hospital grounds and then there were occasions when he'd go missing for several days at a time but he would never confide his whereabouts to Carole. If she needed to get hold of him, and he made it explicitly clear that those occasions would be strictly medical emergencies only, she could page him or leave a message with his mother. Evidently he checked in with her every day.

That was another thing Carole found odd, each time she'd asked Fitch how his mother was he'd cut her short and quickly change the subject. He had made it clear he didn't want her prying into his private life so she'd given up trying to get to know him and just worked for him instead. Strictly business, end of story!

CHAPTER THIRTY-FOUR

CAROLE wasn't expecting Fitch to arrive until around lunchtime; he had two private patients to see that day and then a ward visit later in the afternoon. So she took the opportunity to busy herself in his office, bring his filing up to date and maybe give the place a bit of a dusting and airing.

As she crossed the room to Fitch's desk she said out loud, "Bloody hell, what a mess!" There was nothing at all sterile about this place. She wondered what his patients thought when they came for a consultation with him.

Fitch hadn't been in for several days and she was genuinely surprised at the cluttered state of the place. By nature, he was a very meticulous man and, although he occasionally left paperwork lying on his desk, it was nothing compared to the mess that hid it now. In fact there was paperwork everywhere. She shook her head, how the hell does he know where anything is? For such a thorough and tidy person the current state of his office painted an entirely different type of individual.

Surveying the mess, she wondered if he'd been looking for something specific, but then he always asked her to pull papers and files for him – even if he was sat twiddling his bloody thumbs at his desk, he still got her to do the donkey work. She stood with her hands on her hips, shaking her head at the disarray, *what on earth has he been doing?* There were boxes of medical papers, general filing and patient notes stacked high on his desk and more piled across the row of filing cabinets that ran along the far wall of his room. He had told her more than once to leave well alone, if he left paperwork on his desk, it was there for a good reason, and not one to be questioned by her. If he wanted his office tidied up, he would tell her so.

She might not like her boss but she still prided herself on being a good PA and she believed that part of her key responsibilities were to make her employer's office and administration run as smooth and slick as a well oiled machine. So, despite the possibility of incurring his anger, she decided to tackle the chaos that was now his office.

After a couple of hours, she managed to bring about quite a bit of order and she was one hundred per cent confident that he'd still be able to put his hand on any patient note or file he might need at a minute's notice. All he had to do was to refer to the clearly labelled drawers of the cabinets where everything was listed alphabetically and chronologically. She stood by the filing cabinets and surveyed the office once again and smiled, pleased with her efforts; *surely he'll find it much easier to work now that he can see his desk again? He might even thank me!*

Finally, she turned her attention to the large stack of medical journals precariously piled high on one of the chairs by his desk. The chairs were meant for patients and colleagues, not for paperwork, so she looked around the office for a suitable place to store them. She considered the possibility of another filing cabinet. She could call down to the Porters office and have a couple of the men fetch one up. Two of the cabinets were almost full and the third one she couldn't get into because it was locked and the key was missing. *Why are the keys to the other two available but this one's kept locked all the time? And where is the key anyway?*

She stared at the locked cabinet and pondered for several minutes at what could possibly be inside the cabinet that Mr Fitch obviously didn't want anyone to see. She went over and pulled at the top drawer, *yes, it's definitely locked*. She crossed the office back to his desk where he kept a small blue marble bowl he dropped paperclips, staples and other bits and bats into and, result, *ha ha,* there was also a small bunch of keys, one of which she hoped might be for *that* filing cabinet.

Inquisitive by nature, she smiled thinking; *why not give it a try? Maybe Mr Fitch might be hiding a horde of grubby magazines* – the very idea made her chuckle as she went back to the cabinet. She couldn't wait to open it!

There were five small keys on the ring and she was about to insert the last one when Fitch unexpectedly arrived at the office. Her back to the door, she was completely absorbed in her quest to find out what *Leonard Fitch* was hiding, and oblivious of the fact that Fitch was standing right behind her, oblivious that was, until he almost burst her eardrums!

"*WHAT THE HELL DO YOU THINK YOU'RE DOING?*" Saliva ran down his chin. His face was almost purple with rage and his small eyes bulged behind his round rimless glasses. Stunned and terrified, she dropped the keys; caught red-handed and now he had her trapped. Her knees trembled and started to buckle as she turned to face him. Her mouth dry, she couldn't speak even if she wanted to; she was struck dumb with fear. Never in all the time she'd been working with him had she seen him look so full of *hatred* and *menace*!

She was desperate to flee from the room but her legs were barely holding her up. She thought she was going to throw up.

"M Mr F Fitch . . . I'm so s sorry, I was just trying to, to, to . . ."

He moved in nearer and when he was close enough to feel her breath and smell her fear, he pointed to the keys on the floor beside her and said, "*PICK. THEM. UP!*"

Fitch had left her no room for manoeuvre; she couldn't move an inch without coming into physical contact with him. So with her back pressed firmly against the filing cabinet, she slid to a squatting position, her legs shook so bad she could barely hold herself up. She struggled to maintain her uncomfortable position for fear she was going to fall face first against his legs. It was impossible; she was about to collapse. She burst into tears, "Mr Fitch, I can't, please . . . you're frightening me. I can't reach the keys, I can't move. You're standing in my way, Mr Fitch." She was humiliated and terrified.

His top lip curled into a snarl as he stared down at the top of her head; she was trembling violently. She was useless, he wanted nothing more than to bring his fists down hard and smash her cranium wide open.

He took just one step back, deliberately leaving the minimum of space between them for her to stand without touching him. Knowing that his closeness was intimidating her, he felt a sudden rush of euphoria, like the druggie who injects and experiences that first indescribable high. The power he had over Carole Worsley at that very moment made him want to reach for her throat and choke every last breath from her body.

The telephone rang out loud, bringing him back to the here and now, "*You're pathetic. Stand up!*"

Thank God! Carole looked sideways, "The phone, Mr Fitch. I need to get the phone . . . "

Inching back again, Fitch raised his arm and pointed to the open door, "Get OUT of my office and don't *ever* let me find you snooping around in here again! Do I make myself clear, *Mrs Worsley*?"

She managed to slide out from in front of him then ran the short distance to the door mumbling tearfully as she went through it, "Yes, Mr Fitch." She pulled the door closed behind her and ran to the ladies room – the urge to empty her bowels was almost beyond control.

Leonard Fitch picked up the small bunch of keys and buried them deep inside his jacket pocket then crossed the room to his desk. As if nothing out of the ordinary had taken place he sat down and began going through the messages Carole had placed in his in tray. There was a message stapled to the corner of a yellow folder marked 'Travel Documents'. He frowned, damn; how could he have forgotten about that? He was due to attend a medical conference in Madrid at the end of the week; he'd be away for four days. He'd have to pay her a visit before he left. The thought excited him and his mind came alive with images of Erin Fallon tied to the beam, begging him to take the rats off her.

The shrill ringing of his telephone broke into his thoughts. One of the hospital reception staff was apologising profusely for having to disturb him, but they couldn't get hold of Mrs Worsley to let her know that his next patient was on his way up for his appointment. Fitch grunted acknowledgement and hung up before the caller had time to finish.

All business again, he took his jacket off, grabbed a coat hanger from the stand behind his desk, and hung it up, smoothing the lapels and brushing stray bits of hair from the collar before straightening his tie as he walked to his office door. Carole was back at her desk, head low, both hands wrapped around a mug of coffee. She froze as she heard Fitch's door open, and as if the incident in his office had never taken place, he said, "Mrs Worsley, please don't put any calls through until I advise otherwise. My next patient is on his way up; he's twenty minutes early. Ask him to take a seat in the waiting area. I'll buzz through as soon as I'm ready for him"

She didn't look at him; merely nodded her head and muttered, "Yes, Mr Fitch."

"Oh . . . and please run along to the cafeteria and grab me a cheese and tomato sandwich." He looked at his watch then spoke to the back of her head again. "In my office at eleven forty sharp, please, Mrs Worsley. And I'll have a small pot of tea, too, if you wouldn't mind." Without waiting for an answer, he closed the door and went straight to the filing cabinet that Carole had been trying to gain access to.

Carole was very clear in her mind about one thing; she never, ever wanted to spend a moment alone with Mr Fritch again. And so not wanting to incur his wrath for a second time that day, she dashed at full speed through the hospital to the cafeteria.

As Carole made her way along the endless cold grey corridors to the canteen, she couldn't help wondering what Fitch was hiding in that locked cabinet. What was in there that he didn't anyone else to find? One thing she was sure about, she had to tell someone what had happened this morning.

For a long time, she had her doubts and suspicions about Fitch and if she ever needed proof that he was suffering from some kind of mental disorder, multiple personality perhaps, she had seen it first hand and had been on the receiving end of it, the ugly menacing and possibly dangerous side of Mr Fitch, a side of him she had never seen until today.

She was still shaken and deeply upset as she barged through the swing doors into the staff canteen and as she waited in the queue with other employees her thoughts raced. Who could she tell? He was a highly respected Consultant – what would she say? *"Mr Fitch caught me trying to open a locked filing cabinet in his office, he went berserk, staring at me like some sort of a mad man . . ."* Who was going to listen to her and take her serious? Could she tell that person that she believed Mr Fitch had something to hide, possibly something serious. And something about him and what he might be hiding had her very worried? His reaction and behaviour when he caught her trying to open the cabinet had been completely irrational; there was *madness* in his eyes, he's definitely unhinged.

She looked along the queue now and realised she was going to have a long wait before she got to the front to pay for Fitch's lunch, and dear God, if that pot of tea and sandwich isn't on his desk by eleven forty, she was likely to face another insane outburst from him.

CHAPTER THIRTY-FIVE

CAROLE could still hear him, he had enunciated every word, his instruction explicit . . . lunch in his office at eleven forty, exactly - not a minute later; the consequences were clear, it was in his tone and no way was she going to push her luck with him a second time. No way! Never again! She glanced at her watch; it was almost twenty five to eleven, even if she ran all the way back to the office she'd never make it back on time. Her heart was racing, she felt hot and light-headed; she had to get out of the canteen quickly. Looking along the queue frantically, she recognised one of the junior secretaries, third in line at the pay point, and decided to jump the line. The thought of upsetting Fitch again was out of the question. What had taken place half an hour ago had changed their working relationship irrevocably.

Her hands were shaking as she pushed towards the front of the queue, much to the annoyance and surprise of others. Some she overheard making comments at the nerve of her but she ignored them; she had no choice. She wasn't in the mood to argue or apologise.

The young secretary was about to pay for a small fruit bowl and orange juice when Carole nudged her and said, "Sorry, Hannah, I'm in a bit of a hurry! Here, pay for this for me." She shoved the sandwich and a handful of change at the girl, who in turn looked a little surprised but didn't refuse. After all, this was Mr Fitch's PA and Hannah wasn't about to say no to her.

Hannah picked up on the fact that Carole was rattled about

something; she looked upset and her hands were shaking as she pushed the money into her hand. As Hannah handed the money to the cashier, she couldn't help showing her concern and asked, "Are you alright, Carole?"

Carole wouldn't look at her; she was watching the entrance to the canteen. She looked *worried*? "Yes, yes! Fine. I'm fine, just give me the sandwich!" She snatched it back from her. Hannah became annoyed and she stared after Carole as she rushed off without so much as a 'thank you', almost knocking people off their feet as she dashed out of the canteen.

Billy Ashcroft was waiting in line behind Hannah and watched with interest as Carole Worsley pushed her way to the front of the queue, collared Hannah and then left in a hurry. He whispered into Hannah's ear, "Looks like that creep Fitch's rattled her cage"

"Shush, Billy! You could get sacked for remarks like that! You know how important Mr Fitch is," she whispered, as she picked up her lunch from the counter.

He chuckled, placed a bag of Golden Wonder crisps and a can of Irn Bru on the counter and idly rummaged around in his pockets for change. He winked at the frumpy middle-aged cashier who was holding her hand out waiting to be paid. It didn't have the desired effect, "I haven't got all day, son! There's a queue behind you, or hadn't you noticed?"

Hannah tutted, impatiently, "Come on, Billy! Hurry up! I'll get into trouble if I'm late back at my desk."

Billy dropped a pile of loose change into the waiting cashiers hand and followed Hannah, whispering into her hair, "Aww, you've got to admit, Hannah, the bloke's a total *weirdo*." He laughed again, squeezing the back of Hannah's neck as they walked out of the canteen. "Something definitely not right there if you ask me. I wouldn't like you to have to work for him, he gives me the creeps, and I don't scare easy!" Nodding his head in the direction Carole had taken he said, "She's upset about something. Did you see how bad her hands were shaking?"

"Hmm, I know. She looked as though she'd been crying, too. Did you notice?" She stared down the length of the long hospital corridor where she could see Carole walking at break neck speed back to Fitch's office.

"No. Just saw how bad her hands were shaking, but I'd say that she was *definitely* worried about something. I was watching her while you paid for her stuff. I wonder if he's had a go at her. Not that she probably didn't deserve it, she's a stuck up cow!" He laughed again.

"Don't say that about her! She's a very nice lady. I like her but I don't envy her position. They couldn't pay me enough to work for Fitch. I actually feel sorry for her sometimes, spending all day alone with only him for company. No they definitely couldn't pay me enough. It's not as though she has anyone else to talk to either, she's completely isolated from the other secretaries and admin staff."

"Goes with the job, Hannah. I don't suppose someone in his position wants her associating with the rest of the admin staff and low life hospital porters like me."

"Don't be ridiculous! At times, you really do say some stupid things, Billy!"

He put his arm around her shoulders and hugged her close, "Yeah, but you love me and you wouldn't have me any other way!"

She blushed and tried to pull away from him. "Don't flatter yourself! You love yourself more than enough, Billy Ashcroft! You don't need any one else to love you." They arrived outside the medical records department; Hannah turned to him. "Do you think I should tell Stella about Carole, I mean about her being upset and everything. They're quite good friends, I'm sure she'd want to know if there was something wrong."

He frowned, "Why would you want to tell anyone? It's not like we really give a damn. She earns big bucks working for Fitch, if she's willing to be bullied by him, that's her choice."

"Hmm, still . . . like I said, I like her so I'm going to have a word with Stella."

"Please yourself. Anyway, I'd better get a move on. I'll call for you at half seven, make sure you're ready, Hannah, I don't want to have to face another grilling from your dad. In fact come to think of it, he's even scarier than old Fitch. Second thoughts, I'll meet you at the Roxy at eight, get your dad to drop you outside, Ok?"

"Billy! Don't talk about my dad like that, he only wants what's best for me."

"I know. I'm just kidding. Course I'll call for you. Half seven on the dot, and make sure you're ready, at the door, waiting for me to knock, okay?" He slapped her playfully on the backside then strutted off towards the lift area.

* * *

Stella was on the phone whispering to someone as Hannah walked in, she turned around so that she had her back to her. Hannah heard her whisper, "I've got to go now. I'll ring you tonight when I get home. Yes, yes, I said I would didn't I?"

She hung up and turned to Hannah, "Did you get me a sandwich?"

Hannah's face fell, "Aww, Stella! I'm so sorry. I forgot. I had to queue for ages, I completely forgot." She dropped her lunch on her desk.

"I'll run straight back to the canteen. There shouldn't be anyone queuing now. I'll only be five minutes!"

Stella was annoyed; Hannah could see it written all over her face.

"Forget it!" Stella snapped. "Anyway, I'm supposed to be on a diet. You've probably done me a favour, it's not as if I'm in any danger of wasting away if I go out without any lunch today."

She turned away from Hannah and started reading through some notes on her desk and without looking at her she said, "Dr Sanderson's secretary's been on the phone, she wants all the case notes on Michael Lawrence." She held out a blue folder with a note stapled to it, "Here you are, patient's details. And she needs them by two o'clock today." She looked at her watch, "You know what Sanderson's secretary's like. She'll have my guts for garters if we don't deliver on time. Have your lunch and then get cracking, Hannah!"

Hannah took the folder and sat down. She peeled back the cellophane wrapper off the fruit bowl and started eating. Aware that Stella was in a bit of a strop because she'd forgotten to get her a sandwich, she wasn't sure whether or not she should tell her about Carole. She glanced at Stella clacking away noisily at her typewriter and decided that now wasn't a good time, she'd wait until she was in a better mood.

Hannah settled back in her chair and idly flipped through a glossy magazine as she ate her lunch. As she was scooping the last bit of fruit out of the bowl her telephone rang. She jumped to attention, sitting up straight in her chair, "Medical Records, Good afternoon, Hannah speaking, how may I help you?"

"Hannah *speaking*? I thought your name was Hannah *Ridgway*?"

Stella moved out of earshot over to the other end of the office to the filing cabinets. She was in no mood for childish banter.

"*Stop messing, Billy*! You're going to get me into trouble," she lowered her voice, almost to a whisper, "Stella's in a foul mood because I forgot her lunch. Anyway, what do you want? And make it quick, Billy!"

"I've just been to the God's," he said, nonchalantly.

"What?" She rolled her eyes impatiently; she didn't have time for his games.

"Fitch's Office."

"Mr Fitch's Office? Why? Not because of Carole, surely?"

"Don't be daft. I told you. I couldn't care less about Fitch and his PA. I took one of his patients; he was lost, couldn't find his way so I escorted him there. But, get this, Hannah, Carole looked as though she'd been crying and to say that she was a bag of nerves would be an understatement. She couldn't wait to get me out of the office, wouldn't even look me in the face."

"Well? What do you want me to do about it?"

"I thought you said you liked her and you'd want to know that's all. Tell her mate Stella, I bet she'll want to know. See you later my lovely. Oh, and if you find anything out, let me know. I love a bit of gossip!"

"Yes I know. You're a busybody, Billy Ashcroft. I'll see you later." She hung up. She decided that, bearing in mind Stella's current mood, she'd broach the matter casually whilst she was pulling the Lawrence case notes, knowing that as Carole's friend, Stella would be pleased she'd told her. In fact, it might improve her temper; take her mind off the lunch she hadn't had!

She eyed the patient details listed on the notepaper Stella gave her and walked over to the huge wall of filing cabinets. Stella was sat on a small stool pulling files from the bottom drawer of one of the cabinets.

"Stella?"

"Yes."

"The reason I forgot your lunch is because Carole Worsley pushed to the front of the queue and – "

"For heaven's sake, Hannah, I told you to forget it!"

"No. That's not what I want to tell you. It's Carole, Carole Worsley. Her behaviour was really odd and she was very upset about something. I think she'd been crying. She pushed her way to the front of the queue, made me pay for her things and then stormed out of the canteen. She almost sent a few people flying as she barged her way out of there. But the funny thing was . . ." She hesitated as she formulated the words in her head. "While she was waiting for me to pay, she was staring at the canteen doors as if she was running scared of someone and expecting them to walk through the doors at any moment. She looked *petrified*, Stella."

Suddenly concerned, Stella stood up and placed a handful of

files on top of the cabinet and turned her full attention to Hannah, "What exactly did she say to you?"

"Nothing much really. She just shoved her lunch and some change at me and told me to pay for it. It was more her . . . behaviour, it was completely out of character. Well, anyway, she was definitely upset and she looked frightened too."

Stella frowned and looked up at the clock above the filing cabinets. A puzzled look on her face, she closed the cabinet drawer slowly and made her way back to her desk saying, "Thanks, Hannah. I'll give her a ring, make sure she's all right."

* * *

Carole was miles away, staring at Fitch's office door and when the phone rang she almost jumped out of her skin, "Mr Fitch's office. Carole Worsley speaking."

"Carole, it's me, Stella. Are you okay?"

She glanced nervously at Fitch's door again. He was in consultation with a patient. "Yes I'm fine." Defensively, "Why shouldn't I be?"

"Well I don't know. Hannah was concerned, Carole. She told me you looked very upset at lunchtime. I just wanted to make sure that you're okay that's all. You are, aren't you?"

Still watching the door, she pressed the receiver hard against her ear and whispered tearfully, "Not really, no. It's him, Fitch. I'm terrified of him, Stella. He's not right in the head. He's a *psycho*." She couldn't help it; she started crying quietly into the receiver.

"What? Mr Fitch? Has something happened, Carole?"

"Yes. I need to tell someone, Stella," she whispered, sniffing back her tears and wiping her nose with the back of her hand.

"Is he there now?"

"Yes. He's in his office. He has a patient with him."

Stella's concern grew and it came across in her voice, "Listen,

Carole, I'm working late tonight. Do you want to come down here as soon as he leaves?"

"Yes. Yes. I'll call you as soon as he leaves and then I'll make my way over to your department. I don't want to stay in this office a moment longer than I have to."

"Okay. But in the meantime, if you need me, Carole, just pick the bloody phone up, do you hear me?"

"Of course I will. Thanks, Stella, I'll see you later." She hung up, grabbed her bag and made her way out of the office to the ladies room to check her make up. She didn't want Fitch to know she'd been crying.

* * *

Hannah only heard one side of this conversation but got the gist; it *was* something to do with Mr Fitch. Billy was right; she couldn't wait to tell him but what could she tell him? She needed to find out first what exactly it was that Fitch had done to upset Carole.

Pretending not to have been listening, she casually called over to Stella, "Did you speak to Carole, Stella?"

"Yes. She's coming down to see me later this afternoon."

Stella picked some files up off her desk and said, "I'm taking these over to Geriatrics. I'll be about twenty minutes." As she was on her way out, she turned back and popped her head round the door and called out to Hannah, "Oh, and make sure you get that file over to Sanderson's secretary on time, Hannah, or don't bother coming to work in the morning, do you hear?"

"Yes, Stella." She looked up at the clock; it was twenty to two. Exactly twenty minutes before she had to hand the file over to the dreaded battle-axe, Ferguson, and now, God help her, she was beginning to worry she'd misfiled it. It wasn't where it was supposed to be. Ferguson would play holy hell with them if Hannah didn't deliver it on time.

As she flicked through files desperately trying to find the

Michael Lawrence notes she was thinking if she hadn't agreed to go out with Billy that evening she could have stayed behind and done a little overtime so that she could find out what had happened with Carole and Mr Fitch. Not that she was nosey; merely concerned that's all, and she knew Billy would love the gossip; he was such an old woman. The thought of him made her smile. Never mind. She'd try and get it out of Stella somehow tomorrow. In the meantime, *where the hell is that Lawrence file?* She checked the time again, it was now panic- o'clock!

CHAPTER THIRTY-SIX

A S the white Consul GT turned into Bleaksedge Lane, DC
Jones glanced at his boss. "According to that dossier Sarge,
perpetrators of sexual crimes are likely to be somebody who
is severely emotionally disturbed. Possibly a person who was
themselves abused as a child."

"*Gerraway, Jonesy*! And here's me thinking we were looking for
someone who'd just graduated from charm school. Don't waste your
time with that rubbish. I told you, the man's a nutter, but a very
clever one. Probably a professional, you know, a dentist or a doctor.
The thing is; why did he miss Fallon's birthday?" Harris was not one
for taking on new ideas and couldn't see the irony in his statement
– he was himself drawing up a profile of the perpetrator, a point that
didn't go unmissed in DC Jones's mind.

"Well, you're saying it's a man, but we don't know that. Could be
a woman, or a couple. Look at Brady and Hindley."

DS Harris exhaled. Jones was right, they didn't know it was a
man. They didn't even know for sure if the crimes were sexually
motivated, as no bodies had ever been found. All they had were
the photographs sent on the birthday of each of the victims to the
grieving parents. This could well turn out to be one of those cases
that would never be solved until some poor sod dug up his patio or
knocked a wall down only to find the gruesome remains of the five
girls ten or twenty years from now. But he knew, deep down, this
was a man, *an intelligent man*, and a professional. Call it a copper's
instinct, or whatever you want, he knew.

"Pull over here, Jonesy," DC Jones applied the brakes a bit too sharp for the Sergeant's liking, causing him to reach out for the dashboard. He tutted then glanced sideways at the Constable and shook his head. *Those platform soles don't help*, he thought to himself. *Like driving with a pair of barges on your feet.*

"This do you?" Jones said, unperturbed. The two of them got out, DS Harris sniffed the air as if looking for clues. Jones lit a cigarette. The smell of burning tobacco passed Harris's nostrils stirring that age-old craving in his mind, sharpening his senses.

"It was somewhere around here. This is where she used to walk home from school. This is the spot where the Ashcroft lad said he tried to kiss her before she ran off." Harris surveyed the area. He pointed, "That side road there, you see it?"

"Yes"

"Do you know where it leads to?"

"Hinckley Village, I think. Nice place, need a few bob to live there."

In his mind's eye, DS Harris pictured a car pulling out of the side road, Erin walking casually along the pavement, the car stopping, Erin talking to the driver – *did she know him?* The driver gets out, grabs Erin and throws her in the back before driving off to . . . where? He thought about the logistics. Erin was only just sixteen but she was a feisty girl according to Ashcroft. She wouldn't have gone quietly, but looking around there were no houses at this end of the lane, nobody to hear her scream. But how could he have kept her still in the back of the car? Three options crossed his mind and he decided to share them with DC Jones.

"He either knew the girl, there were two of them, or he subdued her in some way."

"Well, most perps in cases like this tend to work alone" Jones chipped in. Harris cringed at his use of American slang but let it go. "I know I mentioned Brady and Hindley before, but statistically they are few and far between. At one point they were trying to pin the first four on Trevor Hardy, remember him? *The Beast of Manchester?*

But he had alibis in all cases and they didn't really match his MO. If these are sexually motivated crimes though, that's the type of person we're after."

"*Oh yeah?* Is that the profile you've got in mind? Wasn't Hardy the one who sacked his brief and pleaded manslaughter, then got life?"

"Well, yeah but . . ."

"Yeah but nothing. Our perpetrator's clever, been active for more than four years and no clues. Okay, let's say it's one person, a man. How would he have known all five victims well enough to know the day they were born? And where would he take them? If they got in the car of their own free will at some point they would have realised they weren't being taken home. He must have sedated them in some way."

"Or tied and gagged them."

"He would need to move fast. I'll bet this is a busy road during the school term, he couldn't risk being seen tying up a young girl. What about the others, where were they taken from, what time of day?"

DC Jones pulled out his notebook and flicked through the pages.

"Never mind, we'll have a look when we get back to the Station. Need to see the locations on a map. I assume they plotted all these disappearances on a map?"

"Err, yes Sarge. It was Sergeant Paisley's case at the time, and you know what he's like."

"Jock Paisley? Ha! No wonder they never got anywhere with it. Took him two months to realise this was possibly the work of a serial killer."

"Yes but he is thorough. Once he saw the connection he had every detail plotted out."

"Right, what're we waiting for? Come on Starsky, move it."

"It's a Ford Consul, Sarge, not a Gran Torino."

* * *

Back at the station, DS Harris opened the map Sergeant Paisley marked up several months ago. Jones was right; Paisley was thorough. The homes of all five victims were indicated although the scale was too small to identify the street. He would have to turn to the individual case notes to see that, but for now this would do; it showed the pattern. He pinned it to the notice board and studied it for a while, stroking his chin as if that might help him understand it better.

Cahill lived in Ackenthwaite and was believed to have been taken shortly after alighting the school bus on her way home, no doubt excited about the birthday party her parents had planned for her. Paisley had also indicated her school, Bleaksedge High – same as the Fallon girl.

Hilton lived in Millhead, a village just outside Carnforth at the time she was taken, but Paisley had again done his homework. He also marked on the map her former residence – Bleaksedge. The pattern was the same though, school bus, this time from Carnforth, long walk home, alone.

Critchley differed in that she went to school in Lancaster, about fifteen miles south of Bleaksedge. No connection with the place either, according to Paisley's map. The only similarity was the school bus and the walk home. It occurred to Harris that this was probably the only way he could get them alone on their birthdays; he was selecting girls not only for their appearance or age but also their availability. This made sense, no point choosing a victim then being unable to take her on the one day he planned to do it. This also filled another gap in the pattern, something that had been bothering Harris from the beginning. The girls had been taken in June, July, early and late September and November. None in August – the summer break.

Finally he turned his attention to Johnson. Her hometown was Helsington, and she went to school in nearby Kendal, about 10 miles north of Bleaksedge. Like Critchley she had no apparent link with the place but the method was identical; the MO as Jones liked to call it. It was like getting all four edges of the jigsaw in place – all he needed now were the bits in the middle.

Jones brought in the box that had been delivered by the Greater Manchester Police earlier that week, then turned and headed off to the kitchen to brew up. The box contained four thick brown folders, each labelled with a serial number and the names of the victims in brackets, as if the names were now secondary. Their lives summed up by the statements and contemporaneous notes taken by the Police Officers, and of course the photographs. *What kind of sick bastard could do that?* It beggared belief.

Harris took out the first file, C45280.72.06-73.08.01 (Gemma Cahill), and untied the ribbons holding the worn folder together. The photographs were right at the front, the first few being family snaps showing a pretty, smiling fair-haired girl on a beach somewhere. Then the school photo, the individual one taken by a professional – a moment for every parent to cherish which ended up in the lasting memory of all those involved in the case and those who watched on television as the mother cried and begged for her child to be returned to her home.

These were all in colour but the one that sent a shiver down his spine was monochrome. Perhaps just as well. It was a Polaroid, the self-developing type that didn't age particularly well, but the detail still clear enough to see that the girl was dead, her vacant eyes staring into space as if looking at something beyond the camera. Her mouth open, in a silent scream, face distorted from the agony she must have suffered in her final moments.

Looking down at her naked body he could see the cuts and abrasions, the burn marks and bruises. His eyes returned to her head, tilted slightly towards the camera, resting on something. A book? But the most bizarre thing was the feet, neatly arranged at the side of her head, toes pointing towards her ears.

"Tea Sarge." DC Jones placed the cup down on the desk next to the folder, taking care not to spill the steaming dark liquid over the evidence. "Not a pretty sight is it? Imagine what she must have gone through."

"What do you make of this Jonesy?" Harris tapped the picture near the girl's head.

"Foot fetish? Can't say Sarge. It's an odd one. He sent it to her mother with a belated birthday card. Obviously killed her on her birthday, I'd say. Exactly a year after he took her."

"And when did he take the Fallon girl?"

"8th of November."

Harris looked up at the calendar on the wall and made the mental calculation. "We've got six weeks to save her life."

CHAPTER THIRTY-SEVEN

STELLA was passing the lifts on her way back to the Medical Records Department, when she almost collided head on with Carole who emerged, like a bat out of hell, from one of the elevators, "*Bloody hell, Carole!* You nearly knocked me into next week! Who are you running from?"

"Oh God! Sorry, Stella! I was just on my way to see you."

Stella linked arms with Carole and said, "You look frightened to death!"

"I am. You wont believe what happened earlier with Mr. Fitch. He's gone now and won't be back until next Monday. I just had to get away from that office."

As they hurried along the sterile corridor, Stella eyed Carole furtively; wondering what exactly had happened between Mr Fitch and Carole for her to be in such a state.

They were almost at the entrance to the records office when Carole turned to Stella and asked, "Will Hannah still be there?"

"Yes. She doesn't finish until five-thirty. Would you rather go somewhere else? We could go to the canteen if you like?"

"No. Let's go to your office, too many busy bodies in the canteen. We'll have to tell Hannah that she isn't to repeat a single word of what I tell you."

"Don't worry about Hannah. I'll threaten her with a transfer to Ferguson's department if she repeats a bloody word to anyone. What the hell's been going on up there, Carole?"

Carole looked over her shoulder again as if she expected to see Mr Fitch stalking her, "I'll tell you in your office, Stella.

* * *

Hannah sat at her desk clacking away at the keys of her typewriter. She didn't look up from the notes she was copy typing, "I dropped the Lawrence file off on the dot, Stella. Scary Mary Ferguson actually *smiled* and *thanked me!* Does that mean I can come back to work in the morning?"

"Don't be facetious, Hannah. You'd *better* be here in the morning."

Hannah didn't know that Carole had walked in behind Stella. It was only when Stella asked her to make two cups of tea that she looked up. "Oh! Hi, Carole. I didn't realise you were here."

"Hello, Hannah. Make mine a strong one will you? No sugar."

"Okay. Yes. I'll go and do it now."

"Oh, and Hannah, sorry about earlier on. Thanks for helping out."

"That's okay. What was the problem? You looked – "

"The *tea,* Hannah"

"Yes Stella, I get the message."

Hannah jumped up from her desk and disappeared behind the wall of filing cabinets where the tea things, including the kettle were stored neatly on top of a small fridge by a washbasin.

As Hannah busied herself rinsing the cups, Stella called out, "Hannah? We'd like a word with you."

"Okay." She reappeared with a cup and a tea towel in her hand and sat down at her desk again. Stella and Carole were sat opposite her at Stella's desk.

"Carole's got a problem with Mr Fitch, right?"

Hannah looked directly at Carole and nodded her head, "Oh, right . . . err, yes. But I don't know what it is . . . the problem I mean."

Stella glanced at Carole, rolled her eyes and turned back to Hannah. "We know that, silly! *I* don't even know what the problem is yet because Carole hasn't told me, have you?"

"No. I haven't."

"What I'm saying, Hannah, is that what you hear in this office, this afternoon, what Carole tells me that is; *you will not breathe a single word of it to anyone, understood?* And I mean ANYONE *including* that shiftless bugger, Billy Ashcroft! It's strictly confidential. And if I find out that you *have* discussed it, I'll personally see to it that you're transferred to Scary Mary Ferguson's office, as her junior and general dog's body, because that's all you'll amount to with her. Now have I made myself clear?"

Hannah nodded her head up and down quickly, looking at both women in turn; Carole also nodded to confirm Stella's threat.

Hannah blushed deeply, she cleared her throat and said quietly, "Erm, yes, Stella. Perfectly clear."

"Good! Now get us that cup of tea, please."

While Hannah busied herself making tea, she became increasingly angry at being treated like a child. *How dare she! After all, if I hadn't told her about the business with Carole in the first place, she'd have been none the bloody wiser!*

She slammed about behind the filing cabinets as she made the tea and deliberately put an extra large spoonful of sugar in Stella's teacup, knowing full well that she was on a diet. *That'll teach her to order me about like a school kid. She can make her own bloody tea in future! She's got no right talking about Billy like that either. I can't wait to tell him what she said about him.*

She banged the cups down onto the saucers making as much noise as possible so that Stella wouldn't think she was listening to their gossip and muttered, *"Bloody bitch!"*

Stella and Carole could hear the din going on behind the cabinets; they rolled their eyes at each other and carried on speaking quietly.

Hannah carried a tray with three cups of tea over to Stella's desk, slamming it down, causing the tea to slop into the saucers. She handed one to Carole, took hers and left Stella's on the tray. Stella pursed her lips and raised her eyebrows, glancing at Carole and then back at Hannah.

"If that was meant to impress me, young madam, it didn't! Grow up!"

Carole looked awkwardly at the junior secretary, she had a soft spot for Hannah, thought she was a pleasant young girl. Hannah didn't deserve the lecture that Stella gave her about gossiping, it's no wonder she was in a mood.

In an effort to diffuse the difficult situation between the two of them, Carole took a sip of her tea and said, "You make a lovely brew, Hannah. Thanks."

"Thank you, Carole." Sulking, she turned and went back to her desk and started sorting through paperwork. She didn't want to appear as though she was remotely interested in their conversation, even though she couldn't wait to find out what Fitch had been up to.

Stella picked her cup and saucer up off the tray, muttered, "Thanks" and turned her back on Hannah and said to Carole, "Come on, get that down you."

"And don't worry about madam over there, she won't breathe a word – she's bloody terrified of Scary Mary Ferguson."

"No, I'm not worried. Hannah's a good girl. I know we can trust her."

"So come on then, what makes you think Mr Fitch is up to something dodgy?"

Carole shook her head and frowned, "I can't explain, it Stella. He goes missing for days and I'm not allowed to contact him unless it's a patient emergency – life or death matters only, his orders."

Stella raised her eyebrows and cocked her head, "What? How are *you* supposed to make that sort of a decision?" She laughed mockingly, "You're his PA for heaven's sake, not a senior bloody registrar!"

"No of course not. That's not what I meant, Stella. If the hospital needs him in an emergency of that kind, of course they can contact him; page him if he's not near a telephone. And believe me, you can never get hold of him by telephone, anyway. I don't even have a number for him, can you believe it?"

"Well that's not what you implied, Carole. In fact, I'm not quite sure I know what you mean. You did say: patient emergency – life or death? Am I right?"

Carole began massaging her temples.

Stella, naturally nosey, thrived on gossip and even though she was a close friend of Carole's she'd never warmed to Fitch – she couldn't say why, but now more than ever, she was eager to find out what he'd been up to.

Not wishing to push Carole too hard, she decided to change her approach, "Carole, have you got a headache, love? Can I get you a couple of Aspirins?"

"No. No thanks. I don't take pills, just a tension headache. It'll go soon. What I was trying to tell you is that . . ." She turned her hands palm up as if what she was about to say was utter madness, "He's hiding something. Something serious, and whatever it is, it's in that filing cabinet. The one I was trying to get into this morning."

Stella chuckled, "What? You mean like a body?"

"Don't be so bloody obtuse, Stella! I thought you were supposed to be helping me, not taking the piss!"

"I didn't mean to make fun. I'm sorry. I really am. Carry on. I promise to listen and take what you tell me seriously."

Carole sat up straight and took a deep breath, "Okay. This is why I think he's into something . . . well . . . a bit *unsavoury,* shall we say? I don't know if that's even the right word to describe what I think he's up to." Stella raised her eyebrows again and peered out over her spectacles.

"Perhaps the cabinet's full of dirty mags, Carole, and he just doesn't want you know that he's into that sort of thing. Let's face it, as far as we know, he doesn't have a wife or girlfriend and you've said yourself that you're convinced he's not batting for the other side. So he has to get his kicks somehow. He's a bloke, he'll have to be getting it somewhere, somehow!"

"It's more than that, Stella. If you'd have seen the way he reacted when he caught me, it was terrifying. He had me pinned up against the filing cabinet. Saliva running off his chin, he was that close I could smell his breath." She shuddered and screwed her face up at the memory. "I thought he was going to attack me, you could see it in his eyes, total evil and menace. He looked *deranged*." Carole glanced at Hannah who appeared to be absorbed in paperwork and not the least bit interested in the conversation.

Although Hannah didn't give the impression that she'd been listening to the conversation, she heard everything and she couldn't believe what Carole told Stella about Fitch. Billy was going to love this; she couldn't wait to tell him. She sneaked a quick look in Carole's direction; she was rummaging in her handbag. Hannah hoped that Carole wouldn't leave before she'd told Stella *everything* so she decided it was time for another brew.

"Carole, I'm having another cup of tea, would you like one?"

Carole glanced at her watch, plenty of time; there was no need for her to have to hurry back to her office, she'd switched on the answering machine so she wouldn't miss any important messages. She looked up and smiled at Hannah, although the smile didn't reach her eyes. "Yes. Thanks, love."

"I'll have another one, please, Hannah. Not so heavy handed with the sugar this time, either."

The phone rang on Stella's desk, "Let me get this, Carole."

Hannah came back with the tea. As she'd done earlier, she left Stella's on the tray and handed Carole's to her, avoiding all eye contact with Stella.

Stella replaced the receiver. She nodded thanks to Hannah as she lifted the teacup and took a sip. "*Jesus Christ, Hannah!* I've scalded my bloody mouth!" She put the cup down, spilling boiling hot tea into the saucer, as she grabbed a tissue from the box on her desk and dabbed it against her mouth. "You'd better not have done that on purpose, madam! Why didn't you tell me you'd only just poured it?"

Hannah spoke out, full of indignation and feigned innocence "Stella! How could you accuse me of doing something so nasty? You can see the steam coming from the cup; I thought you might have waited until it had cooled. Tea's meant to be served piping hot, anyway!"

"That's enough, Hannah! You're becoming far too lippy for your own good lately. Spending too much time with that idle swine, Billy Ashcroft. Does your father know you're knocking about with that good-for-nothing?"

Hannah was fuming now. "Yes, he does as a matter of fact and he likes him, very much!" She lied. "And anyway, it's my business who I go out with!"

Stella turned her back on Hannah and called out of her shoulder "Likes him? Hmm, I bet he does!"

"Right, Carole, you were saying?"

"Erm . . . yes, where was I?"

"The third filing cabinet? Did you manage to open it?"

"No. I was about to insert the key when he caught me. I wasn't expecting him in the office until just before lunchtime. I didn't even hear him come in; he crept up on me and yelled into my ear. He almost burst my eardrum. My legs turned to jelly and my knees buckled. Oh, Stella, it was dreadful!" Tears began to well in her eyes again.

"Did he *threaten* you, Carole?"

"Not exactly, no. But it was there in his eyes, if you know what I mean. I think, in different circumstances, he is definitely capable of it. It was the way he spoke to me, in a sort of a quiet, calm but menacing way. His eyes were full of hatred and . . ." she threw her hands up at a loss to convey her thoughts and articulate her fear.

Stella called over her shoulder, "Hannah, there are some biscuits in the tin back there, can you fetch them in please?"

Hannah's top lip curled as she stomped away from her desk. *Just when the conversation was getting really good!*

CHAPTER THIRTY-EIGHT

"ERIN, wake up." Neive knelt by Erin's side, tugging at the worn woollen blanket. Erin stirred slightly and mumbled incoherently. How long had she been sleeping? Where was she?

Still pulling on the blanket, "Please, Erin wake up!"

"Neive?" Erin struggled to open her eyes. Her vision was blurred and foggy. Neive was kneeling beside her bed, her warm baby breath fanning her face. Erin reached out to touch her "*Neive? Is that you?*"

"It isn't time yet, Erin. You have to go back, it's not time."

Erin struggled to focus again, but the more she tried the more confused she became. Through the foggy haze, Neive started drifting away from her. She called out to Neive, "What are you doing here? Am I home, Neive? Please don't go, don't leave me . . ."

Her vision cleared. Neive had gone. She was still on the filthy mattress in the corner of the room. Apart from the soft amber glow of the moon coming in through the window, casting a ghostly glow inside the room, the hallway and beyond was shrouded in darkness. She was alone. She had no idea how long she'd slept. The blanket covering her did little to keep her warm, she started shivering. She was sore everywhere and just about every part of her body was aching. The apparent sight and the thought of Neive, so close and so real, made her cry. Tears flowed down the sides of her face, soaking the dirty mattress.

For days she drifted in and out of consciousness. No one heard her rambling and constant moaning. When she came round again, the result of a terrible and blinding headache, her lips were dry and cracked and her throat was unbearably sore – she couldn't swallow. Her heartbeat was abnormal, beating at a rapid rate, sweat pumped out of her. She shivered uncontrollably yet her body felt as though it was on fire.

Desperate for water, Erin tried to pull herself upright. As she did, a searing pain down below brought her knees up to her chest. She waited for the pain to subside then reached under the blanket putting her hand between her thighs. She wretched noisily as her hand moved over a cluster of sores. Her fingers were wet and a nasty odour fanned from beneath the blanket. The bites at the top of her legs had become infected.

Matted strands of hair stuck to the side of her face with dry acrid smelling vomit, the vile stench made her retch again. The pain from her broken ribs was so intense she screamed.

Perhaps this time he had left her to die. She hoped so.

CHAPTER THIRTY-NINE

L IAM and Sean were tormenting the life out of Neive, yanking her ponytail and making up silly songs about her as they strolled through the town centre on their way back to the bus station. It was half term and they'd been to the cinema to see the new Disney film, *The Apple Dumpling Gang*. Neive stormed off ahead of them. They'd messed about during the film and had been told off several times; the usher had even threatened to throw all three of them out if they didn't behave themselves. It wasn't her, she wanted to watch the film, it was Liam and Sean being idiots and annoying people. It wasn't fair that she'd had a telling off. *Just wait until dad finds out.*

Realising they'd probably gone too far, Sean called out to Neive to wait for them. She turned around and shouted back at him, "Get lost and leave me alone! When we get home I'm going to tell dad you two nearly got us chucked out of the pictures. I hate you both!" She turned her back on them and ran off.

"Aww, shit, Liam! Come on. Dad's gonna murder us if she gets the bus home on her own." They set off running after her.

As she turned the corner onto the busy high street, she slowed down; she had a stitch and was out of breath. The bus stop was just ahead of her. Holding her side, she made her way to the empty bench just inside the shelter. Relieved, she sat down and began rubbing her side. She grimaced, *not had a stitch so bad in ages.* As she waited for her brothers to catch up, she looked out across the road at the numerous shops and stores. A light drizzle had started to fall – the rain always made her feel miserable, that and her two stupid brothers.

Neive was fascinated by the countless shop windows advertising brightly coloured *Autumn Sale* and *Massive Discounts*, when her gaze came to rest on the back of a tall, slim copper haired girl looking in the window of the *'Chelsea Girl Boutique'*. *Erin?* She screamed, *"Erin!"* Disbelief and tears of pure joy welled in her eyes – *she'd found Erin*. The pain in her side forgotten, she screamed from the top of her lungs, "ERIN! ERIN!" And without looking, she ran straight off the kerb, into the path of an oncoming car.

Liam and Sean turned the corner just as they heard tyres screeching and people began yelling and screaming and running from every direction. Neive's body had been tossed into the air and thrown several feet, landing on the opposite side of the road into the path of an oncoming wagon, which managed to stop within inches of the stricken girl.

All hell broke loose, shoppers and store workers ran into the road and surrounded Neive's body. Constant calls from within the gathering crowd could be heard up and down the busy high street, "Call an ambulance! Has anybody called an ambulance?" A huge circle of people gathered around Neive; women and children crying above gasps of, *Oh dear God in heaven. Help her, somebody help her!*

The driver of the vehicle that hit Neive was on his knees, his head in his hands, howling like a wounded animal, "She ran out, she just ran out into the road! I had no chance. She ran out straight in front of me!" No one was taking any notice; it was the little girl they were interested in.

Liam and Sean stood on the edge of the crowd trembling, tears streaming down their faces. Liam grabbed hold of Sean's hand, *Sean! Sean! It's our Neive, oh, God, Sean . . ."*

Desperate to reach Neive, Sean yelled, "Come on!" He dragged Liam along with him, pushing through the sea of onlookers that was growing by the second.

It was mayhem, people yelling at once. "Where's the ambulance?

Oh my God! NO! DON'T move her! Is she still breathing? She's in a bad way; she's losing a lot of blood! I think she might be dead!"

When Sean and Liam reached the immediate crowd surrounding Neive, Sean tried to push between two men, one of whom turned around and grabbed Sean's arms, and held him back, "Whoa! Whoa! Where do you think you're going? Get back, son!"

Sean fought back using all his strength to free himself, "GET OFF ME! LET GO! SHE'S MY SISTER!" he yelled at the top of his lungs, "NEIVE!"

The distant sound of sirens drew closer. Liam, inconsolable, kicked the man holding Sean back, in the shins, "Let go! Let go of my brother! It's our Neive! She's our sister!"

A tall well-dressed man carrying a black bag forced his way through the crowd, making his way to the centre where Neive lay motionless. His tall, stern no-nonsense manner had the desired effect as the crowd parted to let him through. "Excuse me. Excuse me, please. I'm a doctor. Let me through, please."

The well-dressed, softly spoken man put his bag down by the side of the injured child; a hush fell amongst the onlookers staring in horror at the twisted and broken body of the little girl. A middle-aged woman tugged at the doctor's shoulder as he checked the child's vital signs, "Don't let her die! Please don't let her die!"

The doctor looked up at the sea of faces staring down at him, expecting him to perform an instant miracle to save the little girl's life. He pushed his glasses up on the bridge of his nose, "Please, move back. I need some space here!" The crowd shuffled back.

The stranger, who had struggled to hold the young brothers back, now had his arms folded firmly across the chests of both boys. He bent down so their faces were level, "Where are your parents, lads? Do you have a telephone number where we could reach them?"

Sean didn't answer; he stared, numb with shock and disbelief at his sister's twisted, bloody body. Liam mumbled, "Our mum's gone, hasn't she, Sean. She left us . . . didn't she Sean . . ." Sean didn't respond; he clung with both hands to the strong hand covering his chest. His eyes vacant, he hadn't heard what the stranger had asked, and he hadn't heard Liam's question.

The doctor pulled a stethoscope and blood pressure monitor out of his bag and began assessing Neive's injuries; her pulse was barely audible and her blood pressure was dangerously low. He noted the open wounds, mumbling to himself "periocular and temporomandibular. Suspected sub-dural haemorrhaging". She was going to require urgent surgical decompression if there was any hope of saving her life. He ran his hands along her body, his long thin fingers gently prodding as he felt for broken bones and other injuries.

The police arrived in droves at the same time as the ambulance and were now busy dispersing the crowd as the two ambulance men worked quickly and meticulously to put Neive onto the stretcher. The doctor spoke rapidly and authoritatively to them "My name is Leonard Fitch, I'm a consultant neurosurgeon at the Royal. I think there may be internal bleeding. We need to act fast."

He stood up and began brushing invisible dirt from the bottom of his expensive suit jacket. As he did, he looked towards a nearby police car where a female constable was gently coaxing two young boys into the back seat.

He called out to her, "Officer!"

She looked over and waved back at the doctor in acknowledgement as she finished buckling the boy's seat belts then she dashed over to Fitch and asked, "Yes, sir, what is it?"

"We need an escort!"

"Yes. Of course." She pointed in the direction of another police vehicle parked a little further along the road, engine running idly. "We have a patrol car waiting, sir."

She nodded towards the car where the two young boys were sitting in the back seat and said, "That one's taking the little girl's brothers home. We're trying to contact their parents."

Fitch glanced at the tiny girl on the stretcher who was being wheeled towards the waiting vehicle. "As soon as you make contact, bring them to the hospital as fast as you can. She has life-threatening injuries." He turned quickly, dismissing her with a wave of his hand and hurried to the ambulance as the medical team were sliding the stretcher inside. He climbed in and began preparing for the high-speed dash to the hospital.

CHAPTER FORTY

D C Jones pulled into the car park off the High Street in the centre of Bleaksedge. The dental practice was situated in the row of shops opposite. Harris gazed out of the window and peered through the drizzle at the flats above the shops. "Might be worth checking those out as well," he said as he unclipped his seatbelt. He never used to bother but since his last experience with Jones it was "Clunk Click every trip" from that point on.

The two detectives crossed the road, running the last few steps to avoid being hit by a speeding ambulance. Harris glared over his shoulder. "Bloody maniac!" he yelled. Jones carried on running until he reached the surgery, swung the door wide and held it open for his senior officer who panted towards him. *Out of puff again and he's only run a short distance,* thought Jones. Stepping into a small vestibule area they went through another door into the main reception-cum-waiting room. Jones took in their surroundings. Eight plastic chairs lined up against a lavender coloured wall and two small teak coffee tables either end holding an array of magazines. Three patients sat waiting to be seen – *can't be accompanying another patient,* Jones thought, *they look scared to death.* Several doors led off the reception area and Jones cringed and shuddered inwardly at the sound of drills, suction instruments and muffled voices beyond. *The sooner we're out of here the better.*

As they reached the counter, Harris flashed his warrant card at the Receptionist. "Detective Sergeant Harris, and this is DC Jones." The Receptionist smiled at each in turn.

"What can I do for you, officer?" she said in a light Cumbrian accent, with a little too much confidence for Harris's liking. He preferred the, *what have I done,* look on their faces when they saw his badge.

"Do you have a Mr *Kra-pi-alis*, working here?" Harris read the name out slowly from the index card in his hand.

"*Karapialis*! Not Krapialis," she said indignantly. "We did. He left about seven or eight months ago."

"Any idea where he went?"

"Back to Greece I think. Set up his own practice in Athens."

"Have you worked here long?" chipped in Jones.

"About eighteen months now. Why? What has he done?" Her eyes grew large at the thought of some misdemeanour. She didn't know him well but remembered him as quite an attractive man and had heard about the affair with her predecessor. She'd had no luck in that direction, though.

Harris ignored the question. "Can we take a look at your Patients Records Miss . . .?"

"Hall, Karen Hall."

"Miss Hall, yes. Your records please?"

"And it's *Mrs*. But you can call me Karen"

"Mrs Hall, could we see your records please?" Harris was getting a little impatient. Karen Hall narrowed her eyes at him as she lifted the flap in the desk to the side of her and motioned for the officers to go through.

"At the back there, pet." She nodded towards the bank of filing cabinets behind her. "They're all in alphabetical order, fully up-to-date. Did it all myself. The last receptionist was a waste of time. I think she was only hired for one reason and it wasn't her clerical skills, if you know what I mean." She let out a coarse laugh. The two detectives ignored the comment and went to the filing cabinets.

Gemma Cahill was the first one they found. Address and date of birth tallied with their records. Erin Fallon and Wendy Hilton were also there, again all details present and correct. But no Critchley and no Johnson. The two from out of town had no apparent links with this dental practice.

"Can you give me a list of names of the Dental Surgeons who have worked here in the past five years, Mrs err . . .?"

"Hall!"

"Yes. Do you have such a list?"

"I can get one for you. Might take a few minutes, mind."

"That's okay, we've got six weeks." Jones replied.

"Sorry?"

"The list Mrs Hall?" said Harris, throwing Jones a sideways glance and shaking his head.

The two detectives made themselves busy giving the office a general once over while Mrs Hall disappeared through a side door into another office. Jones picked up a note pad and thumbed through the pages. Harris turned back the pages of the calendar on the wall, humming as he did so.

After about five minutes Karen Hall returned with a list in her hand.

"Like I say, I haven't got . . . *put that down!*" she said, snatching the note pad from DC Jones. "That's personal that is."

"Sorry"

"Now then, like I said, I haven't got a forwarding address for Vlasis, but this is a list of all our dentists over the last five years and where they are now, if they're not still here, if you follow me?"

"Yes that's perfectly clear, Mrs Hall. Thank you for your help." DS Harris put the in the inside pocket of his jacket. "That will be all for now."

"Aren't you going to tell me not to leave the Country or anything like that?" A sly grin tugged at the corner of her mouth. Harris paid no attention.

"Please feel free to leave anytime you like" Jones said as he brushed past her and Harris in order to grab the door handle.

When they got outside, Jones stopped to light a cigarette. "No surprises there" he said, blowing out smoke as he did. DS Harris feigned a coughing fit and waved the smoke away. "Sorry Sarge. Might still be worth checking out these dentists though. See if there's a link with the other two towns."

"Definitely. Get onto that when we get back, Jonesy. Check out the dentists in Kendal and Lancaster, see if any of these have worked there." Harris handed the list to Jones and began to cross the road. Sirens could be heard in the near distance and a second later a police Panda car raced past followed by an ambulance, causing Harris to jump back again.

"Mind yourself Sarge."

"Christ Almighty! If you don't get me going, why not try when you're coming back? That where you learned to drive Jonesy?"

"Actually it was BSM"

"It was a rhetorical question."

* * *

Back at the station DC Jones pulled out all the directories and Yellow Pages for Kendal and Lancaster. He knew this was a waste of time. The perpetrator was not a dentist. He'd also studied those photographs; the grotesque way the killer had arranged the feet. All four were the same, toes pointing towards the ear. But that wasn't what stood out in his mind; what he noticed was the neatness of the cut. The feet hadn't simply been hacked off; they had been surgically removed. The person they were looking for was not a dentist but a *medical surgeon*.

CHAPTER FORTY-ONE

S EVERAL days passed and the investigation was stalling again. The dental surgeons had all checked out, there were no links to the victims. Jones had also checked out local GP's. None of the doctors could be linked, either. DS Harris was getting frustrated, so DC Jones decided it was time to test his theory.

"You know what I think, Sarge?"

"I've no idea! Go on, enlighten me why don't you?"

"The person, persons or man doing this is very meticulous, right?"

"Right"

"He also has a lot of patience. He plans what he's going to do and then waits for his chance. He watches his victims, knows their movements. Each girl was taken on a special day for the family, her birthday."

"Apart from the last one."

"Yes, apart from Erin Fallon. But then her birthday fell on a Saturday last year. He knew he wouldn't get the opportunity to catch her alone. This time he had to wait."

"Because he knew his best chance was when she got off the bus and began the long walk down Bleaksedge Lane." Harris saw another piece of his jigsaw fit into place.

"Yes but in this case, he took her on the way *to* school. I checked the records; she wasn't there for registration that day. The last time any of her friends saw her was on Bonfire Night, the day before her birthday."

"You have been a busy boy, Jonesy. So go on, where's this leading?"

"This man doesn't just take people at random, when he feels like it, yeah? He *'earmarks'* them. Selects them from their medical records because of their age and forthcoming birthday AND where they live."

"*Earmarks* them? Interesting turn of phrase; wonder if that's what the pictures are all about?"

"Well maybe, but the pictures are also a bit of a giveaway."

"Go on, I'm intrigued."

"Check them again. The feet have been surgically removed. The last one he took, the Johnson girl, you can see it clearly on that one."

Harris took the lid off the box and rummaged through the folders. He took out the Johnson file and hastily untied the ribbon. The photographs, like all the others, were at the front. Spreading them out across the table, he picked up the Polaroid and studied it. Being a recent picture, this one was clear as a bell and in colour. Jones was right; the feet were not just hacked off as though by some deranged maniac, the cuts through the flesh were clean and the perpetrator had cauterised the limbs to halt the bleeding, suggesting that the victim was alive at the time. The bone, which was just visible on this picture, was neatly trimmed. Whoever did this had access to surgical equipment and knew how to use it.

"You know what, Jonesy? You might have something there!" DC Jones couldn't help smiling; praise from Harris was rare. "Okay, let's run with this for a while." DS Harris was back in charge. "We're looking for someone with a medical background, probably a surgeon, with access to the records of all five girls. The main hospitals in the area are . . ."

"Bleaksedge Royal, Westmorland General and Lancaster General."

"Do we know whether these girls attended any of these hospitals?"

"Well, remember when we visited the Doctors' Surgeries of the missing girls?"

"Yes, and none of the GP's could be linked to all five girls."

"That's right, but I managed to get copies of the medical records of all of them. Well, all apart from Critchley. We didn't follow that one up because we'd drawn a blank with the others. Look at this Sarge." Jones pulled a pile of papers from out of his briefcase. He'd obviously been doing some homework on this and was eager to show what he'd discovered. "All four attended hospital within six months of being kidnapped. Cahill had her tonsils out in January 1972 at Bleaksedge Royal, as did Hilton a year later."

"Fallon banged her head playing netball and was admitted to The Royal wasn't she?" Harris chipped in.

"That's right. Johnson, appendix operation at Westmoorland General, May 1975."

"And you can bet your life Critchley attended Lancaster General at some time in 1974. Jonesy, if we can find one man who worked at all three hospitals, I reckon we've got the bastard. How did you get all this information anyway?"

"I used my charm and wit, as usual."

"And they still gave you access? *Unbelievable.* Anyway, you know this would be inadmissible in court."

"Yeah I know, but if it leads us to our man and possibly saves Erin Fallon's life . . . "

* * *

The next few days were spent going through the records of all of the surgeons who had worked at the three hospitals over the past five years. It was a daunting task. Firstly, there were the different types of surgeon. Harris had commented that it didn't need a specialist to remove part of a limb, just someone with the equipment and

191

knowledge. After all, it didn't matter if the operation wasn't entirely successful; the patient was as good as dead and not likely to sue!

Whilst Jones accepted the point, his profile of the killer had him down as a specialist, possibly an orthopaedic surgeon or a gynaecologist. Somebody who spent their everyday working life healing people or helping to deliver life, but during their spare time they delighted in taking life away in a long drawn out and painful process. The duality was, for Jones, an important thread in this case – the person they were looking for had serious issues in his or her personal life, but like most serial killers, this would not be evident to those close to him or her. Their perpetrator had a split personality, not the popular misconception of a schizophrenic but a pure psychopath. Possibly the most difficult person to find because, in their everyday life, they appeared decent human beings.

He pondered on the birthday cards; all sent to the mothers of the victims - never the fathers. This was somebody with a complex about his or her mother. He had read about Oedipus and Electra, and the hatred of the same sex parent that could result. Was this an indication that the perpetrator was a woman?

Jones decided to take a chance on this. He narrowed his search to the female surgeons and came up with, what he thought was a lead. '*Mrs Olivier Horton FRCS*' appeared in all three lists. She worked at the three hospitals in question between January 1972 and the present day; currently she was a consultant at The Royal.

* * *

"Are you mad?" DS Harris yelled. "Olivier Horton? *The* Olivier Horton; the paediatric surgeon who saved the lives of hundreds of children?"

"But Sarge, she fits the profile, she worked at – "

"Profile my arse, Jonesy! Look, I don't know her personally, but I can guarantee that a female doctor who spends her life looking after teenage kids is not going to keep one of them locked up for twelve months only to brutally beat and kill her, then chop off her feet and take a picture for the family album."

"What if she has an accomplice? What if it's her husband, and she just helps out with the surgery? Look at Brady and Hindley. She was just a young, innocent kid who became besotted by a monster."

"*She was also as thick as pig shit!* Olivier Horton, your latest suspect, is a *Mrs*. Not a lowly Doctor. She's a *Fellow* of the Royal College of Surgeons, not a mere *member*. They don't get much higher than this, Jonesy."

"Jack the Ripper was most likely an eminent surgeon as well."

Harris sighed. "Okay, we go with this for now, see where it leads us, but remember, softly softly . . ."

"Yes Sarge, I know, *softly softly catchee monkey*."

CHAPTER FORTY-TWO

HANNAH shifted in her seat, "I can't believe we're doing this. What if he spots us? We must have been following him for about half an hour, now. Don't you think he would have noticed by now that he's being followed?"

"Nah. I've hung back every so often and shifted lanes. It's the M6, Hannah. He's hardly going to notice us amongst all this traffic, and anyway it's getting dark. His car's easy to spot – it's a status symbol, tells us all he is a man of means! Ours is a bog standard, Ford Cortina, nothing special. There must be thousands of this make and model on the road. Anyway, what makes you think he's gonna be clockin' us?" He squeezed her hand. "You worry too much, you know."

He checked the rear-view mirror and moved back into the inside lane. He was behind Fitch again. He glanced at Hannah; she was chewing her nails. "Stop worrying! We'll be okay. Just think of it as a bit of an adventure, you and me sort of like . . . *McMillan and Wife*, a pair of sleuths!"

She laughed. "You're mad, Billy! And anyway, you look nothing like Rock Hudson." She studied him side on, "Actually, I'd say you were more like Mr Hudson, the Butler in *Upstairs Downstairs!*"

He burst out laughing and slapped her knee, "Cheeky! Okay, since we're exchanging insults, you look nothing like Susan Saint James – more like *Sid* James."

Hannah turned and stared at him, full of indignation, as he laughed out loud at his own joke.

"Aww, come on, Hannah, don't look like that! It's just my idea of a little joke, that's all. And anyway, you know you're gorgeous – you don't need me to remind you."

She blushed at the compliment and turned to stare through the passenger window, hoping he hadn't noticed her embarrassment.

Billy settled back in his seat and began singing along to '*I'm Mandy, fly me*' on the car radio – he turned the volume up full blast and shouted to Hannah over the din. "10cc. I love 'em! Brilliant songwriters! One of the best bands ever!"

Her face creased with concentration, "Turn it down, I can't hear a word you're saying!"

He did as she asked, "I was just saying, 10cc – "

"Yes, I know. You're favourite band. How much longer are we going to follow him? I'm starving, now." She glanced at her watch. When they set off almost an hour ago they had no clear plan. Billy's idea was to follow Fitch after he left the hospital grounds and neither she nor Billy had any idea where they were going. Nor for how long they would be following him. Hannah began to worry. *Where is this leading?*

It was Friday night. Hannah had told her mum and dad she was stopping over at her best friend's house until Sunday. She'd primed her friend, Coleen, in case either of her parents checked up. Coleen and Hannah had been friends since nursery school and there wasn't much Coleen wouldn't do for her, it'd been that way all throughout their childhood, but Coleen had expressed concern over this one. "Are you mad?" she asked. "Sleeping in a tent with *him*."

"Aww he's not as bad as everyone makes out, Col. He's really nice when you get to know him." Hannah hated it when people badmouthed Billy. "I can't tell Mum and Dad, they'd hit the roof! You know my dad can't stand him."

Coleen had agreed to keep their little secret on two conditions – that Hannah phoned the moment she got back on Sunday evening, and that she took her own sleeping bag and kept it well zipped!

Hannah bit her lip as she gazed out of the window. She caught Billy's reflection in the glass, illuminated by the glow from the dashboard, as he tapped the steering wheel to the music on the radio, singing away wildly out of tune.

She turned to him again and said, "Come on, Billy, you must be a bit peckish as well by now. How long do you plan on following him? Because for all we know he could be going to Scotland. Have you even thought of that?"

He didn't answer straight away; he eyed the clock on the dashboard and considered her question. She was right, he hadn't given much thought about where Fitch might be heading or how long they might follow him for. He could still see Fitch's car cruising along in the nearside lane, still heading north.

Hannah shifted constantly in her seat, twisting strands of her long blond hair between her fingers. Billy glanced sideways at her; she was doing it now, messing with her hair and biting at the corner of her bottom lip. He had to admit, she did have a point, what if Fitch was on his way to Scotland? They couldn't possibly travel that far north. The idea was to follow Fitch, see where he ended up then they would head into Bleazedale Forest, find somewhere nice and secluded to pitch the tent, and spend the weekend taking long walks and in the evening they could sit round a fire with a couple of glasses of beer; a nice romantic weekend without interference from friends and family. It was about time he and Hannah took their relationship to the next level. He took his hand off the steering wheel and checked the inside pocket of his jacket. The unopened pack was still in there.

He'd packed a tent, two sleeping bags – he still had his fingers crossed in the hope that one might become superfluous to requirements – a Calor Gas stove and plenty of food and beer as well as Hannah's favourite tipple, Cherry B, enough to see them over the weekend. Everything they needed was in the boot of the car but best of all, he had Hannah all to himself until Sunday afternoon – he couldn't have planned it better! He looked at the petrol gauge; they still had three quarters of a tank left,

With his eyes still on the road and one hand on the steering wheel, he stroked her hair. "Tell you what, we'll give it another thirty minutes. No more, I promise. And if he doesn't pull off anywhere during that time, we'll leave him to it and head up into the forest, find a decent place to camp. What do you say, Hannah?"

"Promise?" She raised her eyebrows and cocked her head to one side, looking at him as if she didn't believe him.

"Promise! Another thirty minutes and, if he's still heading north, we'll forget it." He checked his rear-view mirror, then his right wing mirror and pulled out into the middle lane. He could still see Fitch's vehicle, just two cars ahead of them.

He muttered to himself, "Follow Fitch? Probably not one of my better ideas."

Hannah looked puzzled, "What did you say?"

"This . . ." He waved his hand in front of the windscreen, taillights coming on with the onset of dusk, "You and me following, Fitch."

She sighed heavily, "I know. I'm starting to feel a bit uncomfortable about the whole thing myself now. What if he has spotted us?"

"I've told you, Hannah, he hasn't! And even if he has, what can he say? He doesn't own the M6 and anyway, we're on our way up to Bleazedale for the weekend. It's got naff all to do with him."

"Hmm, I suppose you're right." She yawned and tried to stretch in her seat. "You don't mind if I have ten minutes do you? I feel a bit sleepy now."

"No. You make yourself nice and comfy." He stroked the back of her head and smiled at her,

"Get some shut eye. I'll wake you up when we get to wherever it is we end up. Think of it as a mystery weekend, Hannah."

She rolled her eyes and said, "Hmm, that's what worries me, Billy. As long as your mystery weekend doesn't turn into a murder mystery weekend!"

She reclined the seat a little and snuggled down in her warm winter jacket.

"You've no sense of adventure, Hannah."

She mumbled something, pulled her scarf up under her chin and closed her eyes.

This stretch of the motorway was completely unlit; almost pitch black with only the overspill from headlights providing what little illumination there was, bouncing off the 'cat's eyes'. Billy massaged his eyebrows with the middle finger of his left hand, gripping the steering wheel tightly with his right. The taillights from the vehicles ahead of him were having a hypnotic effect and he was beginning to feel the strain. Struggling to keep Fitch's car in view, he was about to nudge Hannah awake to tell her he was going to abandon their mission when Fitch's left indicator light started blinking. Billy pulled himself up, ramrod straight, leaned forward and peered through the windscreen. The sign up ahead said, 'Bleazedale Forest'. *So that's where you're going is it?* He was suddenly wide-awake again. He flicked on his indicator and began to move into the exit lane where he found himself directly behind Fitch's car. Not so cock-sure of himself now, the adrenalin flowing and his heart racing, he sank lower in his seat, peering over the top of the steering wheel. Breaking a little and easing off the accelerator, he put a little distance between the two cars. *Don't want Fitch recognising me through his rear view mirror.* No other cars were on the slip road, making Billy even more conspicuous.

Coming up to a roundabout, Fitch indicated left again, still following the signs for Bleazedale Forest, turning onto a narrow tree lined lane that was blacker than the motorway. Billy hung on at the roundabout, not sure what to do next.

He decided it was time to wake Hannah; he shook her gently, "Hannah, wake up. We're here."

She wriggled in her seat as she stretched and pulled herself up straight, yawing and rubbing her eyes, "Where are we?"

"Well, Fitch is heading down that lane . . ." He indicated to the left with a nod of his head, "Straight into Bleazedale Forest by the looks of it. I'm not sure about where we're heading now though."

"What do you mean? I thought the idea was to see where he goes?"

As if she was some sort of imbecile, he said impatiently, "Yes, it was, *is*. He's just turned down there." Billy pointed towards the left now with his index finger, "There are no lights, Hannah, and if I carry on following him now, he's going to get suspicious, as there's no other traffic on the road."

"Oh. Right. I see. So what are we going to do then?"

He checked the rear view mirror; nothing coming up behind him. "We'll get off this roundabout, give it a few minutes or so then we'll head into the forest. We probably won't see where he's gone but at least we can set up camp for the night; after all, it's what we planned isn't it."

Before she could answer, he leaned across and kissed her lightly on the mouth. He set off, took the second exit, the opposite direction to Fitch to make sure he didn't see their headlights. He swung into the lay-by and turned off the engine. Both hands loosely draped over the steering wheel, he turned to Hannah, "Well? Are you still up for a bit of an adventure this weekend, my lovely?"

Chewing nervously at her thumbnail, she said, "Hmm, I don't know now . . ."

Billy frowned, "You don't know? What do you mean?"

"Billy, my dad would murder me if he found out where I was and who I was spending the weekend with."

He tutted and shook his head, sighing loudly, "Well he's not going to is he? You said Coleen was covering for you, so why should you be worried?"

She stared straight ahead and didn't answer.

Stroking the side of her face, he said, "Don't go all soft on me now, Hannah. We've come all this way and now you're having second thoughts?"

She bit down on her bottom lip. "I don't know . . . it just feels sort of – scary, following Mr Fitch like this."

Billy sighed and turned away then looked over his shoulder in the direction Leonard Fitch had taken.

An awkward silence lay between them now. Billy looked straight ahead through the windscreen into the darkness, chewing the side of his bottom lip.

Hannah didn't blame him for being annoyed; after all, it was her idea as much as his to embark on this daft trip to find out where Fitch disappeared to for days on end. "Okay. You're right. I suppose I was just as much up for this as you were." Feigning cheeriness she definitely no longer felt, she added hurriedly, "Well let's not wait here too long, I'm starving, and we've got to find somewhere to pitch the tent."

He leaned towards her and kissed her again. Cupping her face in his hands, he said, "That's more like it, Hannah. Don't worry about Fitch. Trust me. *We* are going to have a fantastic weekend!"

She pulled his hands away, "I do trust you, but can we please get going now? Because we're going to have a helluva job pitching a tent in the dark."

He smiled, "That's better. I hate it when you go all grumpy on me!"

He started the engine again, checked his rear view mirror and did a U turn, heading back to the roundabout where he exited onto the black narrow lane that Fitch had taken.

Adjusting the headlights to full beam, he said, "If we can't pitch the tent tonight, we could recline the seats and kip in the car, just for tonight. I've got sleeping bags and a couple of blankets in the boot. It'll be nice and snug."

Hannah strained to see beyond the soft pale yellow beam of the headlights, she knew what he meant; it was pitch black out there. "Okay then. Besides, I think I'd feel safer in the car. This place is starting to give me the creeps."

"There's nothing creepy about it, Hannah." He sounded exasperated again, "When you wake up in the morning and see how beautiful the landscape is you'll feel different about it." And like a parent convincing a young child, he continued, "We'll be perfectly safe. I promise to look after you and let no harm come to you. Okay?"

She ignored his patronising tone and asked, "How do you know it's beautiful, have you been here before?"

"No I haven't. But a few of the lads at work have been on weekend camping trips up here, they said it's fantastic."

Listening to Billy being all positive and enthusiastic made her feel as though she was becoming a bit of a wimp and a killjoy.

She apologised, "Sorry, Billy. I'm such a coward. I know you'll look after me. And I'm sure you're right about how lovely this place is. So I say, let's go for it!"

They'd been following Fitch for more than hour and Billy's eyes were starting to sting with tiredness. Using the heel of his palm he rubbed hard at each eye then tried to focus again into the darkness. There was no sign of another vehicle in the distance ahead, no taillights, no main beams lighting up the trees. They'd definitely lost Fitch.

"You okay, Billy?"

"Yeah, just a bit tired. I think we'll have to find somewhere to camp pretty soon. It's so dark . . .it's a killer when it's like this." He shook his head as if trying to shake off the tiredness.

"Yeah, I know. You did remember to bring a torch, didn't you?"

"Yeah, of course I did. Considering how dark it is out there and the fact that there's no lighting whatsoever, it'd probably be better if we sleep in the car after all - just for tonight. And in the morning we'll look for a good site to pitch the tent and get everything set up for the weekend. Is that okay with you?"

"It'll have to be okay, Billy. I don't fancy the idea of stumbling around in the dark with a tent and everything else."

"Right then. The first exit we come to along this road, I'll pull off and we'll park up. I'll get the blankets out of the boot and I'll grab us a couple of drinks and something to eat. I'm really sorry about this, Hannah, I didn't plan on us having to sleep in the car; it's just the way things have turned out. I'll make it as comfy as possible for us."

She didn't say anything. She was thinking about home. She'd never spent the night in a car before, and in a forest, too! Her dad would be incandescent with rage if he knew what she was up to this weekend – and that she'd lied about where she was going and with whom.

Billy saw a clearing on the right and pulled over. If they were going to stay in the car overnight, he didn't want to be seen from the road, so he looked for a place where there was some cover. A mass of what looked like rhododendron bushes appeared in the headlights, so he pulled up behind them and killed the engine.

Stretching and yawning noisily, he said, "Here we are. This should do us for the night."

"At last. Get the food and drink out, I'm famished!" Fiddling with the lever at the side of her seat, she added, "Are you sure these seats go all the way back?"

He leaned across to her, "Err, well I've never actually tried, but they always do in the films don't they? Here let me have a go."

"Yes, but this isn't a 1960's Chevrolet, it's a 1970's Cortina." Billy was impressed at her knowledge of cars but slightly embarrassed that she'd pointed out the flaw in his plan.

He struggled with the lever; Hannah's seat only went back about a foot or so. He tried his. Same thing. Trying not to sound disappointed at the thought of having to unload the entire contents of his boot he said to her, "Okay, the tent it is then."

"But it's pitch black out there, Billy. How can we pitch a tent in the dark?"

"We've got headlights on the car and there's that big torch in the boot as well, what more do you want?"

"Go on then, I suppose we've no choice have we!" She sighed

noisily, unfastening her seat belt, "But you'd better not drain the battery, Billy. Don't want to be stuck here for God knows how long do we?"

Billy gave her a sideways glance, which Hannah read as; *do you think I'm stupid?* He got out of the car and walked around to the rear and popped open the boot lid. "Come on then, give us a hand!"

"Yeah, okay, I'm coming."

The tent was much bigger than Hannah had imagined. It was a large heavy canvas one which Billy had bought from the Army and Navy Stores a couple of years ago. It had a musty smell about it; Hannah screwed her nose up in disgust as he heaved it out of the boot.

"This it?" she said, not really wanting to touch it, let alone sleep in it.

"What's wrong with it? It was good enough for the Desert Rats, it'll be good enough for us."

Billy pulled out the wooden poles that were about three feet long and handed them to Hannah. He untied the lengths of rope that held the roll together, and spread the tent out on the ground in front of the car where the headlamps illuminated a flat patch of grass. In a matter of minutes, the tent took shape as Billy began pounding the pegs in with a rubber mallet.

"Gently Billy, noise travels in the night. Don't want to alert Fitch."

"Good thinking. Pass me that rag then, please." Hannah handed him a piece of towelling that had fallen out of the roll. He placed it over the peg and began knocking it into the ground once more.

"Right, that's it." Billy said. "Let's get the sleeping bags."

"And don't forget the headlights, Billy. You don't want to –"

"I know, I know, drain the battery. I have done this before you know." Hannah pulled a face behind Billy's back and mocked him.

As soon as he switched off the car's headlights, the temporary campsite was plunged into darkness; so black that Hannah couldn't see a thing. The Moon was a thin sliver, offering no light whatsoever. She felt a shiver run down her spine. "Quick! Come on, Billy, hurry up, it's so dark here."

"Ten out of ten for observation" Billy, remarked sarcastically, before emerging from the back of the car with the sleeping bags, blankets and pillows, trying to switch on the torch at the same time.

"Ouch!" he yelped as he stubbed his toe on one of the pegs, tripping in the process. Hannah managed to suppress her laughter but couldn't resist a smile as Billy struggled to keep his balance and carry the load. Her eyes were slowly becoming accustomed to the darkness; she could just make out his silhouette against the pale fabric of the tent.

"Give us a hand then!" Hannah grabbed the torch off him and thumbed the switch on. The narrow beam was enough to light the way to the entrance of the tent. They were soon settled down for the night. Billy had fetched in the coolbox, which he'd loaded with food and cans of Colt 45, and a few bottles of Cherry B for Hannah.

"Bring out the goodies! I can't wait to see what you've packed for us."

He handed Hannah two cellophane wrapped Melton Mowbray pork pies, then went into his rucksack and pulled out a couple of bags of Golden Wonder crisps and a large pack of ready salted peanuts.

"Tucker time! Let's get stuck in."

She squealed with delight. "Hmmm, Melton Mowbray! My favourite."

As he removed the lid from the small bottle, he said, "Here, Hannah, another favourite of yours – Cherry B! Get one of these down you, it'll warm you up and put a smile on your face. All giddy-like, just how I like you!"

She giggled as she took the bottle from him, "Oh, Billy you really do know how to treat a girl."

"Yep, I certainly do! Bottoms up, sweet cheeks!"

Tapping his beer can against her Cherry B bottle, he added, "Here's to a great weekend full of laughter, pork pie, crisps, nuts, and speaking of nuts, Leonard Fitch! Down the hatch, girl!"

After an hour or so, they were snug and relaxed. The bicycle lamp that Billy had attached to the tent pole was beginning to fade as the battery started to die.

"I think it's time to call it a night. Shall we turn in now?" Billy said, reaching for Hannah's hand and kissing it. "I'm knackered!"

"Thought you'd never ask." She turned and kissed him before snuggling down inside her sleeping bag, pulling the zip up as far as it would go, remembering what Coleen had said.

Within minutes, Billy was fast asleep. Although tired, Hannah just couldn't get off. The forest was a world unfamiliar to her and all her senses were affected by this. The first thing was the darkness. It was like black velvet; no shapes, no shadows nothing; just a black nothingness. Then there was the noise; or to be more precise, the lack of it. Back home there was always a hum, the background noise of distant factories and traffic, but here there was nothing apart from the individual noises of animals scurrying around, looking for food. At night the forest comes to life but it was not the kind of life a townie like Hannah was used to.

When senses are heightened, as Hannah's were now, panic and anxiety kicks in causing a rush of adrenalin and the fear and tension builds up. She lay in her sleeping bag absolutely rigid with fear and unable to control her increasing heart beat.

Somewhere in the distance she heard a scream. She sat bolt upright almost leaping from her sleeping bag. She turned to look for Billy, groping along his sleeping bag. He was dead to the world, snoring his head off. Seconds later she heard it again. "Billy!" she whispered frantically. No reaction. "Billy, wake up!"

"Wha . . . what's up? What is it?"

"I heard a scream . . ." She nodded towards the entrance of the tent, "Out there . . . there's someone out there, Billy."

He rubbed his eyes, but in the pitch black it made no difference. There was absolutely nothing to be seen. "Eh? A scream? It'll be an owl or something."

"Billy, it was *human*! Listen." He listened. Nothing. He screwed up his face, as if that would help him hear better, but still nothing.

"It's your imagination." He rolled over to face Hannah but he couldn't see her.

"Billy, I heard it! I'm telling you, it was human!"

"Come here, snuggle up close to me. I've told you haven't I? I'll protect you, Hannah. You've got to believe me or else you wont sleep a wink all night long; it was an animal you heard. Now try and settle down – count sheep or something . . . or even the number of handbags you've got, that should send you to sleep. Come on, hutch up, we've got an early start tomorrow."

"I can't sleep. You've not stopped snoring since your head hit the pillow, it's pitch black in here and someone out there is screaming." She was about to snuggle down against him when she sat bolt upright again, "What was that?"

"What?"

"That noise. It's outside the tent." Billy sat up. He could hear rustling and a sniffing sound.

"Do they have bears here?"

He laughed. "No love, they don't have bears. It'll be a hedgehog or something."

"It's the *something* bit I don't like, Billy."

"Well the biggest thing it could be is a fox."

"Foxes kill things don't they?"

"Chickens, yes. People? No, definitely not. Now try and go to sleep, Hannah."

He settled down again. Hannah snuggled up close to him and pulled his arm around her, gripping his hand tightly.

She closed her eyes and tried to drift off but after a few minutes her eyes fluttered open again. Even though she was dog-tired she just couldn't get off to sleep. She couldn't get that awful scream out of her head. It was going to be a very long night.

CHAPTER FORTY-THREE

IT was eight am and the sun was just beginning to warm the side of the tent. There was a heavy dew and Hannah felt the dampness on the canvas causing a rivulet of water to run down the inside. She had managed to get some sleep, albeit fitful and, although still tired, she was relieved it was daylight.

Billy was already up trying to light the Calor Gas stove with damp matches and cursing as another attempt failed. Hannah smiled smugly to herself as she snuggled deeper into her sleeping bag; her nose was cold but it was nice and warm in there. "Try rubbing them together" she called out, lazily. "Were you never in the Scouts?"

"Tried it once but got mugged on the way. Two lads nicked my subs but no one believed me. When it happened a second time, that was it, they chucked me out."

She chuckled, "Have you just made that up or did it really happen?"

"No, I'm not making it up and yes it did happen." Billy shouted.

"Poor you. Have you got it working yet?"

"Just about. Hope it doesn't blow out, I'm down to my last two matches." He put a pan of water onto one ring and empted the contents of a tin into a pan on the other, then stepped a few yards away from the tent and surveyed their camp area, *not a bad job considering how dark it was when I put it up*. Although he never quite made it in the Boy Scouts, he had done his fair share of camping with his mates and it appeared to have paid off very well in his opinion.

"Where do you think Fitch might be, Billy?" Hannah called out.

"Dunno. Can't be far." The water was about to boil and got the cups out of his rucksack. "Tea or coffee?"

"Oh, coffee please! Are we going to walk from here?"

"Yeah, can't risk him hearing or spotting the car. If we're going to find out what he's up to we need to take him by surprise."

The rich smell of coffee forced Hannah to drag herself out of the warmth of her sleeping bag. She stuck her head out of the tent as Billy was spooning beans and sausage onto two small tin plates.

"Hmmm, yummy! Heinz Beans and Sausages. I haven't had them in ages."

"Right, well get your backside out here and let's tuck in. I'm bloody ravenous! Must be this fresh country air!"

After they'd eaten and had a couple of mugs of coffee each, Billy started packing things away in the boot.

"Are we going to take the tent down?"

"No, we'll leave it where it is. It'll be fine. It's not as though there's anyone else knocking about. I'm just putting the stove, cups and plates away. You roll the sleeping bags up in the tent for us."

When they'd got everything tidied away, they got dressed in jeans, thick jumpers and walking boots. Billy packed his rucksack with another two small pork pies, a large bottle of water, four bags of crisps, a couple of bananas and some Cadbury's fruit and nut bars. To say that he'd thought about their stomachs and come well prepared was an understatement!

He caught the look of amusement on Hannah's face as he was stuffing the provisions into his backpack, "*Always be prepared. That's my motto, Hannah.*"

She didn't comment, she was busy rummaging about in her small overnight bag.

Billy stood with his hands on his hips looking impatient, he sighed noisily. "Come on, Hannah! What are you looking for now?"

She replied absently, "My lipstick."

"Hannah, you don't need lipstick. We're in the middle of a bloody forest, it's not like we're off to a wedding or a night out on the town!"

She tutted and fastened the bag then threw it at Billy to put in the boot of the car. "Yeah, yeah! Okay then. I won't bother."

Billy hugged her to him, "No sulking, please. You're gorgeous without make up. Now come on, let's get moving, see if we can't locate the strange Mr. Fitch."

As they set off into the forest, Billy looked back. He decided that the car was far enough off the road to avoid being seen by a passing motorist and before they'd set off he'd used some broken branches to wipe out the tyre tracks. Hannah was impressed at how Billy thought of just about everything!

As the road disappeared beyond the tree line it became little more than a dirt track. The evergreen Douglas Firs gave the track shelter from the low angled sun, giving the morning air quite a chill. Hannah could see her breath in front of her and pulled up her collar for extra warmth. "Don't you think we should get off the road, you know, in case he drives past us?" she asked.

"Good idea. We'll nip through that clearing over there" They took a right turn through a wooded area, where the sycamores had begun to shed their leaves, allowing daylight through onto the dense forest floor. The dry leaves crunched noisily under their feet as they walked.

Every few seconds Hannah looked back over her shoulder, her eyes darting everywhere. She wrapped her arms around herself, defensively.

Billy frowned as he watched her. "What's the matter now, Hannah? You look frightened to death!"

"I don't know. I don't like it, Billy. It's creepy, and the noise we're making crunching along on these dead leaves, well it's . . ."

"Well, what?"

"Well, someone might hear us! And what if Fitch is hiding out here, he's going to know that we're here isn't he?"

Billy laughed, "What? You mean like he might be hiding up a tree or something? Like a Japanese sniper?"

Hannah snapped, "Don't be so ridiculous, Billy! You know I didn't mean that. What I mean is . . . Oh! I don't know what I mean! It's just creepy that's all!"

He pulled her to him. "Listen, we're two people who have come camping for the weekend. We're not doing anything wrong. We're simply enjoying a walk in the forest. And, even if we did come across freaky Fitch, what the hell can he say? It's not his forest, it's a free country and we can go where ever the hell we like, when we like."

Hannah thought about what he'd said. She smiled now, more at her own stupidity for worrying about being heard taking a walk in the forest. "Well I suppose if you put it like that, Billy, you're quite right."

He hugged her again. "That's my girl. Now! Show me those teeth again!"

He felt her body relax against his as she laughed out loud at his way of asking her to smile.

Still hugging her to him as they walked on he said, "That's more like it. It's the first thing that attracted me to you, Hannah. Your gorgeous smile!"

He pinched her cheek playfully. "Ouch, Billy, that hurts!" She pulled away, punching him in the arm.

They continued walking, hand in hand, sometimes chatting about this and that and sometimes in silence as they enjoyed the chill autumn air and the peace and tranquillity of the forest with it's amazing shades of red, burgundy, gold and green. All thoughts of Fitch seemingly gone from her mind, Hannah relaxed; she was happy again, actually enjoying being there, just the two of them surrounded by the natural beauty of the forest.

"What time is it, Billy?"

He let go of her hand and pushed the sleeve of his jacket back to look at his watch. "It's almost half eleven." He took her hand again

She sounded surprised. "That means we've been walking for almost two and half hours. We will find our way back alright wont we?"

"Yes. Of course we will. We have the Sun. I've got a compass and I've got a plan."

She looked at him, a puzzled expression on her face. "Oh? And do you plan to share it with me . . . your *plan*, I mean?"

"Well it's pretty simple really. We won't get lost, if that's what you're worried about. I've got the compass and I know which direction we have to take to get back to our camping ground. We can also use the position of the Sun, for that matter. Trust me, Hannah, I will not let anything happen to us and we won't be sleeping under the stars tonight. We'll be snuggled up in our sleeping bags!"

"Yes. Okay. But how long do you intend for us to keep walking. My only concern is that we turn back before it begins to go dark."

"The Sun doesn't start to set until about six o'clock. We've got hours yet. We'll keep on walking for another couple of hours or so and I estimate that we'll probably have to turn back at about two o'clock."

"Promise?"

"Yep! I promise. But in the meantime, where do you think Fitch might be holed up?"

She shivered. "Urgh! I'd forgotten all about him. I've absolutely no idea where he might be holed up and I don't care. In fact, I'm not bothered about finding him now. I'm quite enjoying just the two of us being here; just like you said last night, Billy, the forest is beautiful. Fitch is such a weirdo, he could be holed up in a cave like a hobbit for all I care!"

Billy laughed out loud. "Fitch a hobbit? Bilbo Baggins? Hardly, Hannah, he's about six foot six! And he's way too gangly. Hobbits eat at least six meals a day and they don't live in caves either, they live in holes in the ground."

"Oooh, hark at Billy Ashcroft, expert on the habits of the hobbit!"

They both burst out laughing.

They continued walking and chatting and generally getting lost in themselves, until they began to climb higher up into the trees, and when they eventually reached the top of a hillock, Billy stopped and pointed into the distance.

"Look Hannah, over there."

"Where? I can't see anything."

Billy pointed again. "Look, in the distance; rings of smoke rising through the trees."

Hannah's eyes followed to where Billy was pointing; he was right. In the distance she could make out the smoke swirling lazily above the tree line.

"*That's* where our man is, Hannah. I'll bet you a pound to a penny!"

They began their descent down the other side of the hillock, going deeper into the woodland walking in the direction of the smoke, hoping to find its source. They continued in silence, both lost in their own thoughts. Hannah became jumpy again, occasionally grabbing hold of Billy's hand, startled by some of the noises echoing from the hidden depths of the forest.

Billy laughed, "You're such a city girl, Hannah! The noises you can here are from the different birds and animals living here, it's their habitat."

"I know, I know. I'm such a coward! I'm not used to this sort of environment. It's so . . ." she searched for a word to describe how it felt to her, "Tranquil, peaceful, until the silence is broken by loud snapping sounds or wild flapping noises." She inhaled deeply, taking in the smell of the damp earth of the forest, "Don't get me wrong, Billy, I do like being here. I love how the sun filters through the trees creating lots of different colours, casting colourful shadows everywhere. If feels magical and mystical. I love it. But I'm scared at the same time."

"See, didn't I tell you you'd enjoy it? We're going to have a cracking weekend, just the two of us and the forest!" He playfully grabbed the end of her nose between the knuckles of his index and middle fingers.

"Ah, Billy! GET OFF!" she pulled his hand away and shook her head as if shaking off his fingers, "You know it ticks me off when you do that! And don't you mean the three of us?"

He frowned and cocked his head to one side, "Three of us? I'm not with you, what do you mean?"

"Well *who* do you think I mean, silly? Mr Fitch? Isn't he the reason for this barmy adventure we've embarked upon? "

"Ah, I see what you mean." Nonchalantly he added, "Nah. All we're gonna do is to try to find where he's staying and just have a bit of a nosey around, see what he's up to. He might have a cottage or something out here, I mean, I can't see him staying in a tent can you?" He laughed at the image he had in his mind of Leonard Fitch in a tent wearing a suit, shirt and tie and his briefcase by his side, laying on his back reading medical files.

"Can you imagine him in a tent? I can't. He'd only get his upper half inside. He's far too lanky; he'd never get those legs inside for a start! I don't think they make sleeping bags in his size either. He'd probably have to kip in his suit!" He laughed again at what he thought was an amusing scene; *Mr Fitch Goes Camping.*

She laughed with him, "And you say I've got a weird imagination!"

They continued further into the forest, quietly enjoying the calm and beauty of the dense woodlands, totally unaware of time. It was beginning to grow dark, the shadows crowding in on them. Hannah shivered.

"You cold?"

"A bit, yes. What time is it? Haven't you noticed? It's getting dark. We've been walking for hours. And we still haven't found where the smoke was coming from either."

He looked at his watch; his face fell, "*Shit!* Jesus Christ, Hannah!"

She stopped dead in her tracks, "What? What is it?"

"It's ten to six! I didn't realise how long we'd been walking." He stopped and looked around, the light was definitely fading, and quickly too. "We have to turn around and start heading back to their tent – right now!"

Hannah picked up on the anxious tone in Billy's voice. "Billy, you're scaring me. We are going to make it back, aren't we?"

"Just give us a minute, Hannah." He took the rucksack off his back and placed it on the ground, knelt, and began to rummage about inside. Frowning, he looked up at Hannah, "I did put that compass back in here this morning, didn't I?"

"The compass? I don't remember seeing you with it, Billy."

"Yeah, I did." He pulled his hand out of the sack and rubbed hard at his temples, trying to remember.

"I emptied the rucksack outside the tent to pack the food and drink in it. I remember the compass fell out . . ." He stopped, his hand falling to his side, and stared up at Hannah's worried face. He *was* worried now and she could see it.

"I don't believe it, Hannah, it's not here. Shit! What the hell are we going to do?" All his bravado and Boy Scout expertise had suddenly deserted him.

Hannah got down beside him, "Here, let me have a look." She pulled the rucksack towards her and tipped it upside down, spilling the contents onto the ground: food, bottled water, a small torch, a bag of boiled sweets, binoculars, a packet of Kleenex Handyandies tissues and two pairs of gloves. The compass definitely wasn't there. They stared at each other.

"What are we going to do, Billy? How are we going to find our way back?" She looked into the trees around them, the sun was setting, and darkness was beginning to crawl over them. She shivered but this time it was more from fear than cold.

He didn't answer her question. Truth was he didn't know how they were going to find their way back in the dark. Instead, he pulled the canvas sack from her and began putting everything back inside. Unable to think of anything reassuring to tell her, he held out one of the small pies, "Here, have this. You must be hungry, I know I am."

"No! I don't want it. I'm not hungry. I just want us to go back, back to the tent and the car."

He offered it to her again, "Come on, take it. It'll give you energy and warm you up. You'll need it for the journey back."

She wasn't hungry but she knew he was right about needing fuel for energy so she took the small pie from him and began to tear the cellophane wrapper off it and as she did, the loud crisp crackling noise of the cellophane seemed to echo around them, she stopped and stared into the trees.

Not in the mood for Hannah's over-active imagination, Billy said, "For God's sake, Hannah, what's wrong now?"

Looking down at the cellophane wrapped food, she whispered, "It's this . . . the noise it's making. It's . . . well, loud!"

He sighed noisily, "It's a bloody cellophane wrapper! If the sound's scaring you that much, eat the pie with the bloody wrapper on it! That way it won't make any sound at all and you'll still be chewing it tomorrow morning!"

Tears sprang in her eyes. She looked away quickly. Billy reached for her hand, "I'm sorry. Come on, Hannah. Don't cry. I am sorry, really I am. I just feel such an idiot for getting us both into this mess."

Using the back of her hand, she swiped at the tears and sniffed loudly. She began tugging at the cellophane wrapper again. "It's okay. It's not your fault. We're both to blame. We should have turned back hours ago."

"I know, I know. But don't worry; I'll get us back to the tent somehow. We'll be all right. It might take us a while but we will find our way back. I know it's a tall order but you've just got to trust me."

She shrugged and sighed, plonked herself down fully on the ground and crossed her legs. "Okay. Let's eat this quickly and then we'll set off again."

"Yeah, okay." He picked up the torch and switched it on; the light shone brightly for a few seconds and then dulled faintly.

He shook it, as if that would make a difference, "Aww, bloody hell!" And then it went out completely. He switched it off and looked sheepishly at Hannah, "I don't believe it! The batteries are low." He switched it back on but the pale yellow beam flickered a couple of times before dying completely.

Hannah was horrified, she dropped the pie she was picking at on the ground beside her, her appetite suddenly vanished, "Aww, *please,* Billy, tell me you're joking? You have got more batteries in that rucksack haven't you?"

He couldn't look at her, "No. You know I haven't, you've just emptied everything out of it. There were no batteries!"

He couldn't believe he could have been so stupid. Even though they'd set out to follow Fitch, they had intended on spending the weekend in Bleazedale forest, camping, and he was at a loss to figure out how he could have overlooked the importance of packing a working torch with spare batteries!

As it was now, the sun had gone down and darkness was all over them like a malevolent fog. He shivered. When he finally looked up at Hannah, she was nodding her head slowly from side to side. He didn't know what to say to her. He'd lost the compass and now they had no light.

Hannah couldn't believe the situation they now found themselves in, her tone low and accusing, she said, "So how are we going to find our way back, in the *pitch black,* Billy?"

He looked up into the trees and with a confidence he didn't feel he said, "The stars, the Plough and Cassiopeia. I can follow the line of the stars to get us back to where we're camped."

She followed his gaze up through the trees into the night sky; it was an infinite sea of blackness. It was so dark she couldn't see where the tops of the trees ended, never mind the stars, "Are you winding me up? *What stars?*"

"Up there." Billy pointed towards the sky. "I told you, we'll follow the line of the Plough. You just need to get your night vision." He couldn't see the stars either but pretending he could was the only way he knew of placating her. What he did know for certain was that they were up shit creek without a paddle.

Well aware of the fact that he was talking through his arse about the Plough and Cassiopeia, he had no desire to continue the discussion so he began putting everything back into the rucksack hoping she wouldn't mention the bloody stars again, or more to the point, the fact that there were none visible to follow!

He returned everything to the rucksack except a small bottle of water, which he held out to her, "Here, drink some. You've not had anything to drink since this morning."

She snapped, "No thanks! I'm not thirsty."

"Hannah, come on! Don't be so childish. You have to drink something, we both do! Now come on, take it!"

She snatched the bottle out of his hand, unscrewed the cap and took a couple of gulps before handing it back to him.

He refused it, "You've only had a couple of mouthfuls, drink some more. There's another bottle in the rucksack."

She did as she was told then held the bottle out to him. He accepted it, took several gulps then held his hand out to her for the cap.

He stood up and offered his hand to her.

"Come on, Hannah, let's get moving. We can't hang about here any longer."

She let him pull her up off the ground. As she brushed bits of broken twigs and dead leaves off her backside, she asked him, "Which way, Billy? Do you know which direction we should take?"

He looked around; he couldn't possibly admit to Hannah that he was clueless. It was eerily quiet and so black he had difficulty reading the expression on Hannah's face. They would have to hold onto each other all the way back, it would be disastrous should they accidentally lose one another. He looked up through the trees again; the moon was a mere sliver, offering little, if any, light at all.

Realising he didn't have a choice, he thought it best to come clean with her, "Being honest, we're going to struggle to make it back to the camp. We've come too far. I think the best thing is to try to locate the source of the smoke, where it's coming from. It can't be that far now, Hannah. It's probably a lodge used by Forest Rangers. I'm sure we'll find it, and when we do they'll give us a lift back to where we've camped, trust me!"

"Oh, and I thought that's what we'd been doing for the last few hours, Billy!"

"Yeah, I know. But I think we just lost sight of it, Hannah. You've got to admit we were enjoying the scenery too much and . . .well, I don't know! Christ, what a bloody cock up! "

She didn't say anything. She was cold and scared. She wished with all her heart that they'd never come up with the stupid idea of following Fitch, in the first place. It was because of him they were in the mess they were in now. She thought about her parents at home believing that she was actually stopping over at her best friend's house, warm and safe with Coleen and her parents. She wanted to cry but knew if she did Billy would probably get angry with her again. Hating him for the mess he'd got them into, she reluctantly took his hand and they set off again, more slowly now, their steps cautious, in what had become a very sinister environment.

Stumbling in mutual silence through the trees, Hannah's grip on Billy's hand grew tighter as they constantly tripped and fell over fallen branches and small rocks. Every now and then, Hannah would cry out, rigid with fear at the sound of bark cracking and rapid movement in the trees. What should have been a lovely weekend camping under the stars was fast turning into Hannah's worst nightmare.

Billy squeezed her hand reassuringly and whispered, "Hannah, it's just birds and small animals, nothing to harm us and nothing to be frightened of. We'll be okay, I promised you didn't I?"

They continued blindly into the heart of the forest, completely unaware of what the night had in store for them.

CHAPTER FORTY-FOUR

JOHN Fallon was becoming increasingly concerned. It was almost half-past five and the boys and Neive should have been at home by now. He had given them strict instructions that after the film ended they weren't to hang about in town they were to go straight to the bus station and be on the first bus home. He knew what time the film ended and he'd told them he'd be there to pick them up when they got off the bus. There was no way he would allow his three young kids to walk all the way down Bleaksedge Lane on their own, especially after Erin had gone missing.

John didn't know why he couldn't shake off the sense of dread that was hanging over him like a black cloud; he shuddered. He had seen at least three buses arrive from the town centre; his kids weren't on any of them. Becoming agitated, he decided to turn back and head home thinking he may have somehow missed them, or possibly one of the neighbour's might have seen them and picked them up. As he drove along Bleaksedge Lane, frantic with worry, he began praying silently. *If they are at home when I get there I'll murder the little buggers for making me worry like this*. As he got to the bottom of the road he turned left into Florence Terrace and that's when he saw it, the police car parked in front of his house. A cold sweat sent beads of moisture down his neck and back. *Oh, God in Heaven, please don't let anything have happened to my kids. Not again, please God, no!*

With his heart pounding out of control and his legs trembling uncontrollably, he pulled up behind the Police car, turned off the engine and waited. Unable to move, he sat rigid, both hands gripping the steering wheel, staring numbly at the back of the police car. That sense of dread he had been unable to shake off was all consuming. Something was wrong, very wrong. As his car door was pulled open, he looked up into the police officer's face. He was saying something but John couldn't hear him. He just felt numb, like an out of body experience, as though he was watching a scene being played out but he wasn't in it.

From the corner of his eye, he saw movement. He turned, his eyes focusing on the police car. He watched Liam and Sean being helped out of the back of the car by a second officer; a female. The boys stood and faced their father, distress and terror in their eyes. It was as if everything was happening in slow motion. He watched and waited for what seemed like an eternity, but in reality it was only seconds, before he realised Neive wasn't with them. In that instant, John knew. *They've lost her. She's been taken. Gone.*

An anguished scream pierced the quiet of the tree-lined avenue. His grief was devastating to witness; the female officer choked back her own tears as she held the two heart-broken little boys, both staring at their father in horror.

CHAPTER FORTY-FIVE

FITCH had no idea how he'd made it to the lodge; he'd driven the entire distance on autopilot. His mind was in turmoil; Fitch had never lost a patient in his whole career as a neurosurgeon and he now found himself strangely affected by the death of the little girl he had try to save. During the high-speed race to the hospital he had fought desperately to keep her alive but she had died in the ambulance before they could make it. Yet it wasn't just the death of the little girl that disturbed him. It was what followed.

At the hospital, Fitch had gone through the usual formalities; time of death, cause, etc. The A&E reception staff had been informed to notify Mr Fitch as soon as the deceased child's parents arrived at the hospital. It was the task of the parents to formally identify the child before she could be taken to the mortuary.

Neive's body was removed from the ambulance to a side room in the emergency department where she would remain until identification. It was some fifteen minutes after the ambulance had arrived at the hospital when the police had contacted the emergency department advising the staff there that they were on their way with the little girl's father, a Mr John Fallon. Apparently there was no mother, just the little girl's father. It was immediately after the meeting with the deceased child's father that Fitch realised the enormity of his error.

CHAPTER FORTY-SIX

NEIVE had sustained fatal injuries to the head and internal organs. Remarkably, though, her face was relatively unmarked, apart from a few scratches and gravel cuts and a slight blue tinge to her lips, she looked as though she was sleeping. She had been covered up to the neck in a white cotton sheet and her thick blond curls fanned out across the pillow, she looked so peaceful, angelic even.

The two nurses tasked with dealing with the body were cleaning the blood from the small grazes on her face; they did so with great care and tenderness as though she could still feel pain. Hardened as they were to dealing with death, when it came to young children they still found it distressing, it didn't matter if they had children of their own or not, a child's death is never easy to comprehend; the tragedy and unfairness of the loss of a young life.

The A&E Sister popped her head round the door and whispered, "Is she ready? The little girl's father is in the family room with Mr Fitch."

"Yes, Sister. We're almost done now."

As the door closed, one of the nurses said, "Doesn't seem right does it, Ange? She's so young and innocent."

"I know, everything to live for. Poor little mite." Angela absently looped a blond curl around her finger. "I'll never get used to this, Sue. Kids. It's so hard, so incredibly sad. I don't think I'll have any myself. I couldn't bear it if anything was to happen to them, the loss . . . you know?"

"No me neither and, yes, I know what you mean. And let's face it, it happens to so many parents, losing their kids I mean. God knows how they cope, live to learn with it. I've only ever lost my Granddad and that was bad enough. But at least he got to see old bones. Ninety six he was."

Angela let the curl fall back onto the pillow and held her hands out in a questioning gesture as she looked down at Neive's small body covered by the large crisp white sheet, "But this? It's just . . . I don't know, I can't get my head around it. It makes you think about whether there really is a God or not." She looked in earnest at her colleague, "I mean if there is, why does he allow things like this to happen to the young and innocent?"

Sue shrugged, "I don't know. Only the good die young? Well that's the saying. And the other one is: *hell is here on earth*. Maybe that's why he takes them, Ange. To save them from this hell on earth."

"Well whatever the reason, it's still wrong. Come on, we're done."

As they stepped over to the washbasin, Sue looked over her shoulder at Neive and said, "She looks so peaceful doesn't she? At least her parents haven't got to witness and remember terrible disfiguring injuries."

"Small consolation, Sue!"

They were washing their hands when Angela glanced over at Neive's body and asked, "Do we know what her name is?"

"Hmm?" Sue was drying her hands, frowning as she tried to remember, "Yes, got it now; the police gave her name when they contacted the department, it's Neive. Yes, that's it, *Neive Fallon*. Her father's name is *John Fallon*."

The colour drained from Angela's face, "NO! It can't be . . ." Prayer like, she covered her mouth with both hands and whispered, "Oh, dear God in heaven!"

Sue screwed her face in confusion, "What?"

"*John Fallon*. His daughter is one of those missing girls, *Erin*

Fallon. Dear Lord how on earth is he going to deal with this? That poor man, this is going to kill him, Sue."

CHAPTER FORTY-SEVEN

JOHN Fallon arrived at the hospital accompanied by the young male constable who had been tasked with the daunting responsibility of breaking the news of Neive's accident to him. The officer told Fallon as much as he knew, and that was that Neive was critical. The officer's colleague had remained with the two young brothers at the Fallon's home; unfortunately there was no other family to take care of the two little boys.

Sister Malone was on duty in the A&E department and was expecting John Fallon, anxiously awaiting his arrival; she knew who Fallon was – she'd seen him on TV and in the newspapers. She'd been following the story for months, hoping that Erin Fallon would be found and returned safe and well. She knew about his wife's disappearance as well, but didn't give a damn about her; she'd heard more than enough gossip about that one. A mother leaving her babies for another bloke, what kind of woman was she?

She approached the police constable and nodded, indicating to him that she would take over now. John Fallon's eyes were dead and his face was the colour of chalk, he was in a state of shock. The worst was yet to come, though, and her heart ached for him; she wished there was something she could do to ease his pain and sorrow. She looked away quickly as her eyes filled; she swallowed and took a deep breath. He needed care and support not her tears. She placed her hand beneath his elbow gently guiding him away from the thankful young officer. "Mr Fallon, I'd like you to come with me, please." He nodded the barest acknowledgment.

She took his hand then and steered him past curtain-covered bays and trolleys laden with medical equipment, towards the family room. He moved sluggishly, wanting to delay the inevitable for ever – the reason he had been driven to the hospital by the police constable, and the reason his little Neive had not come home that afternoon with his two boys. If he could take his own life to spare Neive and Erin, he would gladly do so right now. Sister Malone stole a glance at him, his eyes appeared empty and lifeless and the bright lights of the A&E department made him look like the walking dead as he made the short distance to the small room where his heart was going to be ripped out again. He appeared to have aged ten years or more since she had seen him on the local news channel only a few weeks ago. The police officer, grateful for Sister Malone's intervention, followed at a distance and took up position outside the Family Room after Sister Malone had led John Fallon inside. He wished like hell now that he hadn't volunteered to come in on his day off.

When the door opened Leonard Fitch stopped pacing and froze on the spot. Sister Malone frowned as she caught a strange look on his face. His expression led her to think that perhaps Mr Fitch recognised Fallon and was shocked to see him, but knowing Mr Fitch as she did, she put it down to nerves. He must have recognised John Fallon from the TV and realised who he was.

She led her charge by the hand across the room and eased him down onto a hard plastic backed chair. He went willingly, like a child. "Here you are, my love. Will you let me fetch you a cup of tea, Mr Fallon?" Again, that almost imperceptible nod; no he didn't want anything to drink. He wanted his darling little Neive. *And Erin.* He wanted his daughters back safe and sound, and the life he once had. The life he had before it had all gone so unspeakably wrong, before Helen had deserted them. He wanted to go back to the time when they had been a family, a complete and happy family. But that could never be now. *Not now. Not Ever.*

The family room was decorated in subtle shades of pale green and soft peach – under different circumstances it could be described as warm and inviting – cheerful even. But those unfortunate enough to be taken into that room would tell a different story. There was nothing remotely cheerful about it. It was the room the hospital staff – doctors usually – used for delivering bad news. John knew this instinctively.

Several chairs were placed around a small Formica coffee table and there was a giant vending machine taking up one end of the room. Sister Malone tried again, "Mr Fallon, would you like a cup of sweet tea?"

This time he raised his hand in front of his face and nodded from side to side, indicating he didn't want anything to drink, and then he dropped his head and stared at the floor, his hands fell to his sides and he began wringing the corners of his jacket. He knew why they'd brought him to this room; they were going to tell him something terrible. Tears began to pour down his face.

Sister Malone bit down hard on her bottom lip and glanced at Mr Fitch. She desperately wanted to leave the room. It wasn't like her, she'd seen so much death and grief throughout her thirty year nursing career and could pretty much deal with anything, but right now she was too close to the edge. She had seen John Fallon begging for his daughter's return, so many times. And now this; his youngest daughter passed away less than half an hour ago. How could any parent endure what this man was going through? She couldn't bear stay in the same room with him any longer. A parent's worst nightmare is to lose a child, but to have it happen a second time was incomprehensible.

She turned again to Leonard Fitch and said, "Mr Fitch, this is the little girl's father, John Fallon. I'll leave you alone now. If you need me, I'll be . . ." She raised her left hand, index finger stabbing at the air behind her, then she hurried from the room without another word.

Fitch was rendered speechless. The moment the man entered the room, he recognised him. He was *that* John Fallon, the father of the girl he had kidnapped, the girl he was holding against her will at his remote lodge.

His legs began to shake, forcing him to sit down opposite John Fallon. Playing for time and desperate to get his thoughts together, he fidgeted in his seat, his long legs struggling for room beneath the small coffee table.

John Fallon continued to stare at the floor; he didn't want to hear it. He wasn't ready to hear whatever it was this doctor was going to tell him. He would never be ready, no matter how long.

There was a conflict going on behind Fitch's eyes as he focused on the box of tissues in the middle of the table. When was the last time he'd had to do this? Never! He had never lost a patient in his entire career! Not until today. Nobody and nothing could have saved her. It was unthinkable that he should be sitting in front of this man.

Fitch shifted his gaze from the box on the table, his eyes hooded as he stared at Fallon for a long moment. There was something about him. He reminded him of someone . . . true, he had only just met him but there was definitely something about him, something that was beginning to trouble him for reasons he couldn't understand.

John Fallon sniffed loudly, bringing Fitch back to the here and now.

Fitch decided to be blunt, direct. No point trying to dress it up, dragging it out and delaying the inevitable. John Fallon was still wringing his hands and staring at the floor.

Fitch drew in a deep breath and said. "Mr Fallon, I'm so sorry but you're daughter passed away in the ambulance on the way to the hospital; there was nothing that I, or anyone else, could have done to save her life. Her injuries were devastating. Had she survived, she would have been profoundly brain damaged. She was unconscious when she passed. I'm so terribly sorry, Mr Fallon."

John's head snapped back as though he'd been shot in the chest. Snot poured from his nose onto his top lip as the tears flowed relentlessly and then he howled with a pain so primal, so not of this world. Fitch sat up very straight and removed his glasses, more for something to do. He turned and looked towards the door, he should get Sister Malone. She would be better at dealing with this sort of situation. He stood up to leave.

John Fallon raised his head again and through his tears, he pleaded, "No! Wait! Please don't go! Not yet. I want to see my little girl, I *can* see her can't I?" He sobbed loudly, "Will you take me to see her, now?"

Unable to think of anything to do or say right now, Fitch stood up and handed Fallon the box of Kleenex tissues that had been placed in the middle of the small table, "Yes, yes of course. I'll take you to her in a few moments. But first, I'd like you to take a few long deep breaths, it'll help."

John Fallon took the box of tissues then began drying his eyes and blowing his nose. Fitch watched him, an unfathomable expression in his eyes; a strange emotion swept over him, an emotion that was quite alien to him . . . or was it an emotion that had been lost to him and suddenly reawakened?

John Fallon looked up at Fitch and whispered "Thanks." as he handed the box of tissues back to Fitch; he flinched at the naked grief and desolation in his eyes. Fitch turned away.

Still sniffing and wiping at the corners of his eyes with a clump of soggy tissues, John stared at the floor said, "When Helen left for another bloke, I thought I'd never get over it. I mean, what mother dumps her kids for another man, eh? It's bad enough that she hurt me, *but to do it to her children?*" He stopped for a moment and drew in a deep shuddering breath. Fitch surprised himself. He couldn't deny the sadness he felt for him, and *blame.* He coughed, breaking the tense silence, prompting Fallon to continue.

For the first time since meeting the stern quietly spoken doctor, Fallon looked up and searched his eyes. Fitch grew suddenly awkward. Unable to hold Fallon's gaze, he looked away and brushed at some imaginary object on his sleeve as Fallon began speaking again. "It beggars belief really. I try to convince myself that the kids and me are better off without her. She was a cold hard bitch. Had me working around the clock, seven days a week to keep up with her spending. I barely got see my kids in the end; they were always tucked up in bed by the time I got home. And now I've lost *both* my little girls. I've prayed every single night since Erin disappeared that she'll come home again . . . and now this, my beautiful little Neive, *gone*!" He started crying again, sobbing quietly.

Fallon slumped back in his seat, his arms hanging loose between his legs, as more tears poured down his face and fell onto his bare hands. Fitch exhaled. What had he done to this man? A broken man expressing his innermost thoughts and sorrow to him of all people, the person responsible for reaping havoc in his life and destroying his peace – it was such a cruel and unexpected twist of fate.

Fitch understood now why the girl's mother had never appeared on the TV news alongside her husband. It was because she simply didn't care. The only person he was hurting was John Fallon and his two sons. Silently observing Fallon, he couldn't help feeling that he actually reminded him of his own father in some ways. Good man married to a bitch of a wife who was also a cruel and loathsome mother.

CHAPTER FORTY-EIGHT

FITCH parked his car in the usual spot, concealed amongst thick undergrowth about a hundred yards away from the chainlink fencing surrounding the lodge. Gathering his coat and briefcase he stepped out of the car and just stood there, staring into the darkness. He wished, for the umpteenth time since meeting John Fallon that afternoon, that he could erase the day's events; the strange twist of fate that had brought him face to face with the girl's father. He couldn't get Fallon out of his head; he could still see his anguished and tormented face. He shook his head slowly, as if trying to empty his mind of the thoughts and images that refused to leave him in peace. How could he possibly carry through his plans now?

It was his mother's fault. If she hadn't delayed him, complaining about the pains in her chest he would have made it to the hospital without having got caught up at the scene of the road traffic accident. She'd insisted that he took her blood pressure before he left for the day. He gave nothing away as he made a mental note of the reading, his expression showed not the slightest concern even though her blood pressure was dangerously high, he had convinced her that she shouldn't worry; the pains were nothing more than a mild case of indigestion.

The truth was he suspected something far more serious, her heart rate was sky high – a cardiac event was on the cards, but he didn't give a damn. With any luck she would be dead by the time he returned to the house. Ten minutes giving in to his mother had changed everything for him. The day's events had unfolded in a way he could never have anticipated and it was he who had been right at the heart of those events.

He moved around his vehicle checking that the doors were locked then made his way out of the undergrowth, walking several yards before climbing a few steps onto a winding path leading to the padlocked gate. As he reached the top of the steps, he stopped and stood for a few moments gazing up at the lodge looming out of the darkness. Its secrets beckoned and tormented him. He didn't want to go inside, though, not yet. He didn't want to gaze upon that face, the image of her father.

He placed his brief case on the ground beside him and sat down heavily, his back against the locked gate. He took off his glasses thumb and index finger to massage his temples; he had a blinding headache. He laid his head back against the cold hard steel wire, mentally exhausted, and closed his eyes. His tension began to ease as the sound of the stream at the back of the lodge broke into his thoughts. Its gentle ripple as it washed over rocks and pebbles had an instant calming effect on him; it was constant and reassuring.

What should he do about the girl? Her birthday was less than two months away. She had no idea what he had planned for that day, either. It wasn't gong to be a celebration of her birth; no, it was to be a day of celebration for him. He would be ridding the world of another bitch and reaping untold pain and sorrow on the girl's mother, but that was no longer the case was it? In fact it never would be because the only people he would destroy if he carried out his plans would be Fallon and his two young sons.

He pulled the collar of his overcoat up over his ears. The temperature had dipped considerably, yet he still had no desire to enter the lodge knowing what he now knew. It occurred to him then as he sat in the dark on the cold damp earth why he had always thought Erin Fallon was somehow *different* than the others; she had never shown any lack of respect towards him even when she was screaming in pain. She had never yelled ugly obscenities at him or called him vile and disgusting names, like the others had. She took her punishment bravely as she prayed and begged God to help her.

He couldn't sit out there all night; it wasn't just his ears and face that was cold now. The thought of a warm drink and his bed brought him swiftly back to his feet. With a heavy heart and conflicting emotions, he removed the padlock from the gate, stepped onto his land and put the lock back in place then made his way up the steps onto the porch. When he reached the solid timber door, he stood for a moment, his mind in turmoil. The girl on the other side of the door was in many ways a victim of a cruel mother, just as he was. He sighed heavily. I cannot punish him any longer.

Pulling a bunch of keys from his trouser pocket, Fitch let himself in. As he stepped inside the small hallway, he shivered. It was cold, nothing unusual about that at this time of the year, but there was something else . . . a smell, a rotten smell.

He dropped his briefcase in the hallway and stepped inside the sitting room flicking the switch just inside the doorway as he entered. The stark light flooded the room and a look of horror crossed his face . . . *and that smell!* Erin was lying on the rug in the middle of the room she was still wearing the same garment she had on when he had carried her back downstairs unconscious and dumped her on the mattress several days ago.

Her long matted hair was covering her face. He couldn't tell if she was breathing. He went quickly across the room and knelt beside her. Her legs were covered in angry deep red patches that spread down between her thighs, and along her legs *Streptobacillus moniliformis*. Rat Bite Fever. In a split second, his professional side took over. He checked her pulse; it was rapid. Her breathing was shallow. Her mouth was covered in dry cracked scabs.

She was severely dehydrated. It wasn't necessary to carry out further examination it was obvious to him that she was seriously ill and needed immediate medical treatment. His eyes narrowed as he did a mental stock take of the drugs he had in the boot of his car. She needed antibiotics; preferably Penicillin. The fact that he was unaware of whether or not she was allergic to the drug didn't matter; he had no choice but to take the risk. Without a powerful antibiotic she would develop septicaemia and die.

He stood up and surveyed the room. It was cold, filthy and it stunk. He looked down at Erin again, she'd obviously crawled off the mattress; she must have been trying to get to the bottled water on the other side of the room. The only thing he'd done when he left her unconscious four days ago was to replace the shackles around her ankles, he hadn't even bothered to cover her up, nor had he bothered to give her a second glance as he'd walked from the room, took his jacket and other personal belongings from the hallway, and let himself out of the lodge, locking it up securely before he went.

Worry creased his brow as he examined her semi-naked body, his eyes lingering on the vivid red patches spreading down her legs. How long has she been lying there unconscious? If he was going to save her life he had to move fast. It was fortunate that he did carry drugs and other medical supplies in the event of an emergency, like the one he had been unfortunate enough to attend this afternoon, yet no drugs in the world could have saved the young child. He rested his gaze on Erin's face; he saw the likeness almost immediately. Not wanting to dwell on that thought, he put it out of his mind. He hadn't been able to save her sister's life but he could save hers if he acted quickly. He turned and left the room into the hallway and straight out of the front door, striding rapidly back to his car.

He unlocked the boot and lifted a bulky leather case out, closed the boot lid, locked it again and almost at a run returned to the lodge, remembering to lock the gate on his way back in.

Back inside the lodge, he locked and bolted the door, removed his jacket and hung it on the coat stand in the hallway and began rolling up his shirtsleeves as he went into the kitchen. He washed his hands thoroughly, filled the kettle and put it on the stove to boil. He would have to clean the wounds and somehow get her to take liquid penicillin; it was faster acting than tablet form. He needed to administer a dose as quickly as possible. He opened his medical bag and took out Penicillin along with painkillers, saline solution, cotton wool swabs and dressings.

He entered the sitting room, knelt beside her again and began removing the shackles from around her ankles then threw the long weighty chain across the room. The loud clinking broke the heavy silence throughout the lodge as it hit the bare floorboards, then he lifted her frail body off the floor. Her head fell back and her long matted hair fell away from her face exposing her damp grey skin; her lips had a blue tinge to them; he didn't like it at all, she was gravely ill.

He should really have removed her from the lodge to a hospital but that was unthinkable. It would soon become apparent that she is one of the missing birthday girls; the police would be called and he would be questioned. Worse, he would be arrested when the girl regained consciousness.

He moved quickly, his long lanky legs taking the stairs two at a time. He strode down the landing to a room at the far end. The door was locked. He laid her down very gently on the floor while he fumbled with a bunch of keys. He didn't know why, but his hands were shaking and after his third attempt, the door swung wide open. He leaned inside and switched the light on and went in.

Compared to the rest of the lodge, this room was clean and warmly decorated. It was comfortably furnished and carpeted, unlike downstairs where there were no carpets, just timber floorboards and an occasional rug. The single bed in the large alcove was neatly made up with a pale lilac and grey silk floral counterpane. The plush carpet was a deep purple colour. His mother had to have everything co-ordinated. Even the bedside lampshade had lilac and grey flowers on it. The room definitely had a feminine feel about it; in fact it didn't appear to belong to the rest of the lodge, it was far too womanly for his liking. It was the room his mother insisted she have as her own whenever she visited his lodge, which thankfully had only ever been a couple of times in as many years.

He crossed to the bed, switched on the bedside lamp and pulled back the heavy counterpane and bed sheets. He shivered noisily. The room may have given the impression of cosiness, but right now it felt damp and uninviting. The bed hadn't been used since his mother was last at the lodge. He frowned at the thought of his mother as he cast his mind back to when she was last here. It was in December last year, it had snowed for days on end and she had pecked at his head incessantly, telling him how much she would like to see Bleazedale Forest in the wintertime. She had some stupid romantic notion about staying at his lodge and it being like a scene from one of her equally stupid Christmas cards. And when they'd arrived she began interfering, asking the same annoying questions over and over again. How long had he had the lodge, what did he use it for, why had he kept it a secret and what exactly did he do there all alone.

He wanted to tell her that he'd bought the lodge so that he didn't have to live under the same roof as her. So that he could be as far away from her as possible and not have to listen to her whiney voice constantly putting him down and expecting him to be at her beck and call seven days a week. But most of all he didn't want to have to listen to her insults and ridicule. Taunting him for being single and still a virgin at forty-six. If only the bitch knew. What she didn't know was what he had planned to do to her. She had driven him to the point of wanting to put his hands around her overly ample neck and force every last breath from her ugly flabby body. If she weren't already dead when he returned to the house, she soon would be. He had plans for her but they could wait, he'd been patient this long, a few more weeks wouldn't matter.

It was no wonder the room felt damp, it had been nine months since it had last been used. The door had been locked until today. He ran his hands over the bed sheets; surprisingly they felt crisp and dry. He wondered what she would say if she knew there was a young teenage girl using her bedroom. He might tell her when he returns to the house in a couple of days, that's if she's not dead of course. As he prepared the room for Erin, his thoughts strayed. He blamed his mother for driving his father into an early grave. He could remember his father hardly ever being at home. He remembered the day the police called at their house with the terrible news. It was just before six in the evening, he was sat at the dinner table being forced to eat another bowl of slop the kind of thing she dished up to him every day, no wonder he couldn't put any weight on, the food was disgusting. The Police explained to his mother that his father had been killed in a car accident. From eyewitness accounts, it appeared he had fallen asleep at the wheel of his car whilst on his way home from work. Strange, he thought, my father died in a road traffic accident, and today I had to break the news of a death, the result of a road traffic accident, to a man who reminds me so much of my father.

His father had been the only person, in his entire life, to care about him. He had always stood up to his wife when she bullied and tormented their son. He recalled now the time his mother had once goaded his father by referring to him as *'that worthless ugly brat you spawned';* his father had raised his hand to strike her. She'd laughed in his face and mocked him, calling him a coward, spineless and lily-livered. He said nothing. He just turned and walked from the room, briefly squeezing his son's shoulder as he went. It was the very last time he had seen his father.

He had chosen his mother's grave. He'd planned it for so long, but when it came down to actually *doing it,* murdering her, he'd lost the courage to see it through. It should have been simple, easy, and straightforward. But she'd won again. He couldn't explain to himself nor understand why he'd panicked and backed out. Was he still really that frightened of her? Did she still have such a cast iron hold over him? She still took pleasure in making him feel ugly, unwanted and *totally worthless?*

A soft moaning broke into his thoughts. The girl was coming round. He approached her slowly. Her eyes fluttered open and she stared up into the face of her tormentor. She opened her mouth to say something but nothing came out. It was difficult, too painful; her lips were covered with scabs and dried blood, they still had that blue tinge. As he was about to bend down to pick her up, she went rigid, a look of pure terror in her eyes.

"I am not going to hurt you. I promise. You're very sick. I'm going to make you well again." Although weak and disoriented, she was suddenly aware that she had on nothing but a cardigan; she tried to pull it down to cover her nakedness. Fitch decided to help her. He went back into the bedroom, took a woollen blanket from inside the large oak wardrobe and went back out onto the landing.

He wrapped Erin in it then picked her up, and as he did, he noticed how thin she'd become. He could feel her bones through the blanket and she was trembling all over; he knew it was a combination of fear and fever. He carried her into the bedroom, gently laying her on the bed.

She tried to speak but he simply hushed her by placing a finger against his lips then put his hands under her thin arms and gently pulled her up the bed so that her head was resting on the soft pillows. She was still shaking from head to toe as he pulled the heavy bed covers over her. He looked away; he couldn't help feeling a profound sense of guilt at the pain he was putting John Fallon through. If he could see the abject terror and confusion in his daughter's eyes right now, what would Fallon do to him? He brushed the thought aside; he didn't want to think about that. His priority was to make the girl well again. But then what?

Avoiding her eyes, he spoke softly to her, "I am not going to harm you. I'm going to treat your illness. I need to clean the bites and treat the infection on your legs and you will need to take some antibiotic medicine. Do you understand?"

She nodded. Terrified of angering him, she would do as she was told. She knew she was very sick and needed his help. But this was a different person; he was being kind, was he playing a different game with her now? She fought to keep her eyes open, frightened of what he was going to do to her, but she didn't have the strength and quickly drifted off again.

He went downstairs to the kitchen returning to the bedroom with the medication, saline, swabs and dressings. He arranged everything on the bedside cabinet then ran downstairs again. He rummaged about in the kitchen cupboards for a small bowl and when he found what he was looking for he filled it with boiling water from the kettle, rinsed it to make sure that it was sterile, emptied it and then refilled it. He grabbed a pack of surgical gloves and went back upstairs to his patient.

Before he began cleaning the infected bites on her legs he had to bring her round again to take a dose of Penicillin. He shook her gently and lightly patted both sides of her face in an effort to wake her. She moaned and then her eyes fluttered open.

"I want you to stay awake for just a few more minutes because I need you to take some medicine. Do you understand?"

She nodded, her frightened eyes staring back at him.

He looked away and busied himself with the medication; unscrewing the cap of a small brown bottle he poured a clear syrupy liquid onto a desert spoon. He turned to her again and slipped a large bony hand under the back of her head, gently lifting her off the pillows. As he cradled her head he brought the spoon to her sore mouth.

"Come along. Open your mouth for me and take this. It's liquid Penicillin. You should start to feel a little better in about forty eight hours." Not known for his bedside manner, he struggled to sound sympathetic.

It pained her to open her mouth as the sores on her lips cracked and started bleeding. She moaned in pain. Tears began to spill from the corner of her eyes.

He tried helping her by easing the spoon between her lips and into her mouth. "I know it hurts but you must try to open your mouth for me. It's important that you swallow this medicine." As if talking to one of his patients, he said reassuringly, "You do want to get well don't you?"

She was confused by the sudden change in his behaviour towards her. She didn't know if she did want to get better. At least if she died he couldn't hurt her any more. Unable to speak but not wanting to anger him, she tried to nod her head, *yes*.

He eventually managed to get her to take two spoonfuls of the Penicillin. She moaned and winced in pain as she swallowed the thick liquid.

"Is your throat very sore?"

She nodded, *yes*, again.

"I'll put some pain killers in a glass of water for you and

something to help you sleep. You'll be out for a while but when you wake up, I promise that you're going to feel a little better. You'll have to take the Penicillin at regular intervals, every four hours." He laid her head back on the pillows and left the room briefly. Back in the kitchen he poured a glass of water and took two sachets out of his medical bag, tore them open and sprinkled the contents into the glass of water giving it a quick stir. He grabbed a bottle of pills out of the bag and went back upstairs, his long thin legs taking them two at a time.

As he sat down carefully on the bed her eyes fluttered open, that naked terror and confusion still there. Gently lifting her head off the pillow again, he said to her, "Listen to me. I am not going to hurt or harm you again, *ever again*! I give you my word. I will not lay another finger on you, except to give you the medical attention you need. Do you understand, Erin?" It was the first time in almost a year of being held captive that she had heard her name spoken. It felt very odd, strange hearing him say it and the way in which he said it, she didn't know if she had imagined it but it almost felt as though he'd said it in a kindly way. In her fevered state, she thought perhaps her illness was making her hallucinate because she wanted to hear him repeat it over and over, hearing her name made her feel human again. Tears welled in her eyes. She didn't know what to believe or what to think; this man had never treated her with anything but perverted cruelty and evil.

He continued, "I know your throat's very sore, Erin, but this will help to ease the pain. Come along, sip it for me." There he'd said it again. *Erin*. In her dazed state, she wondered if he might be telling the truth? He promised didn't he? He said he wasn't going to hurt her again. Maybe he might let her go when she's better? She tried to say something once again, but nothing came out, it felt as though she had broken glass at the back of her throat. Instead, she did exactly as he asked. She drank the liquid; it took her a while to empty the glass, especially when he insisted she take a couple of tablets as well, the mere action of swallowing the small pills caused her to cry out in pain. She began crying softly again, she had never felt so ill in her life. She wanted her mum and dad.

"Well done! You'll be asleep in no time and, as I said before, when you awake you'll feel a little better. But you won't be fully recovered for some time yet; you're going to have to stay in bed for several days. I won't be far away. I'll take care of you. Now, go to sleep."

He laid her head back on the pillows and said; "You will feel much better in a few days time, Erin. Sleep is good for healing the body."

She closed her eyes and within minutes she slipped into a deep slumber.

He got up off the bed and stepped across the room to the window. It was pitch black outside yet he could still make out countless branches swaying on the night breeze. He shivered then glanced back at Erin, she looked ghastly; she appeared so tiny now, she had lost far too much weight. John Fallon's wretched face flashed before his eyes, what would it do to him to know that his missing daughter was here with *him*, Mr Fitch, the highly respected surgeon – the same man who had fought to save his youngest child's life earlier that day. What would he say if he knew she was dangerously sick but still alive? Lying beneath the heavy blankets, she looked so small and very young, nothing like the vivacious sixteen-year-old girl he had abducted all those months ago on Bleaksedge Lane. He dismissed the thought and turned his mind to more practical things.

The room still felt damp and cold, that wouldn't do. Her immune system was fighting hard against the infection and she was very susceptible to additional health problems. He worried she might develop pneumonia, sepsis even, so before he started cleaning the infected wounds on her legs, he decided to light a fire in the small fireplace.

He left the room; quietly pulling the door closed behind him, and went downstairs. There was a small closet at the end of the hall where he kept several winter coats, jackets and walking boots; he took out a large padded anorak and pulled it on then went outside, locking the door as he went. He made his way around the back of the lodge to a large timber shed. A strong wind was blowing now. It had definitely turned much colder he could feel the biting autumn chill through the padded anorak. Moving quickly, he gathered an armful of logs and a pack of firelighters, locked up the shed and returned to the lodge.

Carrying the logs and firelighters upstairs, he pushed the door open with his foot. He wasn't worried about making a little noise, she was out cold; he'd given her a strong sedative and knew she would sleep deeply for some hours before he had to wake her up to administer another dose of Penicillin. Over in the small fireplace, he arranged the logs and firelighters in the grate then remembered the matches. He went back downstairs and rummaged about in the closet in the hallway. The large box of Cooks Housekeeper's matches was where he'd left them in the far corner of the shelf above the coat hooks.

As he climbed the stairs for what was probably the sixth time since he'd arrived, he thought about the last time he'd done something similar; back and forth up and down the stairs repeatedly. Not since his bitch of a mother had stayed at the lodge and had run him ragged, fetch me carry me every five minutes. He should have thrown her down the stairs and broke her neck. But this situation is different; the girl upstairs is . . .is what? Not like the others? She's John Fallon's daughter that's who she is and right now she needs his help and he intends to see that she gets it.

Back in the bedroom he began arranging the strong smelling paraffin soaked lighters and logs in the grate. When he'd finished he lit one of the extra long matches and held it under the firelighters. The effect was instant and in just a few minutes he had a cosy fire burning. The dry logs hissed and crackled loudly as the flames shot up and danced between them. He reached for the small mantelpiece above the fireplace and pulled himself up slowly then turned to look at Erin; she was sleeping soundly. The warmth and the soft glow of the fire relaxed him a little, he yawned and stretched fighting a strong desire to go to his room, he needed some rest but knew he couldn't just yet, not until he'd cleaned and treated the infected bites on her legs.

He hadn't planned on stopping over night at the lodge, he hadn't known *what* he was going to do; his mind was in turmoil. Since leaving the hospital, he'd thought of nothing else throughout the journey up to Bleazedale Forest but John Fallon and his daughter, Erin. He had no idea now what he was going to do about her; one thing of which he was certain, from the moment John Fallon had left the family room to see his youngest child for the last time, was that he wouldn't harm Erin Fallon again. He had made a terrible mistake when he had chosen her as one of his victims. Her mother would not feel any pain at the loss of her daughter according to John Fallon; her mother never cared for her or loved her from the day she was born. In many ways Erin Fallon was a lot like him, unworthy of a mother's love.

As he watched her sleeping, he wondered what he should do about her. He knew he'd have to let her go at some point but that presented many problems for him. How, where and when should he let her go? He was fully aware that releasing her would mean he could no longer continue with what had become a very necessary part of his life. It was the only way he knew how to get back at those he considered to have made his life pointless and empty. *Women*. He hated them. But not this one, she was *different*.

If he let her go, it was guaranteed he'd spend the rest of his life in prison, and he didn't need to ask himself what his life would be like if that were to happen. He shuddered at the thought. Three choices came to mind; end his life? What did he have apart from a good career in the medical profession? Nothing! He could keep Erin locked up here in the lodge, indefinitely. But the longer she's missing the longer John Fallon suffers and deep down he didn't want that. He could release her and leave the country. His new passport was in the safe back at the house. He sighed heavily, took his glasses off and began massaging the bridge of his nose with his long bony fingers.

It had been a long day full of unexpected and unwelcome events; he was still reeling from the shock of meeting the child's father and finding out that the girl he was abusing and planned to butcher was innocent. The only thing she was guilty of, in her mother's eyes, was being born, just as he was guilty of the same thing in his mother's eyes.

The desire to leave the room, turn out the light and close the door on Erin was overwhelming but he couldn't go just yet, he still had to treat the infected wounds on her legs, he couldn't leave it until morning. He left the room and went into the bathroom where he washed his hands thoroughly before returning to the bedroom.

He sat down on the side of the bed and pulled the covers back from around her legs. The angry pus filled bites and the spread of the infection was worse than he'd initially thought. It was pretty serious; it had spread from her thighs and down both legs. Pulling on a pair of surgical gloves and using an antibacterial wash, with great care, he began cleaning pus and dead matter from the wounds. He took his time, careful not to apply too much pressure on the festering sores. He worked meticulously for about fifteen minutes and when he had finished cleaning the affected areas he applied antibiotic cream to large gauze dressings and placed them over the wounds then bandaged them securely in place. The dressings would have to be changed regularly and, bearing that in mind, he knew he wouldn't be able to leave the lodge for a few days. She was too sick and he wasn't going to let her die, not now. She was a victim, just as he was.

Such was the extent of the infection, the bandages on her legs looked like cream coloured tights. *What a mess*. He shook his head as he pulled the bed covers over her, tucking the blankets snugly under her chin.

Rising slowly from the bed, he switched off the bedside lamp and left the room, closing the door softly behind him. Back in the bathroom, he scrubbed his hands thoroughly for several minutes, his mind still working at a rate of knots. *What am I going to do about her?* As he was drying his hands he looked up from the washbasin and caught his reflection in the mirror, a gaunt and tired looking middle-aged man stared out at him. Folding the towel over the end of the bath he continued to stare at the face looking back at him, as if he didn't recognise the man in the mirror. He spoke to the reflection, "What do you intend to do now? You should have realised months ago there was no grieving mother. How could you have been so stupid?" He raised his fist and punched the mirror. His reflection multiplied as the glass splintered. Blood from his knuckles ran into the washbasin and along the bathroom floor as he made his way out along the landing, past what was now Erin's bedroom, to his room.

He ran his hand along the top of the dust covered doorframe and found the key; he unlocked the door and went inside. It was pitch black, he flicked the light switch but it didn't come on. The bulb must have gone, so he made his way blindly across the room to his bed where he sat down and began groping around the neck of the bedside lamp for the light switch. Through exhaustion or lack of concentration, or both, he was unable to find the switch so he gave up, took his glasses off and sprawled out fully on the bed.

He couldn't be bothered to undress, besides it was too cold and having no energy or inclination to start building a fire in the small fireplace, he yanked at the corner of the heavy counterpane and dragged it across his body. Lying in the dark, he waited for his body temperature to rise then finally drifted into a deep and troubled sleep.

CHAPTER FORTY-NINE

HE woke around eight o'clock. Lifting his left arm out from under the cover he held his wrist close to his eyes, squinting to make out the time on his watch.

"Damn! She's not had her medication!" He threw back the counterpane and swung his long legs off the bed and shivered, "Hell it's freezing in here!"

He spent the early part of the morning in Erin's room cleaning the bites, administering drugs and other meds, applying fresh dressings and preparing food for her. He was determined that she make a full recovery, *and soon*. He could make her better *physically* but he knew he would never be able to repair the mental and emotional scars he'd inflicted upon her, and as he poured the thick steaming Heinz tomato soup into a small bowl, he cursed at the injustice and the unspeakable pain and sorrow he'd visited on her father. Much to his surprise, he was deeply affected emotionally and psychologically by John Fallon, drawn to him, feeling his pain and sorrow. Was that the reason; that he reminded him *so much* of his own father?

After tending to Erin's needs, he went back downstairs and began a clean up of the room where Erin spent her long lonely days and nights. The room was dirty and smelled. The first thing he did was to get rid of the filthy stained mattress and the clothes that were piled in the corner. He took everything outside and disappeared behind the lodge where he lit a fire in a large steel bin then threw in items of girl's clothing and shoes. He folded the dirty mattress in half and forced it down inside the steel bin then poured paraffin over it, leaping back suddenly as flames shot up above the top of the bin. If he was going to bring his mother to the lodge in the next few days, he must get rid of a few things and get the place cleaned up. There was no question about it, Erin was now a serious problem for him; he was faced with a serious dilemma. It was time. He knew what he had to do.

He retired to his room and changed into his nightclothes; exhausted once more, needing to sleep and knowing he would have dressings to change and drugs to administer during the night, he climbed into bed and settled down under the weight of the thick woollen blankets and satin counterpane. The room was warmer than the previous night, having had the fire lit for most of the evening, but that was just a pile of embers now, crackling and sparking every now and then.

The light flickered in his bedside lamp, he concluded that the generator might be about to pack up so he turned it off and settled down to sleep.

After endless minutes of tossing and turning and staring into the dark, he sighed noisily. Sleep continued to elude him; he was irritable and troubled. Grunting loudly, he threw back the blankets and pulled himself up off the bed into a sitting position and fumbled around on the bedside cabinet for his glasses, then got up and went across the room to the window, opening it wide to allow the fresh night air in and the musty odour of his room out. He shivered as a cold wind brushed his face as it swept through the trees and around the lodge; the *whoosh,* as it passed by, caused the creaking and cracking of branches to break the peculiar quiet of the night time forest. His secrets were safe; only the forest knew of the crimes he'd carried out. Nobody had witnessed the horror he had buried out there.

Standing by the open window staring into the dark, he let his mind wander. He counted them. In this part of the country, he'd taken four so far, they were buried within a few short feet of each other; he was creating a small cemetery that he intended to grow. He was clever, a master in everything he did. He could never be caught; after all, a man in his profession and position would always fall under the radar, wouldn't he? He intended to carry on for a long time – it was his mission in life. Then he remembered the sleeping girl in the next bedroom. *She* knew his secret. He closed the window and began pacing. He was restless.

She doesn't know everything. She doesn't know about the others. What about the clothing? She had asked him once whom the clothing had belonged to. He'd punched her in the face for being insolent. Oh, that was wrong! What would John Fallon think if he knew what I had done? He couldn't switch off the thoughts and questions that were tormenting him, racing back and forth in his head. He decided to get dressed and go out, to walk, to think his problems through. He needed the solitude of the forest.

He left his room, locked the door and put the key back on top of the doorframe and went downstairs to the closet in the hallway and put on a large padded anorak, then grabbed a torch from the shelf above the coat hooks and left the lodge, locking the front door behind him.

The cold night air stung his face; he pulled the collar of his anorak up around his mouth, zipping it up all the way to the top, and set off walking. At the gate, he removed the padlock let himself out then replaced the lock and headed into the trees. Before he completely lost sight of the lodge he stopped and looked back over his shoulder, in the pale foggy moonlight he could see the smoke, rising and curling into the scattering of clouds, at the back of the lodge where Erin was sleeping.

He wasn't daunted by the shadows and strange sounds of the forest after dark, he'd spent many nights out there digging graves and engaging in necrophilia, the only way he knew how to overcome his feelings of isolation and lack of self-esteem. He could find his way to and from the lodge no matter what time of day or night and tonight was no different; he wandered through the trees thinking about how he was going to deal with the horrendous situation in which he now found himself. He headed in the direction of the graves where he had already begun digging the next one, earmarked for *Erin Fallon*. When he arrived at the site, he pulled the torch from his pocket and switched it on; the dim light shone over the area and as he moved the light across his latest dig, he froze. Surely he must have imagined it?

He killed the light and stood, rigid, not daring to breathe. His eyes already adjusted to the darkness, searched the shadows. Dread prickled his skin as he waited, straining to listen through the thick silence. Seconds later, his worst fear was confirmed. *He wasn't alone*. He was about to reach out to the solid trunk of a nearby tree for support, when he heard it again; it was a male's voice, it was close by and he was calling out to someone.

Pressing his body firmly up against the tree in an effort to conceal himself, his mind went into overdrive as he tried to think of what he would say if he was found at the gravesite. How the hell would he explain his presence, dressed as he was in suit pants, shoes - as opposed to walking boots – and a shirt and tie beneath his anorak? He realised that his appearance and the fact that he was standing by a gaping freshly dug hole would require some serious explaining. He looked around and considered making a move, to head back to the safety of the lodge when he spotted something; a shaft of moonlight glinting off the long silver handle of the spade. He couldn't believe he'd been so careless, he'd obviously left it there by accident. That was sloppy of him, *very sloppy*, and that carelessness worried him now, even more – *what other mistakes have I made?*

Fear and panic was getting the better of him; his legs were trembling and he had an overwhelming urge to sit down. Adrenaline kicked in elevating his heartbeat and his blood pounded in his ears. What if it was the police or a search party out looking for someone? Who? Erin Fallon? The others? Unable to stand a moment longer, he slid to his knees. Careful not to make a sound, he crouched low beneath the branches of the tree, doing his best to make himself invisible as he watched and waited for signs of any movement close by.

Crouched as he was against the tree, his legs began to go numb. He reached up above his head and grabbed one of the branches and began pulling himself upright when he heard a male voice calling out. This time it was much closer and much clearer. He could hear clearly now. Someone was calling out the name Hannah. He no longer thought it was the police or a search party; there were snoopers in his territory!

CHAPTER FIFTY

BILLY let go of Hannah's hand and ran ahead of her, going further into the trees and calling out over his shoulder, "There's the smoke, Hannah. Come on! I told you we'd find it!" In his excitement, eager to find the source, he continued running through the trees, naked branches whipping him in the face as he stumbled over mounds of soft vegetation and small rocks, panting as he ran, his cold breath hanging in the air like a heavy fog.

The smoke danced invitingly above the trees ahead, making Billy think of a log fire, warm food and drink and a cosy and comfortable bed for the night. Surely, whoever was staying there would want to help them. He was convinced it had to be a forest ranger's lodge. *People don't actually live in forests do they?* He chuckled at the idea as he turned excitedly to look for Hannah but she was gone.

He panicked, running blindly amongst the trees, tripping and falling in the pitch black, frantically calling out, "Hannah? Hannah, where the hell are you?"

When he had let go of her hand and raced off ahead of her, Hannah had tried to follow him, to keep up with him, but she quickly lost him. It was too dark, it was almost like being blind and she had taken a completely different direction to Billy. She called out to him but her voice was lost on the wind and the rustling of the trees.

Terrified and alone, she yelled as loud as she could, "Billy, where are you? Please don't leave me!" She froze. A sudden movement behind her made her want to pee. Maybe Billy was playing stupid games with her. She turned slowly, tears in her eyes. A pair of yellow-green eyes peered out at her from inside the trees. She let out an ear-piercing scream and ran, her teeth chattering with fear and cold. Stumbling in the pitch black, she slipped on a mossy rock and tumbled headlong down a small hillock, hitting her head as she went. At the bottom she lay momentarily stunned. Her head hurt like hell and she could feel something wet running down her face.

As she waited for a fleeting wave of nausea to pass, she became aware of the sound of fast running water. She lifted her head to try to see where she was. Where was he? She tried again, "Billy? Where are you? I'm hurt!" It was no use. She could hardly hear her own voice over the rush of the nearby water as it drowned out every other sound. Terrified of whatever it was that had been watching her, she struggled to her feet and moved slowly back through the trees, trembling from head to toe, muttering Billy's name over and over unaware that she was moving further away from him – heading in the opposite direction.

* * *

Fitch could hear the girl; she was crying softly and mumbling incoherently. She was close, almost there. He came out of the trees, moving with the stealth of a cat to the open grave and lifted the spade out of the hole and raised it in readiness. He could only just make out the male's voice, now; it was fading in the distance as it was carried on the wind in another direction.

The slender form of a female came staggering blindly out of the trees directly into his path. Like a rabbit startled in headlights, Hannah froze just as the silver blade hit her full in the face. The frenzied second powerful blow was the one that shattered her face and head. He heard the bones crack and snap on impact before she slumped to the ground.

Breathless from the force of the attack, he staggered back against the tree, took his glasses off and wiped beads of sweat from his head and face on the sleeve of his jacket, then quickly put his glasses back on and peered into the trees waiting and listening intently. Things were really out of control now. He had to act fast. He wondered about the girl's companion, he couldn't hear him at all now, so he got to work on disposing of the body.

He squatted beside her and felt for a pulse, it was there, faint and slow. Without a second thought he grabbed her ankles, noticing as he did, that one of her trainers was missing. No point worrying about that right now, he had no time to waste. He dragged her near lifeless body to the edge of the recently dug grave, the grave he had been digging for Erin Fallon.

He firmly believed now that the God's were conspiring against him. Strange events and coincidences; nothing seemed to be going to plan any more, and now this! His face twisted with fury as he looked over the girl's body. Apart from her clothing, she would be impossible to identify if she were found; forensics would have to confirm her identity. But that was out of the question wasn't it, because if she was found *that* would potentially spell catastrophe for him. He got down on his knees and rolled Hannah Ridgway into the gaping black hole. Her body landed face down in the earth; her legs splayed wide, her arms buried beneath her. His eyes lingered a moment longer on her feet and her footwear. *Where is the missing trainer?* He would have to look for it later. He got back to his feet and began filling the grave. This was the last thing he expected to be doing tonight. Serve the stupid bitch right for being where she wasn't wanted. Full of life and youth one moment and in the next, *gone,* as simple as that!

He worked quickly, stopping every few minutes and listening keenly for any sound or movement close by. Silence had descended over the forest like a thick blanket and the forest was completely still, as though frozen in time. He went back to work, shovelling great piles of earth in to the grave, working at a frenzied pace and all the time wondering where the girl's companion could be. The more he thought about the faster he worked. Anxiety creased his face as a terrible thought occurred to him. What if the girl's companion has found his way to the lodge?

Beads of sweat ran off the end of his nose and his shirt was plastered to his body. His glasses kept slipping to the end of his nose as covered the grave with broken bark, dead leaves and fallen branches. He had come into the forest tonight to do some thinking, to try to get clear in his mind what he was going to do about the Fallon girl, not in his wildest imagination would he have believed what had taken place in the last couple of hours. Buried *alive*! This was a first, even for him. She wouldn't have been aware though, unfortunately. He couldn't believe that he had just murdered another girl – right out of the blue at that, and it had taken him all of a split second, totally unplanned and unexpected. He silently congratulated himself in the knowledge that the world would be a better place without her.

He shrugged, picked up his coat and the shovel set off, moving quickly through the trees back to the lodge, stopping occasionally to listen, waiting for the sound of another human being. He had had no choice but to kill the girl and more worryingly he realised that her being missing could potentially bring him some very unwanted attention. The girl's companion is bound to want to find her, even if he waits until daylight. He had to find him before he found the lodge and the missing trainer. What if her friend finds it before he does? That will surely alert him to the fact that something sinister may have happened to her and that would bring even more unwanted attention into the forest and into his territory. His movements became more rapid as he made his way back to the lodge. In the morning, he would go in search of the girl's companion and when he found him he would deal with him in the only way he felt appropriate. They had left him with no choice. But in the meantime, he had a patient to attend.

CHAPTER FIFTY-ONE

BILLY couldn't see his hand in front of his face as tried to fend off the sharp branches that whipped his body as he fought his way through the trees calling out Hannah's name, not realising that he was moving further and further away from where he'd last been with her. She wasn't answering his calls and in his frantic search for her he stumbled and fell head long over a rock, twisting his ankle. He rolled onto his side, grabbed the injured ankle with both hands and moaned and cursed loudly. Bloody hell, he was in agony! Biting down hard on his bottom lip he rocked on his side, waiting for the pain to subside.

He tried to stand up but a searing pain brought him back to his knees, "Aww, fuck!" The pain shot threw his ankle and up his shin. It was a fuckin disaster and it was his entire fault. It was a total nightmare. He cursed repeatedly, frustrated and worried out of his mind for Hannah. If only he had listened to her when she'd said they should probably start making their way back to their campsite, they wouldn't be in this terrible mess now. They'd be tucked up in his sleeping bag – well that had been his plan anyway. Where the hell was Hannah? Knowing how scared she felt about being in the forest, he hoped to God that she was all right.

There was no way he could put any pressure on his ankle, not right now, maybe if he rested it for a little while, he could try again. He began crawling on all fours, pulling himself along the ground, reaching out and feeling for something to rest against as he went. He finally found a hollow in a tree. After struggling to get the rucksack off his back, he placed his hands either side of his thighs and pulled himself along on his backside into the opening, sighing as he rested his head against the damp smelling bark. His stomach rumbled loudly in the silence. He and Hannah had been walking for the best part of eight hours or more and they'd not had much to eat or drink and now the freezing night air was taking its toll, he was starving. There was food and water in his rucksack but he was too tired to struggle with it in the dark. I hope Hannah's found somewhere safe to sleep. Maybe she's found a warm bed for the night at that lodge. He pulled the rucksack up onto his knees and hugged it close to ward off the cold that was seeping into his bones. He curled up in the hollow and dozed off, dreaming of Hannah.

CHAPTER FIFTY-TWO

HE craned his neck and looked up as he came out of the trees into the clearing. The smoke he'd observed earlier, curling above the trees, had vanished completely into the night sky. He searched with his eyes, his hearing straining for any sound that was out of the ordinary, out of character with the forest at night. He would know instinctively if there were anyone snooping around.

Before he went into the lodge, he disappeared around the back and hid the spade beneath the decking surrounding the lodge then he stood for a few moments and looked around again, squinting into the dark and listening intently. Where was he, the girl's companion? He exhaled loudly; his fears and concerns were growing.

He let himself in, threw his coat just inside the kitchen door onto the worktop and slipped out of his shoes, leaving them by the front door in the hallway. He was too tired to be bothered about putting things away, putting them in their rightful places. He climbed the stairs heavily, and as he reached Erin's bedroom door, he stopped and turned the knob very slowly and very quietly until the door opened a slither, enough for him to peep inside. The fading embers of the fire bathed the room in a warm orange glow and he could just make out Erin's face as she lay in a deep sleep, curled on her side facing the door. This girl wasn't a bad girl; how could she be? She was John Fallon's daughter.

He glanced at the fireplace again; the fire was almost out. He opened the door a little wider and slipped inside. The dying embers in the grate were keeping the room at a cosy temperature. Erin appeared to be comfortable and peaceful as she lay sleeping, but Fitch knew better; she still had some way to go before she was fit enough to be moved. He stepped across the room and stood by the bed; spoke quietly to her as she slept. "The problem is, my dear, we don't have much time, not now. Things have, shall we say, gone awry."

Taking great care not to disturb her, he pulled back the blankets and moved his hands over the dressings on her legs. There was no unusual heat coming from them and as far as he could see in the dim light, they looked clean, no leakages. "I think these will be all right until morning," Then he placed the back of his hand on the side of her face, her temperature was still a little high, but nothing too worrying. He pulled the covers back over her and left the room, closing the door behind him.

CHAPTER FIFTY-THREE

BILLY woke with a start; he rubbed vigorously at his eyes with the heel of his palms, confused by his surroundings. Curled foetal like, with the rucksack wedged up against his chin, he stretched his legs out fully, he was as stiff as a board. His lower back ached, he groaned loudly, "Argh, Jesus Christ!" His ankle hurt like hell. Day was breaking and the rays from the early morning sun shimmered and danced as they touched the autumn leaves fluttering to the ground on the light breeze.

He looked at his watch; it was almost half past seven. Bloody hell, I've slept right through the night! He lurched forward, banging his head on the tree trunk, "Hannah!" Her frightened face flashed before his eyes. His mind raced, filled with thoughts of how Hannah might be injured, terrified, lost! I'm not leaving this forest without her. No matter what! Her Dad's gonna kill me if he finds out about this.

He set his hands down firmly against the dew soaked ground and pushed forward on his backside out of the hollow, shoving the rucksack off his lap as he turned on all fours and got up onto his knees. He took a deep breath and stood up, tentatively, easing his full weight down onto the injured ankle. The pain prevented him from sustaining that position for more than a few seconds. He wanted to vomit. He moaned out loud. "Argh! Bloody hell!" Sweat and tears ran down his face as he fell back to his knees, his hands clutching his forehead. He wasn't going anywhere. His brow touched the ground, his tears pooling in small circles in the damp sour smelling soil, the pain and the smell made him wretch.

How the hell am I going to find her if I can't walk? The sturdy walking boots he'd proudly purchased from the Army and Navy store on London Road, in Manchester, had probably prevented anything more than a bad sprain, but nevertheless the pain was excruciating.

Unable to put any pressure whatsoever on the injured ankle, he crawled to the nearest tree and sat with his back against it. The ankle was screaming at him. He needed painkillers. Did he pack any? He couldn't remember. He grabbed the rucksack opened it and emptied it onto the ground. After a lot of silent praying, he spotted the small blister pack of Paracetamol. He didn't know how long the painkillers had been in the rucksack, nor did he care. What harm can they do if they're out of date anyway? At worst they'd make him sick, but right now he needed pain relief in order to walk, to find Hannah and get out of this bloody forest. He couldn't sit up against a tree for the foreseeable.

He popped two tablets and washed them down with the bottled water. Give it about twenty minutes and then try walking. Whilst he waited for the painkiller to kick in, he opened a packet of crisp and began wondering again where Hannah could possibly be. If she hadn't made it to that lodge last night, perhaps she's gone there this morning. Maybe got the forest rangers out looking for him right now. He didn't want to think anymore about her being frightened and alone. He silently asked God to please make sure she was unharmed and safe. The thought of Hannah being hurt turned his stomach. He put the packet of crisp back in the rucksack. He had no appetite. The food can wait; I'll share it with Hannah when I find her.

He checked his watch; it was almost ten to eight. Grimacing, he banged the heel of his hand against his forehead several times and muttered, "What a fucking mess!"

Impatience finally got the better of him; he couldn't sit there and do nothing. He got up slowly, scared of putting his full weight down on the bad ankle. He did it bit by bit, putting a little more weight on it each time. He looked around for a stick of some sort, something to help support him so that he could walk instead of hopping on one leg. He spotted the end of what turned out to be a thick branch partially covered beneath dead leaves. It was probably too long for his needs, but it would have to do.

He tested the branch as a walking stick; it was okay. Without it, he wouldn't be able to walk at all. With it, he could at least hobble, painful as it was. He put the rucksack on his back and looked around, completely at a loss as to which direction he should take.

He looked up at the sky; the sun was in the east but he quickly realised that that didn't help him much because he didn't have the slightest clue of where he was in relation to the source of the smoke they'd been trying to get to last night. He needed to head for a clearing in the trees or some higher ground so he could get a good view of the surrounding area if he was to locate the place. He tested his makeshift walking stick again, tightened the straps of the rucksack and set off along what he considered was the easiest, flattest route.

CHAPTER FIFTY-FOUR

FITCH had a restless night, he'd tossed and turned and had woke up repeatedly. He switched on the bedside lamp and squinted at his watch. It was five to six, not quite daylight yet. He threw back the covers and got out of bed. He couldn't stop thinking about the other person, or persons? Surely whomever the girl had been with would be out searching for her? The police would be brought in to help with the search. And there's that missing trainer as well. The idea that his game might be up crossed his mind. He had never contemplated being found out.

He spoke quietly to his reflection in the mirror as he buttoned his shirt, "No. Never. I'm too clever for them, been doing it for years and they still haven't got a clue. And they never will!" He studied his reflection more closely and tugged at a rogue hair protruding from his left nostril.

Dressed in a clean blue and white check shirt and navy corduroy trousers, he put on a pair of slippers and left his bedroom, locking the door again and putting the key back in its usual place. It was time to look in on his patient; she was due to have her next round of medication.

When he entered the room, her eyes fluttered open and shut; she moaned as Fitch approached her bedside. Seeing the fear in her eyes, he spoke reassuringly to her, "You must trust me. I am not going to harm you. I am going to make you well again, and when you're fit enough, you can go home – to your family. You have my word."

Erin moaned again, as though she was in pain. Fitch had brought his medical bag into the room with him; he pulled a thermometer from it and slipped it into Erin's mouth. She closed her eyes as he sat down on the edge of the bed and began his routine checks.

"BP and temperature still a cause for concern," he said more to himself than to Erin. "Best place for you would have been in hospital but I'm afraid that option isn't available to us." He pulled the bedclothes back and began removing the dressings. Erin watched him, as he worked. She was confused and frightened. Fitch glanced at her and said, "I need to check that the infection isn't spreading, it could develop into septicaemia. But, looking at these sores now, it seems you're on the mend. The wounds don't look as angry and the inflammation appears to be receding."

He pulled the covers over her and said, "I'll be back in a moment to change the dressings and give you your medicine. Then I want you to try to eat a little something for me." Erin shook her head; he saw the panic in her eyes. "I know your throat is still very sore, but I'd still like to get some food inside you. A bowl of soup, nothing to chew or hard to swallow."

He left the bedroom and went downstairs to the kitchen. Provisions were basic to say the least. His intention was only ever to keep his victims alive, not to fatten them up, so he provided them with dried fruit and cereals but that was no good right now. She needed something she could swallow painlessly, something warm..

He went to the locked cupboard where he kept his own provisions and took out a tin of soup. Usually when he came up for the weekend, he would pack a game pie or some fresh fish for himself, but food had been the last thing on his mind on his way out here two days ago.

He opened the can, poured the contents into a saucepan and lit the gas ring beneath. Within minutes, the soup was boiling. As he poured the soup into a bowl he looked out of the barred kitchen window and wondered how long it was going to be before someone tried the locked gate.

He loaded up a tray with the soup and a glass of water and made his way upstairs to Erin. The room was warming as the early morning sun shone through the window. Erin had drifted off again. Fitch placed the tray on the bedside table and shook the girl's arm to awaken her. He had more medicine to administer and he was running short on time. "Erin. Wake up! You need to take your medicine."

As her eyes fluttered open, he slipped his hand behind her and lifted her head gently off the pillow. "Come along, take this, it'll ease the soreness and fight the infection." She cried out as she swallowed the liquid penicillin.

He poured more of the syrupy red liquid onto the spoon, "I know it's painful but you have to take another spoonful then you can have this soup. It's Heinz Tomato soup, my favourite and full of goodness." Erin did not respond she stole a quick glance at him before looking down at the spoon he was holding in front of her. The fear was still in her eyes. She didn't trust him, and why should she after what he'd done to her and what he had put her through.

"As soon as you finish the soup, I'm going to give you something to make you sleep again." He continued talking softly to her as he administered the medication, "Sleep is good for the body and soul and will help to make you well again. So I'm going to keep you sedated for much of the next few days. I'll wake you when it's time for your medication and you'll also need to drink too. But don't worry about that now. I'll take care of everything."

As soon as Erin had finished the soup and was sedated again, he pulled back the covers and began carefully removing the dressings from her legs. Using sterile swabs he bathed the area again and applied clean dressings to the infected wounds. As he pulled the covers back in place, he became aware of how cold the bedroom had become now that the sun had moved and no longer filled the room with its warm glow, so he went to his own room and fetched extra blankets.He thought about lighting a fire in her room but then remembered watching the smoke curling from the chimney into the clouds. He couldn't risk lighting another fire it would surely attract unwanted attention to the lodge.

* * *

Erin drifted in and out of consciousness. She was confused; the man treating her, and calling her by her name when he spoke to her was the same man who had kidnapped and abused her. Is this a different game that he's playing? And did he say I could go home? Did he say home? The drugs he was giving her must be making her hallucinate because she felt better than she had felt in many months. This has got to be a dream.

CHAPTER FIFTY-FIVE

GASPING for breath, Billy scrambled on all fours up a steep hillock and as soon as he made it to the top he dropped his makeshift walking stick, threw his rucksack off, rolled onto his back and rested for a few minutes until his breathing returned to normal. He cupped his hands over his forehead and grimaced at the pain shooting along his foot.

He'd spent the last two hours wandering aimlessly through the trees, completely lost, but still clutching at the hope that he would find Hannah, or at least another human being who might help him search for her.

His ankle ached like hell. It was swollen and he had had to untie his laces in order to loosen the heavy walking boot.

He dragged himself up into a sitting position and tentatively tugged the boot off the injured foot; he rolled his sock down to his toes and inspected his ankle. The dark blue swelling confirmed his worry, it was a bad sprain and last thing he needed if he was going to find Hannah and get out of the forest before nightfall.

With that thought, he pulled his sock up and carefully slid his boot back on. He took two more painkillers and swilled them down with water before lacing up the boot and pulling himself to his feet using the stick for support.

Under different circumstances, the scene from the top of the hillock would have been something to behold; he could see for miles into the dense landscape and as he took in the vast array of trees and their striking autumnal colours, he suddenly remembered the binoculars at the bottom of the rucksack.

At first he couldn't see a thing, just blurred light, unfathomable shapes. Adjusting the dial, those shapes became trees, and then in sharp focus he could make out the fine detail of the leaves. He began scanning the area, his head moving from side to side as he tried to pinpoint exactly where he was, continuously adjusting the focal length as his view went further into the distance. Then something grabbed his attention. Nestled deep inside the trees, he caught sight of what appeared to be the apex of a building. Excitement ran like an electric current through his body, invigorating him – *that's it!* He knew it, the lodge where he and Hannah had seen the smoke rising. He grimaced and smacked his forehead with the heel of his hand; I must have been wandering round in circles for the past two hours. He shook his head and muttered, "Idiot!"

Forgetting his pain, he hastily shoved the binoculars back into the rucksack and moved as fast as his injured ankle would allow, down the other side of the hillock into the trees taking the line in the direction of the lodge; he checked his watch, it was almost ten o'clock.

After limping through the woodland for a while, he looked at his watch, it was ten past eleven, surely he can't be that far from the lodge now, probably just a few hundred yards or so at the most. He moaned out loud with each step, the pain in his ankle was worse than ever. Reluctantly he decided to stop and rest for a few minutes, take the weight off, pop just one more painkiller. Leaning against a thick tree trunk for support, he was about to lower himself to a sitting position on the ground when something caught his eye. Lying on the ground in front of him amongst the bracken and dead leaves, was a white trainer, and from where he was standing he could see that it looked almost new – he spotted the Adidas logo on the heel and suddenly went cold.

His heart was beating ten to the dozen as he hobbled over and picked up the trainer. Inspecting it closely, he could see that it had hardly been worn, still looked just as new as when she'd bought them for the camping trip just three days ago; he had no doubt whatsoever, it was Hannah's.

Dread prickled his skin; he was convinced more than ever now that something terrible had happened to Hannah. Looking around anxiously for something – he didn't know what, his eyes came to rest on what he recognised instantly as Hannah's scarf; it was tangled in the lower branches of a nearby tree. But that wasn't all. From where he was standing, he could see clearly that there was blood on it. He limped over to the tree and began tugging it free from the branches. With the blood stained scarf in one hand and the trainer in the other; he had a sudden urge to empty his bowels.

With the trainer and scarf tucked inside his rucksack, he moved through the trees, looking frantically in every direction, half expecting to find Hannah badly injured, unconscious even. Thoughts crashed round his head: how the hell was he going to be of any help to her if she was unconscious? Maybe she made it to the lodge? Maybe whoever lives there has found her and is taking care of her? His mind was full of fear and conflicting thoughts, but one thing he knew for sure – he was in one hell of a lot of trouble if he didn't find her. How in the name of God was he going to be able to explain the trainer and blood stained scarf? What the hell was he going to tell her parents? What should have been a weekend of fun and laughter was turning into a living nightmare.

Stumbling blindly through the trees and muttering incoherently Billy stopped dead in his tracks. Deliberately hidden out of sight in the dense woodland was an expensive looking car – and not just any car. Billy stared incredulously; *it's Fitch's car!*

"What the fuck . . .?" he whispered as he looked around. He'd never noticed the vehicle in daylight before, and now he was transfixed by it. A perplexed expression crossed his face, *there's something about this car – what is it?* As he continued staring at it, he couldn't help feeling uneasy, for a reason, or reasons he just couldn't fathom and then it hit him full on – a flashback. It was the number plate and the GB sticker on the bumper. As he slowly backed away from the vehicle, he remembered now where he had seen the car before, and at that moment a vision of Erin Fallon flashed across his mind and almost knocked him off his feet.

His mind flashed back to the times he'd walked Erin to the bus stop, along a lonely and almost deserted, Bleaksedge Lane and on several of those days, it was *this car* that had slowed right down each time it had passed them; the lone male, staring fixedly at Erin. Billy recalled shouting out after the driver, "Pervert!" The driver had sped off, but Billy's memory was clear now; he could see him, the gaunt looking middle-aged driver – it was *Leonard Fitch*!

Remembering the blood stained scarf and trainer in his rucksack, he moved carefully back towards the car and peered inside. Nothing had been left on show. He didn't know why but he went to the rear of the car and tried the boot – it was locked; he tried the doors, they were locked too. He felt like a coward and a thorough bastard, for leaving without Hannah but instinct was telling him he couldn't waste anymore time looking for her, he had to get to a police station as fast as possible – and knowing that he was probably only a few yards away from the lodge and Leonard Fitch, he made up his mind to follow the tracks the car had made on the way into the forest, knowing that by doing so it would lead him straight back to where he and Hannah had set up camp two nights ago – it was his only chance of getting out of there before nightfall and getting help for Hannah.

Before he set off, he decided to take another painkiller, he didn't know how long it was going to take him but he had to be able to move fairly quickly, and his injured ankle was going to be a serious setback. He got down, sitting with his back against Fitch's car, and began rummaging impatiently for the pills listening all the time for any sign of movement nearby – the last thing he needed now was for Fitch to find him. With the contents of his rucksack scattered on the ground beside him, he took two tablets out of the pack, probably more than he should have done so soon after the last two, and swallowed them with the remaining water, before tossing the empty bottle into the trees. Time to get a move on he thought as he hastily shoved everything back into his rucksack.

CHAPTER FIFTY-SIX

THE last couple of days had been dry, making it easy for Billy to follow the tyre tracks left by Fitch's car. His progress was slow as he tried not to dwell too much on the pain from his swollen ankle – but it was with more confidence than he'd felt in the last twenty-four hours that he believed he would actually find his way back to where he and Hannah had made camp.

He'd been walking for a good hour or two when the mid-day sun broke through the trees – in fact there were fewer trees now and within a few minutes of that realisation, it was with heart pounding relief that he found himself walking on *tarmac*! He'd made it back to the road and the edge of the forest where he knew he would find help.

His mind worked rapidly, estimating about another fifteen to twenty minutes before he reached his car and maybe twenty minutes up to Penrith and the nearest police station. He muttered repeatedly with every agonising step along the tarmac, "*Please, please, God, let her be okay. Please!*" He prayed that he could convince the police to get to Fitch's lodge before nightfall. Otherwise it meant another night for Hannah, alone; or maybe she wasn't alone. He shivered. He rubbed his forehead as he limped along the tarmac repeating his mantra, "please let her be safe!" The disturbing thought that Fitch might do something to her, brought tears to his eyes. He moaned out loud "*Please, God, keep her safe!*"

CHAPTER FIFTY-SEVEN

A S Fitch was getting ready to leave the lodge he had just one thing on his mind, the girl he'd unexpectedly bludgeoned to death last night – she had a companion. Fitch was sure he'd heard her calling out the name, *Billy*. And for the first time since owning the lodge and his own piece of the forest, he was deeply troubled and uneasy. The chance of someone coming onto his property and revealing his crimes was inconceivable.

Changing his MO by carefully choosing his victims and abducting them on their birthdays had become a very gratifying and vital part of his existence – that he had the power to reap indescribable agony and sorrow upon the girls mothers was infinitely more rewarding than the pain and misery he visited upon their little girls.

He closed the front door, locked it and hesitated for a moment on the porch as he stared into the trees. There was a potential threat to him and his existence somewhere out there. He had to find it and eradicate. He stepped off the porch and made his way to the gate where he removed the padlock. He sighed and looked up at the sky; it was a cloudless bright blue. Under different circumstances, he would have relished a solitary walk in the forest on such a beautiful day – but not *this* day!

He put the lock back in place and was about to head into the trees, in the direction of the gravesite, when he remembered the hunting rifle in the boot of his car – he could use it, get rid of the companion with a single bullet. Got to find him, can't let him leave the forest.

He went through the pockets of his overcoat and pulled out his car keys as he made his way around the back of the lodge, continuing until he came to a large thicket where his car was completely hidden from view – or at least he thought it was.

He looked around as if expecting someone to come out of the trees, the thought made him break out in a cold. Stepping to the rear of the vehicle his movement was suddenly halted by the sound of something crackling under his foot. He lifted his foot and stared at the ground. It was a foil blister pack with the word "Paracetamol" written across the back. Definitely not a painkiller he carried, it had to have been left by someone else. His heartbeat increased. He bent down, picked up the foil strip and examined it. The pack had been emptied. Somebody is in pain.

As he was turning the foil pack in his hands, he spotted something else near the rear tyre. He dropped the empty pack and stooped down to pick up a plastic bottle, Evian Water, obviously left by the person who took the tablets.

Someone had been within yards of the lodge. His face twisted with fury at the very idea that he had company, unwanted company at that. It had to be the girl's companion. What if there are others? What if they're still here searching for the girl while somebody else has gone to fetch the police? Whoever it was had been here just a short while ago. The bottle and the blister pack had not been there before, it hadn't been there yesterday he knew that for certain. He looked around for more clues.

The footprints in the dried mud were very clear and he followed them for several yards before he realised that whoever had left them was using the tracks left by his car to find their way out of the forest. He stopped briefly and studied the prints. They belonged to someone wearing heavy boots, definitely a male – too big for a female. They have probably made their way back to the road. Back to civilisation – and most probably, to the police. The nearest police station was in Penrith. He didn't have much time.

If he brings the police back they'll want to search the lodge. What am I going to do with the Fallon girl? As he let himself back into the lodge, he was considering a number of options. He was used to working under pressure, making quick decisions. Deliberation in his line of work could be fatal and failure to act quickly now could be *fatal* for *him*.

Back in the kitchen he paced back and forth as he considered his options, thinking out loud, "The likelihood is that the girl's companion has gone running off to tell the police that his girlfriend is missing." He stroked his long chin as he spoke to himself. "At best he could possibly lead them to the car, except the car won't be there will it? No, I'll be long gone by then. Did he actually get close to the lodge? Did he see it through the trees? Possibly. Could've seen the smoke last night."

He stopped in front of the kitchen window and stared out, searching his mind for a solution. Still so much to do and so little time left to do it. It's time I put my contingency plan into action. I need a diversion, something to buy me some time. He continued staring into the trees, not really seeing them as his thoughts came together. A key part of his contingency plan was his mother, and how she was going to help with his escape. Not willingly or even knowingly, but she would be his 'get out of jail card'.

He spoke out loud to make sure his plan sounded feasible. "I'll put a call in to Penrith Police Station. Explain that I was camping overnight with friends when we became aware of a disturbance late last night. Tell them about the woman repeatedly screaming – what was the name again? Billy? Then total silence. Tell them that she sounded as though she was in some sort of danger, and then I'll send them in the opposite direction to the lodge. That should buy me enough time to get mother here." It sounded good. It would work if he didn't delay getting on with matters But first he head to go and check on Erin.

CHAPTER FIFTY-EIGHT

THE Medical Records Office was located on the first floor of the old Victorian hospital. As the two detectives entered, Stella Oldham stood up and walked over to them.

"Detective Sergeant Harris, and I am Detective Constable Jones." Jones made the introductions, his words bouncing back of the stark walls and the high ceiling.

"Mrs Oldham." Stella said, offering her hand to both. "I've been expecting you."

"Really? I don't remember making an appointment," said DC Jones, shaking her hand politely.

Stella looked confused, "Have you not come about Hannah?"

"Hannah?"

"Yes, Hannah Ridgway. She hasn't returned to work today; she went away for the weekend and nobody's seen or heard from her since."

"Well no." Harris looked sideways at Jones. "We're investigating a missing person or should I say persons. We wanted to look at the records of one of your surgeons, a Mrs. Olivier Horton?"

"Oh, I thought ... but what about Hannah, is someone looking for her?"

"I'm sorry we don't know anything about that. Have the police been informed?" asked Jones.

"Her parents phoned I think. It's just that it's not like her; she lied about where she was over the weekend. She said she was staying with her best friend but when her mother telephoned after she failed to return on Sunday night, she hadn't been there at all. I think that feckless porter, Billy Ashcroft has something to do with it, she –"

"Sorry?" said Harris raising his eyes, his brow creasing, "Did you say *Billy Ashcroft?*"

"Yes, Hannah was going out with him. I think she must have been with him because he's not shown up either. Wouldn't surprise me if they haven't driven up to Gretna Green for a quick wedding."

Harris turned to Jones. "Maybe Paisley was right," then looking back at Stella, "We'll make enquiries back at the station, Mrs Oldham. While we're here, can we see your records for Mrs Horton? We'd like to know if she has any connection with three girls who were treated here between 1972 and last year."

"Well I don't know if I can; patient confidentiality and all that. They're getting very strict on it nowadays."

"We don't want to know what treatment was provided, just to see if she came into contact with three girls who went missing over that period," said Harris.

"We have reason to believe there is a connection between these girls and two others from nearby hospitals and Mrs Horton," added Jones.

"You're welcome to look but you won't find anything like that. You see; Mrs Horton is a consultant. She is responsible for patient care, but she doesn't actually perform operations, she has a team of doctors under her, they do all of that."

Jones looked at Harris. "Maybe we just bring her in, ask a few questions? She may – "

"I could make an appointment for you to see her." Stella said. "She's very busy as you can imagine, having to cover Westmoorland General as well. That's where she is at the moment."

"No, that won't be necessary." Harris looked at his watch. He didn't believe in coincidences and *Ashcroft's* name cropping up again made him think it was time to talk to Sergeant Paisley. "We need to get back to the station."

CHAPTER FIFTY-NINE

SERGEANT John Paisley, or *Jock* as he was known, was forty-eight years old. The son of a Glasgow shipbuilder, he was as tough as they come. His thick Glaswegian accent had mellowed a bit since his migration south of the border some twenty years earlier but he still had that unique way of saying "*Murrrderrrer*" something that never ceased to amuse his colleagues, not that they dared show it to his face. Nor did they hear it that often. Murder was rare in Bleaksedge; robbery and drunkenness were the usual offences the local police had to deal with. Hardly surprising then that he had missed the link between the four murders in as many years but it still rankled with him that they had to bring in these detectives.

He had no time for the CID and he let them know it at every opportunity. Now *he* sat there facing DS Harris, the files – *his files* – piled high on the desk and *his* map on the wall behind.

"You always thought Ashcroft was behind the Fallon disappearance didn't you Jock?"

"Aye, he was a cheeky wee scamp as a lad; the sort that would end up on the wrong side of the law at some point in time. Always chancing his arm." He leaned across the desk and raised a finger to emphasise the point. "You mark my words, he knows more about it than he's letting on."

"But he would have been only twelve or thirteen when the first girl went missing" Harris interjected.

"Ye see, there ye go again. *Assuming* there's only *one* killer at large."

"Well we know one man, or person, kidnapped and murdered the other four. All four killed on their birthdays. Fallon went missing just two days after her sixteenth birthday – "

"Never heard of copycat killers?" Paisley was becoming quite animated now as he slapped his hand down on the desk.

At that point DC Jones entered the office with three mugs of tea and a pile of McVitie's chocolate digestives on a tray. He jumped as the *thwack* echoed around the room, spilling tea onto the biscuits.

Harris couldn't help noticing that Jones appeared a good deal shorter today and looking down he saw that he had ditched his usual platform soles for a pair of Italian style winkle-pickers. His big fat tie had also been replaced by a thinner one, which was tied loosely at the neck of his plain white shirt. Gone was the pink penny-round collar of yesterday. *My God,* thought Harris, *there's been a bloody revolution overnight, and I'm back in fashion!*

DC Jones placed the tray on the desk, pulled up a chair and sat down next to Paisley. This was intentional to make Paisley feel more relaxed, less defensive. Something he'd read in an article about body language in a Sunday Times supplement at the weekend. "We thought about that. Copycat Killers. Trouble with it is, apart from the 'Birthday Girl' thing, none of the details of the case have ever been leaked to the press. Nobody, apart from the investigating officers and the families of the victims knows about the severed feet, for example."

"Aye, that's true. But who's to say this latest missing person has had her feet cut off?" The brutality of his words shocked Harris but he knew he had a point. The thought that Fallon was not connected to the other girls was a hard one to come to terms with.

"Thanks Jock but we'll stick with the serial killer theory for now" he said as he picked up a biscuit and dipped it into his tea.

"So why the interest in Ashcroft if you don't think it can be him?"

"When a name keeps cropping up during an investigation you've got to ask yourself why?"

"It seems he may be linked to another disappearance over the weekend" said Jones. "A girl by the name of Hannah Ridgway. Do you know about that one?"

Paisley eyed the young DC sat next to him and offered a wry smile. "Aye, we know about it. The mother was interviewed last night but she said nothing about the wee lad Ashcroft."

Harris took his chance to get one over on the Scot. "Oh, didn't you know they are going out together? Yeah, very close, they are. In fact, you might want to check the register at Gretna Green."

Jones could sense the tension building. His approach was very different to Harris's but he knew that this was his boss's show. On the other hand, he had his own way of working things out and he knew that Billy Ashcroft was not their killer. Nevertheless, it was an intriguing situation. He turns up in the investigation into the disappearance of Erin Fallon and now another disappearance and his name crops up again. And both Ashcroft and Ridgway worked at The Royal. There had to be a link.

"Can you tell us a bit more about Ashcroft?" Jones said. "You obviously knew him as a youngster but what was he like?"

"As I said, a cheeky scamp, always up to mischief as a wee laddie."

"Did you ever have cause to arrest him or caution him?" asked Harris.

"No, never managed to pin anything on him."

"So he was just a Jack the Lad."

"Well . . . ye could say that."

"But hardly serial killer material?" Jones asked.

"I questioned him over the disappearance of one lass, now it looks like I'll be doing the same over another." Paisley scowled at Jones. "You're the one harping on about serial killers. No' me Sunny Jim!"

Just then the phone rang. Harris picked it up.

"DS Harris . . . Sergeant Paisley? Yes he's here. For you." he said, handing the receiver across the desk.

"Hello. Paisley speaking."

There was a long pause. The two detectives could hear the muffled sound coming out of the earpiece but couldn't make out any words. Paisley uttered the odd "Aha" but nothing else. Then a wry smile crossed his face.

"I see. Well we'd better get ourselves over there right away." Paisley handed the phone back to Harris. He couldn't help milking the moment for all it was worth. Harris held the phone to his ear but the line was dead so he placed it back in the cradle, looking across the table at the now very smug Police Sergeant.

"Seems our wee friend Billy Ashcroft has shown up at Penrith Police Station *with his girlfriend's trainer and a blood stained scarf*."

CHAPTER SIXTY

HARRIS concluded his conversation with the Desk Sergeant at Penrith, stood up and grabbed his coat. "Come on Jonesy, we're off to the Lake District."

"So when did he turn up?" asked Jones as they walked across the car park.

"Yesterday. Kept him there overnight for questioning before anyone thought to call his local station. They say they had a call from a hiker who was camping in the fells about a disturbance on Saturday night. They've had the local plod traipsing all over the place, no doubt destroying vital evidence, trying to corroborate Ashcroft's story "

"Which is?"

"Claims he and his girlfriend . . ."

"Hannah."

"That's the one. They went off into the forest to find a man who works at the hospital. A surgeon there, name of Fitch; ring any bells?"

DC Jones opened the passenger door of his white Ford Consul and held it open for DS Harris. "Fitch?" The hairs stood up on the back of Jones's neck. He knew the name all right. It had cropped up on one of his lists and was one he intended pursuing had he not got so hung up on his theory of the female doctor with the Electra complex.

"Err, no Sarge, can't say it does." Jones opened the driver's door and eased himself behind the wheel.

The drive to Penrith took them around two hours, during which time DS Harris passed on all he knew from the briefing he had over the telephone with the desk sergeant there. Jones listened intermittently, at the same time thinking about that name. *Leonard Fitch.* He was so close to nailing him. A surgeon who worked at the Royal and Westmoorland Hospitals, he just hadn't got round to checking out Lancaster.

When they arrived at the station, they were immediately herded towards the interview room.

"Yes two coffees please, one white no sugar and one black with two." Jones told the constable who led them to the door. As the door opened they saw Billy Ashcroft sat at the desk, hair dishevelled, a good four days of facial growth and a very pale complexion. His eyes were sunken and reddened.

"Better get him one too" said Harris, nodding his head in Billy's direction.

Billy looked up, his eyes squinting in the stark light from a single bulb hanging from a chord in the centre of the room.

The two detectives sat down opposite Billy. Harris looked him squarely in the eyes as Jones took out his cigarettes, offering them across the table. Billy's eyes lowered onto the golden pack of Benson and Hedges. He shook his head.

"Filthy habit," Harris said as he pushed the ashtray towards Jones. He was a forty a day man until a year ago and ever since has taken every opportunity to condemn all smokers as pariahs. "So Billy, tell us your story. From the beginning if you don't mind."

Billy sighed and dropped his head, closing his eyes, then throwing it back and shouting up towards the high ceiling. *"For fuck's sake!* How many *more* times! We've been through all of this. Why aren't you out there looking for Hannah?"

Jones lit a cigarette and took out his notepad. Flicking through the pages he stopped at one particular page where the corner was turned down. "I understand you work as a porter at The Royal?"

"Yes, I told *them* that," Billy replied nodding in the direction of the door.

"And your girlfriend Hannah, she works there as well?" asked Harris.

"Yes, she works there as well."

"So what made you come out here, late October?"

"Leonard Fitch."

"Go on"

"He was up to something."

"Like what, exactly?"

"I don't know, or at least I didn't, that is until Sunday morning."

Billy put his head in his hands, he'd been over this so many times now and nobody wanted to believe him, but once again he told them about Fitch's behaviour at the hospital and how he had ripped into his PA, Carole Worsley when she tried to get into his personal filing cabinet. He told them of their plan, Hannah and his, to follow him and to find out what he did at weekends, to try and find out his secret. He told them how they'd followed him into the forest and made camp for the night, and the next day had gone in search of his whereabouts. He told them how they lost their way and ended up arguing and how Hannah had stormed off. Finally he got to the part where he found Hannah's trainer and the blood stained scarf. He looked up at the two detectives, expecting a barrage of questions, a cross examination about Hannah. Nobody so far had believed his story, the Police were convinced he'd murdered the girl following the row and was now trying to cover his steps.

"Tell me more about Fitch." Harris looked at him sympathetically. "You say you didn't know what he was up to until Sunday morning? What did you discover then?"

Billy was relieved and grateful that, *finally*, somebody was listening. "It was the car."

"What about the car?"

"It came to me immediately I saw it parked there. I don't know what it was at first, but then it was just like a light going on in my head."

Jones looked up from his notepad, which was rapidly becoming full of scribbles. "Take your time Billy, it's important you get this right."

"The car parked up there like that. I'd seen it before. I know we'd been following it the Friday before but we were some distance behind it and anyway it was dark. This time was different, though. It was like a flashback to twelve months earlier. I was walking a girl down Bleaksedge Lane to catch the bus to school. I fancied her but she wasn't interested. Probably too young anyway."

"That girl, Billy. It wouldn't be Erin Fallon would it?" Harris interrupted

"*Yes!*" Billy felt he was getting somewhere at last. "Yes that's right, *Erin Fallon.* The girl that went missing."

"Okay, let's get back to the car, Billy. What was it about the car?"

"It was the same one, the one that pulled out of Hinckley Road and slowed down as it passed us. I remember the creep looking at us; he was *leering* at Erin, and then he drove off. It never occurred to me before but that man, that *creep*, it was him."

"Who Billy?"

"Fitch. *It was Leonard Fitch.*"

CHAPTER SIXTY-ONE

FITCH took the stairs two at a time as he rushed to look in on his patient before he left; she was still sleeping. Briefly putting aside the morning's events, his professional side took over and while Erin slept, he checked her temperature and pulse and noted with some relief that she was definitely improving.

He removed the dressings and checked the bites on her thighs; the penicillin was doing the job. The wounds looked much cleaner. There was no smell now and the inflammation had receded further. Mr Fitch, the medical professional, was pleased! She was recovering very well but she would need another forty-eight hours or so on the medication before she was fully recovered. He didn't have that much time. His plan required him to be out of the lodge and on his way to his new life in a little over twenty-four hours.

As he was applying fresh dressings to her legs, his thoughts returned to John Fallon, he sighed and looked up at Erin she was like her father. He shook his head and tried to concentrate on what he was doing but he had to admit to himself that he was tormented by his own conscience now. John Fallon had never had a moment's peace since he had taken something so precious from him and his young family.

Worse still he had also been the bearer of the news that Fallon's youngest child was dead. But as he finished tending his patient he made a silent vow to make right the wrong he'd done to John Fallon – *he shall have his daughter back*!

As he was collecting the soiled dressings and other medical paraphernalia from the top of the bedside cupboard, Erin stirred and moaned softly. Her eyes fluttered open. Fitch saw, not for the first time, the look of confusion and fear in her eyes.

"Are you feeling a little better, dear?" He spoke with a kindness that bewildered Erin. She nodded slowly.

"Good. I'm pleased to hear it." He nodded at the contents in his hands and continued as if this was a perfectly normal situation, "I'm going to take these away then I want you to take some more medicine. Just for a couple more days, and then you can go home – to your family."

After he'd given her the regular dose of Penicillin, Erin finally found the courage to say something. Not wanting to make eye contact with him, her voice small and weak, she said, "I don't understand. Why are you letting me go?"

"Don't you want to go home, Erin?" he asked.

No one had called her by her name for as long as she could remember, she felt like a human being again. It was too much for her. Tears sprang in her eyes, "Yes. Yes, more than anything. I want see my dad and my sister and brothers." She sniffed loudly and took a deep breath, "You will let me go won't you?"

"Erin, I'm not sure if you remember this but when I found you, very sick, several days ago, I gave you my word that I would not harm you again, ever – and nothing has changed that. I will treat your illness. Make you well again. And then, yes, you will go home to your Father . . ."

He looked away and finished too soft to be heard, "And your brothers."

Erin didn't know whether or not to believe him but she thought that he must have been telling her the truth. Why else would he want to make her better, to treat her with such care and kindness? It made her cry all the more, the tears leaving wet patches on the pillow.

Fitch pulled a handkerchief from his trouser pocket and handed it to her.

"Come along now, Erin. Dry your tears." Fitch found it hard to deal with the situation; being 'nice' wasn't really in his nature when it came to females but after years of practice as a surgeon, caring for sick people, he had learned to fake it.

Erin was quiet, lost in thought as she wiped away the tears. After almost a year of psychological torture, physical abuse and degradation, he had finally given her hope . . . something to live for.

He broke into her thoughts, "I have to leave now but I'll be back early in the morning. When you've finished eating I'm going to give you something to make you sleep again. And when you wake tomorrow we'll make the necessary arrangements for you to leave."

She dutifully accepted the two small white pills that Fitch had fetched her with a glass of water. "These will make you sleep for several hours and I assure you, you'll feel much, much better tomorrow. You'll be fit enough to go home." He was so calm, so matter of fact about the situation like she was a convalescent patient – spending a couple of months at his country lodge – relaxing and rehabilitating.

Exhausted, she settled back against the soft clean pillows and closed her eyes. She could now dream that beautiful dream. *She was going home . . .*

CHAPTER SIXTY-TWO

FITCH stopped off at a service station on the M6 to make a couple of phone calls, one to Penrith Police and the other to his mother. The call to the police was an easy one, *'Billy'* hadn't shown up but they would 'look into it'. *Useless pricks!*

The call to his mother was more difficult. He didn't get past, "Hello dear –" before she interrupted him with a tirade of abuse and accusations, "OH! It's *you*, is it? Finally bothered to find out if I'm all right have you? I could be lying dead for all you care! Where have you been? Call yourself a son?"

She always made him feel worthless. As usual, his fear of her got the better of him and his nervousness came across in his voice, "Mother, please . . ."

She picked up on his uneasiness and used it to ridicule him before he could get another word in, "You're spineless and selfish! I should have crossed my legs and strangled you at birth! What do you want, boy?"

He almost stuttered now, "Err, yes. Right, erm . . .I'm on my way home to see you. Mother. I, err . . . wondered if you might like to come and stay at the lodge for a couple of days?"

She didn't give it a second thought and she didn't come up for air either, as she let rip at him, "No, thank you, I don't! The place is too cold! Something about it, can't say what, but I don't like the place – gives me the *CREEPS*! It's too isolated. No, thank you. I'll decline the invitation!"

He went in for the kill now, "Please, mother. There's someone special, I'd like you to meet, it's . . ."

Oh, she was listening now and it showed as she interrupted him cackling loudly, " WHAT? Have you got a MAN friend, Leonard?" She howled with laughter at her little jibe at him.

It was all he could do to stop himself screaming down the line at her to *drop dead and burn in hell!* But he was determined to see his plan through and so he continued, this time with more confidence, "No Mother, it's a young lady. I'd like you to meet her. I've got the place all nice and cosy for you and, err . . . besides, I think you'll like her."

She couldn't resist it! *Leonard had got himself a young lady?* Now this she had to see, even if it did mean foregoing the luxuries of her beautiful big house for a couple nights at his grotty lodge.

She often forgot the fact that the house was actually owned outright by Leonard. Emily Fitch had leached off his father until he had died at the wheel of his car and she'd been leaching off her son ever since he was able to earn a living. At seventy, she was a sprightly old woman who was perfectly mobile and lucid but she leaned heavily on her son for everything.

This time she concealed her amusement, "Very well then. When are we going?"

Yes! She's agreed! "We'll leave very early tomorrow morning, Mother. I'd like to avoid the heavy traffic. We could get up there for about eight o'clock, that way we'll miss the rush hour on the M6. I'll see you in about four or five hours, Mother. I have to sort out a few things first. See you later, dear." He hung up without giving her a chance to say anything else.

As he got back to his car he checked his watch, it was mid-day. Excellent. Everything was going to plan. Just one or two people I need to see before I get back home to the bitch. A few things to pick up for the long journey ahead. Should have done it years ago.

Fitch managed a smile at his reflection in the rear view mirror, before setting off on the next leg of his journey. From disaster he had managed to manipulate a situation that would change his life forever, allowing him to continue unchallenged.

CHAPTER SIXTY-THREE

WHEN he arrived home, there were lights on everywhere; the house was lit up like Blackpool Tower and it really annoyed him. "Wasteful bitch!" he mumbled to himself. But then he wouldn't have to worry about her extravagances for much longer because he had plans for her and he was eager to see them through.

Standing in the wide hallway at the bottom of the grand winding staircase, he called out to her with a mock kindliness, "Mother? Where are you, dear?"

"I'm up here, in my room! What do you want?"

Trying to hide the sarcasm in his voice he said, "Oh, nothing really. It's just that there are lights on all over the house, I wondered if you might be entertaining friends." He knew damn well that she didn't have any friends – she was a loner, just like him. Nevertheless, he couldn't help having a swipe at the bitch.

"I'm in bed!" She yelled. "You said we were leaving early so I decided to come up and read for a while. Take my mind off the excitement to come."

Touché! Don't worry Mother dear; it will be the most exciting moment of your life. The adrenaline flow will be to die for. "Yes, it will be nice to spend some time together."

Fitch went around the house turning lights off, tutt-tutting several times at the sheer waste. "Do you really need all these on Mother? The lights? You can only be in one room at a time can't you?"

"I like to leave them on for the burglars!"

"That's very thoughtful dear, but there is an energy crisis you know?" Not that you'd care about that!

He went upstairs to his room at the far end of the large house and unlocked the medical cupboard where he kept a supply of samples from pharmaceutical companies. Pulling out several boxes and tossing them on to his bed, he found what he was looking for. *Vecuronium Bromide* – a nuromuscular block, used to prevent spontaneous movement of muscle during surgical operations.

Unzipping his medical bag, he carefully placed the ampoules into an inner pocket, along with a bottle of distilled water. He grabbed a handful of hyperdermic needles and threw those in as well. Just as he'd finished packing everything he needed, he heard his mother yelling at him from her bedroom.

"Coming dear!" he called out with a fake cheeriness. "Just collecting one or two things for the journey. You know how nausious you get on those winding roads." He dashed over to his bedside cabinet and pulled out a packet of Kwells. Don't want the bitch puking all over my car.

He zipped up his bag and hurried along the landing into her bedroom. She was sat up reading.

"It's late mother and we have an early start tomorrow. Shouldn't you turn off the light and get some sleep, dear?"

She was smirking as she pretended to read, "Tried, Leonard. I can't. The excitement about meeting your *lady friend* has got the better of me!"

He ignored the sarcasm this time, "What did you want me for, Mother?"

"I remembered when I heard you come in, I need some Kwells for the journey. Have you got any?

"Yes, I've fetched you some. Here take two of these as soon as you wake in the morning," he said tossing her the box. "Chew them, don't swallow them whole. Don't want you choking now, do we?"

And on that note he turned his back, wished her goodnight and went back to his room.

CHAPTER SIXTY-FOUR

DURING the drive to Bleazedale Forest, Fitch refused to tell his mother anything about his *lady* – he didn't even tell her that she was already there, he let her think that she would be arriving later that day. Much to his relief Emily Fitch slept for almost the entire journey.

They arrived just before ten. As soon as they entered the lodge, Fitch used the excuse that he needed the bathroom and dashed upstairs to check on Erin. She was fast asleep. Standing over her, he thought how very fragile she looked, her pale skin and long copper hair fanned out against the crisp white pillows. She looked so young and defenceless – just how he liked them but not this one, not any longer – she was different. He had to let her live, for the sake of her father. He quickly dismissed his train of thought and crept out of the room closing the door quietly behind him.

His mother was in the kitchen making a cup of tea. She turned to him and asked grumpily, "Well? What time is she arriving?"

He didn't answer her straight away instead he walked from the kitchen into the living room and spoke casually over his shoulder, "She's upstairs, sleeping."

"What did you just say?" she asked as she followed him into the living room. "Did I hear you right then? Did you just say that she's here, upstairs? Sleeping? What's going on, Leonard?"

"Ever the busy body aren't you Mother?" he said ignoring her question. "Why don't you run along and finish making the tea, dear. I'm parched."

The look on her face was *priceless!* She reminded him of a guppy, her mouth opening and closing, nothing coming out. For the first time he could ever remember he'd actually rendered the old bitch speechless and it felt sooo good – he turned his back to her as he struggled to suppress the laughter bubbling up inside him. He finally had her completely at his will and his mercy.

He mocked her now, "Why don't you go and have a little peek at her while she's still sleeping? I'm sure she won't mind, dear!"

Incredulous, she turned and walked slowly from the room and began climbing the stairs.

Not wishing to waste any more time taunting her, he placed his medical bag on the desk in front of the window reached inside and took out two ampoules of Vecuronium and the distilled water, and began to make his preparations. Seconds later, he heard her coming down stairs and was more than ready for her.

"What have you done? She's a CHILD! My God, Leonard, *are you out of your mind?*"

Fitch kept his back to her but could imagine the look on her face, he was finding it difficult to hide his amusement as she continued to berate him.

Emily Fitch was disgusted and outraged, "Of all the things, Leonard. How could you? Is this what you've been sneaking away for, all this time? Messing with *young girls?*" She spat out, " There's a name for men like you, Leonard – you're a Paedophile! You're sick. Do you hear me, Leonard? You're sick!"

He finally turned to face her, the syringe concealed in his hand behind his back, and said matter of fact, "You've never liked me have you mother? Not even as a child. You've harboured a profound hatred for me all my life haven't you?"

"*That*, up there has nothing to do with how I feel about you!" She said pointing up at the ceiling. "What you're doing is depraved and criminal! You'll go to prison for this, Leonard!"

"Criminal? *Me? A criminal?* Ask yourself then, *Mother dear,* who I inherited *that* particular trait from. Would you like to know how many I've murdered, hmm? I've been doing it since I was nineteen, Mother dear. Now let me see . . . " He pursed his lips and stared fixedly above her head, then stabbing his index finger in front of her face, he said proudly, "I've tortured and murdered *TWELVE*! Twelve to date, Mother dear!" He poked her hard and maliciously on the forehead, "And as for you, you should have been sterilised at birth, you cold-hearted *bitch*!"

Pointing towards the ceiling, he continued animatedly, silencing his mother with a raised hand each time she tried to interrupt him, "Now then, the girl upstairs, she was to be next. I've already dug her grave in readiness. Close to the others. I prefer to keep them all together, at least the last few – didn't have the opportunity with the earlier ones."

He poked her hard again on the forehead, she cried out in pain and fear and tried to back away from him. "But I've recently found something out about her. She's not like you. She's not like the others. She loves her father. But does she love her mother? No! Her mother is just like you. Lazy, hateful, greedy, cold-hearted – and a *whore* too! She deserted her family to fulfil her selfish needs, for sex and material gain!"

Emily Fitch clutched at her throat, her eyes wide with horror, "Leonard, please, *I beg you!* You don't know what you're saying. You're a good, decent man, a *Doctor! Doctors don't take lives, Leonard.* They heal and mend lives! Please, Leonard, please let's stop all this nonsense. You're just saying these things to frighten me. You don't really mean it!"

He moved towards her, slowly, relishing the fear in her eyes; for every step he took towards her she backed further away, out into the hallway. She glanced quickly at the solid timber front door, her only means of escape, but realised immediately that it was pointless, he'd secured the gate on their arrival, putting the heavy padlock back in place. He'd also locked the main door and removed the key.

When he spoke to her next, his tone was sinister and mocking.

"Oh, yes I do, Mother! I'll explain clearly to you shall I? You treated my father and me with utter contempt and cruelty. And what's more, you are responsible for my father's death. You worked him into an early grave. My Father was forced to work around the clock, *seven days a week* to keep up with your incessant selfish demands!"

Emily Fitch glanced up the staircase, wondering if the girl had woken up yet, and as she continued to back away from her son. She had never seen him like this before, *ever*. She had always had the upper hand, always able to intimidate, bully and ridicule him so that he cowered in her presence. But the man standing before her, now, was anything but intimidated, it was *she* who now felt afraid of *him* although she didn't dare to let him know and, with a bravado she didn't feel, she interrupted him. "You don't know what you're talking about, Leonard. You have no idea what your father –"

"*DON'T* interrupt me, *Mother*! I haven't finished with you yet!" Like a hissing cobra, his head sprang forward as he towered over her, spraying saliva in her face.

She continued to back away from him and was standing just outside the kitchen. As he approached her, he absently rolled the syringe in his fingers.

"I loved my father, and he loved me. Oh, yes, Mother, why look so surprised? Yes he did, my father loved me very much and when he died, I never felt more alone in my entire life – he was the *one single person* in my life to ever have shown me kindness and love! *You*, on the other hand, have made my life a *misery* with your constant mocking, ridicule and humiliation. Oh, and let's not forget the *physical abuse* you subjected me to throughout my very lonely childhood. *You* should have died not him. No matter that, against all the odds, after being bullied, ridiculed and emotionally and physically abused at the hands of you and *others like you*, I still made something of myself and succeeded in life. I've made it to the very top of my profession, yet you *still* treat me with a total lack of respect. You still *belittle and* humiliate me and you continue to *take, take, take*, just as you did from my father. Well not any longer, Mother!"

Emily Fitch's heart was racing; she clutched her hand to her chest. Perspiration soaked her face and she trembled with fear. He could hear the fear in her voice now as she pleaded with him. "Leonard, please, listen to me, you must stop this nonsense. Have you lost your mind?"

In a desperate attempt at self-preservation, she tried a different approach, using a more gentle tone, "Leonard, please. There's really no need to drag the past up. Of course I'm very proud of what you've achieved, Leonard . . ."

He seemed not to be listening to her now, his eyes locked on hers appeared vacant as he edged closer to her as she backed into the kitchen. She glanced quickly over her shoulder, scanning the room for something, anything to defend herself with but there was nothing to hand, nothing that would stave off the deranged giant of a man coming towards her with undisguised hatred in his eyes.

Her voice timid and shaky, she whispered, "Leonard, what is it? What have you got behind your back? *Please, Leonard*, there's no need for this. You're frightening me, son!"

"*Son?*" He spat out the word. "Oh, I'm your *son* now am I? You want to know what I have behind my back do you?"

The menace in his voice shook her to the core. She raised her hands up in front of her, pleading and defensively, but she was too late.

"This is for you, a bit of your own medicine!" It happened quickly, Emily Fitch was powerless. He raised his arm above his head then brought it down fast, thrusting the needle into the side of his mother's neck.

"*Leonard! What have you . . .*" She clutched at her throat as she fell backwards into the kitchen, sending the door slamming against the wall. He caught her just before she hit the floor and lifted her non-too gently, throwing her over his shoulder, then carried her up the stairs as he calmly and professionally explained what was happening to her.

"The injection I've just given you is a paralysing agent. Don't

313

resist, just let it take its effect. Soon you will start to feel weak, faint even. But you won't pass out, oh no, you'll be wide-awake and able to see everything going on around you. I'm afraid I haven't brought my anaesthetist along, so unfortunately, you'll be able to *hear and feel* everything as well."

The drug was fast acting, her body started twitching and a moment later she was limp, a dead weight. She desperately wanted to plead and beg him to stop whatever he was going to do, but she was unable to speak. She couldn't move a single muscle yet she was aware of everything that was happening and what her deranged son was saying to her. He carried her along the landing, past the bedroom door where Erin was still sleeping then dropped her outside his bedroom door.

"Just make yourself comfortable. Won't be two ticks."

CHAPTER SIXTY-FIVE

F ITCH knew it was just a matter of time before the police search party found the lodge – they were closing in fast. Somewhere in the distance he heard the rapid *thud, thud, thud* of helicopter blades.

He kept Erin sedated; she would be totally oblivious to his grand exit, his explosive departure from the scene. He carried her to the car wrapped in a heavy woollen blanket, and laid her gently on the back seat, closing the door but not locking it. His heart racing, he made his way back to the lodge; the sound of dogs barking in the distance was getting louder, as was the sound of voices calling out to each other.

"Over here! Think we've found something! The dogs are going mad! Hurry! Hurry!" Fitch realised they must be at the gravesite, several hundred yards away.

On his way back into the lodge, he stopped at the lockup and took two cans of petrol out. Back inside, he began dousing the strong smelling liquid around the kitchen, living room and hallway. Whilst in the kitchen he turned the gas on for good measure. Taking the second can, he unscrewed the cap and made his way up the stairs, deliberately slopping the liquid as he went. When he got to the top, his mother was still slumped against his bedroom door. The horror in her eyes was clear to see. She couldn't blink, speak or move. He stood for several seconds smiling at her and then realising he had little time left to waste, he grabbed her by her hair and dragged her into the room where Erin had been sleeping, picked her up and threw her on the bed.

As she lay, fully aware of everything that was happening, Fitch vigorously shook the can, spilling the petrol all over the room the room and onto the bed, before emptying the remains all over his mother.

Satisfied that he had used every last drop of fuel, he threw the can into the corner of the room and took a Zippo lighter from his pocket. He flipped the lid open and placed it in his mother's open hand, forcing her thumb onto the serrated wheel. He stood back and admired the scene, trying to picture how the police would see it when they finally arrived.

As if addressing an audience, he spread his arms in a wide sweeping gesture and spoke to his mother for the last time, his voice calm and clear, belying the racing heart in his chest, resting his gaze on her eyes. "Do you see what I have done here mother? Have you got it yet? All my life you put me down, forced me to believe that I was worthless. You regretted giving birth to me, but having spread your legs and allowing me to breathe my first natural air, you had little choice but to raise me. It was what my father wanted.

"Well Mother, this is it; it's time for us to go our separate ways, for now at least. I am sure we shall meet in Hell, if such a place exists, and if it does it was surely created for the likes of you and I."

As he backed slowly from the room he couldn't tear his gaze from the look of horror in his mother's eyes and it filled him with an indescribable joy, a euphoric sense of fulfilment unlike anything he had experienced before.

He took the box of Swan Vestas from his pocket, struck the first match and threw into the room, aiming for the bed where his mother lay. It was instant. The flames ran rapidly along the satin counterpane and up his mother's legs. She was going to burn alive and she would be aware of every second, unable to move or even scream out in pain. "No less than you deserve!"

He struck a second match and tossed it across the room, the bedroom floor ignited. He turned his back on his mother and hurried along the landing to the staircase as the flames quickly spread outside the bedroom, chasing him as he fled.

The fire grew much faster than he had anticipated. He could feel the heat on the back of his legs and as he stepped onto the top step, he slipped on the wet liquid and fell head first down the stairs, landing hard against the front door of the lodge, his head hitting it with a sickening thud. Petrol fumes filled the air, burning the back of his throat, mixing with the smell of rotten eggs from the kitchen as the propane leaked out. He was lying at an awkward angle, his long legs twisted beneath him and his right arm trapped behind his back; he tried to pull it free. A wave of nausea swept over him and he became disoriented. He had to fight it, had to get out before . . .

CHAPTER SIXTY-SIX

THE scene outside was one of utter chaos. Police sniffer dogs had traced the scent of Hannah Ridgway to the makeshift burial ground, where officers were now digging frantically and it wasn't long before they realised that there were more bodies buried in the area.

"The dogs are going crazy, Sarge," the dog handler shouted.

"Quick, over here!" another yelled. Two uniformed officers stopped uncovering Hannah's body and dashed over with their spades to where the dogs were now digging.

D C Jones paced back and forth angrily, running his hands repeatedly through his hair "*Fucking hell, Sarge! The sick bastard's* – "

The explosion was deafening. Flames shot up and danced above the trees and the splintering and cracking of wood could be heard from every direction. Jones and Harris were within a hundred yards of the lodge when the thunderous boom almost threw them off their feet. The smell of burning timber filled the air as the smoke began to billow out towards them.

"What the fuck –" DS Harris was suddenly cut short as two young Bobbies came running out of the trees towards them, shouting excitedly, "Sarge! Sarge! We've found her. We've found the Fallon girl! She's alive, sir! She's alive!"

CHAPTER SIXTY-SEVEN

Hindthorpe, November 1978

FOLLOWING the death of his beloved Neive, John Fallon had lost all hope and had never dared to believe that Erin would ever be found alive, but here she was celebrating her birthday. He stood in the doorway of the cosy sitting room watching the scene unfold before him, his eyes brimming with tears of sadness and joy.

Erin was surrounded by many of her closest and dearest friends. Caitlin, Erin's first and life-long friend, was helping her open the huge pile of birthday cards – her eighteenth, a birthday Erin thought that she would never see, and although she was faced with a long journey to making a full recovery from her ordeal – and much, much longer to come to terms with the death of her little sister, a smile lit up her beautiful face as she read the countless well wishes, many from people she didn't even know. The story of Erin's abduction had been played out on national TV and in the press right up to and beyond her release.

John quickly wiped the tears from his eyes, shook his head and winked at his sons as they smiled and rolled their eyes at the level of chatter and giggling from the excited females surrounding Erin.

Caitlin whistled, "Wow, *look* at this, one Erin! The envelope alone looks really expensive! And this sticker, '*Par Avion*', whatever that means." She handed it to Erin, "Here . . . open it, it looks a bit special. I wonder if your Mum's sent it, Erin?" The girls suddenly went quiet; an expectant hush fell across the room.

"No. I don't think so, Caitlin." Erin was puzzled as she took the envelope from her friend. She'd already opened the cards from Sean, Liam and her dad as soon as she'd come downstairs that morning, so she knew it wasn't from any of them. It wasn't from her grandmother either because she wasn't arriving until later that day and she'd told Erin in a 'phone call earlier that week that she wanted to be there when she opened her card. God only knew what she was going to bring as a present this time. *I hope she's not been knitting again*, she thought with a degree of sadness. Because the last time she had celebrated a birthday in this room, Neive had been there too.

Sadly, she knew the expensive envelope had not been sent from her mother so she dismissed that thought very quickly. She hadn't even bothered to turn up at Neive's funeral, so why bother with a birthday card now?

The suspense was killing them. John Fallon laughed, "Come on then, darlin', put us all out of our misery will you? Me and the boys are dying to know who it's from, aren't we lads?"

"Yeah, come on Erin!" Liam and Sean went and sat down beside her on the arm of the settee, "C'mon, Sis! Open it!"

She smiled; it was the happiest day of her life and one she never dreamed she'd see. Hands shaking with anticipation, she tore the envelope open and pulled out a beautiful card with the words, *"SPECIAL BIRTHDAY WISHES TO A VERY SPECIAL PERSON!"* Then as she opened the card to find out whom it was from, the blood drained from her face. "No! It can't be . . ." The card fell from her hands, and it was Liam who picked it up.

He proudly read out the words. "Happy Birthday, Erin. Hope you're well . . . *Leonard?"*

ABOUT THE AUTHOR

I was born in Manchester into a large family of seven brothers and five sisters. As a child our playground was Belle Vue, one of the largest amusement parks in Europe. There are many stories I could tell about those days, and maybe one day I will. I have always been known as a storyteller. As a very young girl, I developed a voracious passion for books, and I read all the classics: Dickens, Eliot, Trollope, and Hardy. During my teens it was Stephen King and James Herbert, and then I got a taste of the political thriller with Daniel Silva's "Moscow Rules". For "Rings of Smoke", I drew on real life experiences, particularly in respect of the protagonist Erin Fallon. With stalkers, a runaway mother and abduction, I had the bones of what I believed was a good story.

ENJOYED
THIS BOOK? WE'VE GOT LOTS MORE!